The Paris Plot

Joseph Aragon

Oakhurst Print

This is a work of fiction. All of the characters, organizations, and events portrayed in this novel are either products of the author's imagination or are used fictitiously

THE PARIS PLOT

ISBN: 0998161209
ISBN 13: 9780998161204

Printed in the United States of America

For Ellen, my Paris muse

For Marc, Conrad, and Andelys
You make me proud each day

ACKNOWLEDGMENTS

For Linda Palmer, extraordinary mentor, writer and valued friend. For Douglas Glenn Clark, ever-insightful and supportive.

PROLOGUE

Paris 10:50 p.m.
l'Élysée Presidential Palace
Office of French President, Amaury Jardin

"Monsieur le Président," said Francois Rambeau, the president's Foreign Minister. "I finally reached magistrat André Malevu, the judge who issued the judicial order. He's on the line."

"Put him through," said President Jardin. The judge's voice came on.

"Bonsoir, Monsieur le Président," said Malevu. His tone was jocular.

"Monsieur," President Jardin said, "There has been a dangerous misunderstanding tonight. A Commandant of the police Préfecture claims to have a judicial order from you directing him to enter Hôtel Marly where the American president is staying. Our French security detail at the hotel fears Commandant Poussin may be attempting to arrest

President Childs. This would be madness and surely lead to bloodshed. Please assure me that no such action was ordered by you.

"There is no mistake." Malevu sounded gleeful. "I have issued a valid warrant for the arrest of the President of the United States."

"My god, man! Do you realize what you've done?"

"I know exactly what I've done."

"No, you clearly don't. Do you want France at war with the United States? As president of the Republic I order you to rescind to this absurd warrant. Contact Commandant Poussin immediately and withdraw the order."

"No, Mr. President, I will not. And I wish to remind you sir that this is France, not some banana republic. France's constitution is clear that the judiciary shall be independent of the executive branch. You cannot just wave your presidential wand and make the French constitution disappear."

Jardin placed his hand against his forehead and realized it was wet with perspiration. His pulse had accelerated.

"I will have you arrested for treason! Recall Poussin now!"

"There is no treason. The order I issued as juge d'instruction was prepared in strict accordance with the statutes of France, the European Union and applicable treaties. I have invoked the well-established doctrine of universal jurisdiction. It gives a magistrat such as myself the judicial authority to order the arrest a foreign official for the commission of war crimes and crimes against humanity - even if he is a head of state. The American slaughter of

innocent French citizens was clearly such a crime. So, with all due respect, sir, even as president of the Republic you cannot undo the warrant. President Childs will be arrested tonight."

1

TEN MONTHS EARLIER

The White House

A perfect day for the White House Easter-Egg Hunt. The South Lawn, bathed in glorious March morning sunlight is filled with the laughter of several hundred children, doting parents, President Leyland Childs, the First Lady and special invitees from the Hill.

Isabella "Izzy" Stone, Secret Service Special Agent in charge of the presidential detail, is trailing Childs as he good-naturedly urges the children to fill their baskets. She'd like to be closer but this morning he wants more space.

Above, the sky is dazzling blue and cloudless. Izzy scans the panoramic vista where, in the distance, a sole bird circles in the peaceful emptiness. She wonders if it has lost its way from the flocks that often make their passage across the Potomac. Well, the bird will find its way back. That's what birds do.

She returns her attention to the president. He's waded deep into the crowd and is holding a baby dressed in a rabbit's costume. The baby is smiling as the president bounces it gently in cradled arms.

Out of the corner of her eye Izzy can see the bird continuing its aimless orbit above the Washington monument beyond the South Lawn. And it occurs to her that the bird must be larger than she imagined, perhaps a hawk, because given the distance to the monument, a smaller bird would be hard to see.

As she watches, Izzy observes a subtle inflection in the creature's airy movement. It seems off, unnatural. Suddenly, It drops almost vertically, and disappears from her line of sight.

Something's wrong!

A survival reflex deep in her reptilian brain is screaming DANGER!

Jesus! It's headed for the president!

Now Izzy is moving fast toward Childs who's buried in the admiring throng.

I'll look like a monkey's ass if I'm wrong.

"Incoming!" Izzy is shouting, her arm pointed upward as the president and other agents turn to her then look skyward with bewildered expressions. She hears the buzzing doppler sound of an approaching motor and frantically hurls herself into the crowd violently knocking parents and toddlers aside as she struggles to reach Childs. Only a few feet away she leaps toward the president, her body in full block mode.

Too late! The drone, loaded with TATP high explosives, detonates with murderous force, sending Childs and the mangled body parts of 200 others flying in a thousand directions.

Dammit!

Izzy Stone awakened in a sweat. Again. She brushed her thick red hair back with her right hand and checked the clock.

Two a.m.

For days she'd been having recurring nightmares like the one tonight.

They all followed the same pattern. The president was going to die and she couldn't stop it because she'd missed something critical, waited too long to act, and now it was too late.

The nausea was back. Izzy made her way to the bathroom and threw up in the toilet. Afterward she brushed her teeth and looked in the mirror.

Am I losing the ability to keep POTUS safe?

West Point had toughened her and years with the secret service had wizened her. Yet she knew the job of protecting the president from the kooks, crazies and terrorists of the world eventually took its toll and had to wonder if she was losing her edge.

As head of the presidential detail it was her job to worry, especially given the upcoming POTUS visit to the volatile Middle East, where everybody seemed to have gone bat-shit crazy. But menace came with the territory, and given the constant threats against POTUS, there was always more than enough to worry about.

Still, something about this particular trip was gnawing at her. She'd read and re-read the trip Intel, but the mandarins of the spy world hadn't identified a specific threat to the president. Even so, whether intuition, clairvoyance or just a feeling in her bones, something wasn't right in the cosmos and that put Izzy into an elevated state of unease and vigilance.

Will I be able to stop the next one? Because sure as hell there'll be a next one.

In the morning she'd have to push CIA, NSA and every other intelligence asset to dig deeper. There was something. But what? She considered the advice she'd often imparted to the members of her detail, "It's a big world with lots of moving parts. Expect the unexpected."

2

Paris

Young Émile, with his special edition Patek Philippe watch, hand-worked English leather shoes, cashmere coat, and bespoke Saville Row tweed suit, stepped onto rue du Faubourg Saint-Honoré and made his way down what many considered the most elegant street in the world.

To the right stood the stately Palais de l'Élysée, official residence of the president of France. At the entrance, four heavily armed members of the president's executive protection service watched passers-by with seeming disinterest.

Beyond the French "White House," rue du Faubourg glittered with the crown jewels of fashion; Fendi furs, Givenchy, Buccelatti, Dolce & Gabbana, Cartier, and many others.

It was Christmas Eve and the narrow street sparkled with garlands of dazzling holiday lights strung across the historic passage. A light snow, unusual for Paris, had dusted lampposts and rooftops with a delicate mantle of white, making the scene resemble a masterful confection.

On the street below, gleaming shops and boutiques awaited the attention of oil-cartel billionaires, mortgage bankers, Chinese magnates, Russian nouveau-riche mafiosi, Beverly Hills trophy wives and, from time to time, an actual aristocrat.

But tonight Émile was not thinking of fortunes or furriers. Instead, the young man with the gold scarf, chocolate cashmere winter coat and aloof bearing was on his way to Christmas Eve Latin mass at the sepulchral Church of St. Roch located in the 1st arrondissement. It was a departure from the ten a.m. morning mass he regularly attended at St. Roch. But tonight's mass was to be very special indeed.

At rue d'Anjou he paused a moment to adjust his coat, tonight heavier than usual.

His choice of rue du Faubourg was not accidental. On the contrary, to follow the path of the narrow cobblestone street was to revisit the greatness of France. Here, Jeanne d'Arc had fought a pitched battle against the occupying English and helped save Paris. Three hundred years later, following his triumphal return from the American Revolution, Lafayette had received the Queen of France at his residence on the same street. Years after, tumbrils would carry Marie Antoinette and Louis the Sixteenth down rue du Faubourg to their bloody appointment with Madame Guillotine.

Émile was a product of that insular club of French families who'd not forgotten their noble lineage or their rightful place in the higher order of things. He considered himself a good Catholic possessing a reverence of France that was now out of step with the majority of the French public. He knew that many of his less privileged friends did not share his romantic nostalgia. To them, his chivalrous notions of "*la patrie*" were nothing more than cultural detritus floating in the wake of the new European order.

Yet the blood and glory of the great patrician families of France still coursed his body and mind and Émile refused to accept the new reality of the twenty-first century.

Honor. Heroism. Sacrifice. Those were the true virtues that rue du Faubourg Saint-Honoré stood for. It was what France stood for - what guided him tonight.

3

Arriving at the unheated, historic church of St. Roch on rue St. Honoré, Émile checked his watch. Good. Not too early. That might invite unwelcome attention. Not too late. He didn't want to lose his hand-picked seat to some lapsed Catholic succumbing to year-end guilt.

He made his way to the fourth row, right-center-aisle chair and sat down, relieved to find it unoccupied. It was a routine he'd developed over the last three months faithfully attending mass at St. Roch.

Émile understood that though relatively new to the staid congregation the regularity of his attendance had made him a weekly fixture at St. Roch. And those who lived in that exclusive district of Paris would have decided that the impeccably attired gentleman with languid brown eyes, delicate features and aristocratic bearing, "*belonged*." He did not fear being drawn into personal conversation. Prying questions about family, career, or political views were unlikely. This was, after all, the center of Paris, home of the Palais de Justice, Banque de France, and the Louvre. In short, the place where powerful people had always understood the importance of discretion. He knew that in the 1st arrondissement, inquiring into the personal lives of others was considered a social *bêtise.*

Begun in 1653 by Louis XIV the massive French Baroque cathedral rivaling Notre Dame had eventually lost its *caché* and come to languish in cavernous solitude, dark and forgotten except for a small, loyal following of wealthy parishioners.

Yet, St. Roch had known great moments. It had witnessed the baptism of Louis XVI, and the daring actions of a young French officer named Bonaparte who brutally crushed a royalist revolt on the blood-soaked steps of the cathedral, thereby saving the young Republic.

These thoughts and many others coursed through Émile's feverish mind as he sat outwardly attentive and devout in the small wicker chair. Those around him could not see his starched shirt collar moistening under the thick cashmere coat. A coat made all the heavier by the weight in the right hand pocket.

Precisely five minutes before the commencement of the mass, Monsieur Jean Louis Abelard, Chief

Magistrate and juge d'instruction of the most powerful and secretive court in Paris, entered the church accompanied by his wife Anais and his two young grandchildren. As was his custom, Abelard proceeded to his reserved seat in row four, left center aisle. Making his way down the aisle, he politely acknowledged the whispered well wishes of parishioners.

"Merci, merci," he replied.

Now in his late seventies, judge Abelard was the most admired jurist in France. His compelling decisions and sense of fair play had made him a national treasure.

As the massive oak and metal doors of the great church of St. Roch began to close, the singing of a Thirteenth Century Gregorian chant heralded the commencement of the Latin Mass.

Émile listened devoutly and drank from the haunting melodies, counterpoint and medieval words of the prayerful monks. The songs spoke to him of ancient traditions, past glories and spiritual atonement. They spoke of sacrifice and redemption, of justice and punishment. And as he listened, he accepted his destiny. He was at peace.

The priest rose: "*In nomine Patris, et Filii, et Spiritus Sancti, Amen.*"

Emile crossed himself and knelt on the cold stone floor as the service began.

Eventually, the communal peace offerings were exchanged. The worshippers stood and began to file by row toward the altar where the priest, holy hosts in hand, awaited.

Émile rose.

He watched as the rows directly across the aisle began discharging their congregants into the center aisle. Soon, judge Abelard stepped into the aisle. Émile quickly moved forward, stepped into the aisle and inserted himself a mere half step behind him.

The parishioners advanced, heads bowed, toward the priest and the sacred expiation. Moments later, both Abelard and Émile reached the foot of the altar, where the priest was dispensing the holy wafers.

With hands cupped, left hand cradled in the right, the frail jurist received the host, whispered "amen," placed it in his mouth and moved on.

Now almost directly behind Abelard, Émile too, extended the palm of his hand and accepted the host, whispering "amen." He placed the host in his mouth and moved forward with a slightly longer step until he was immediately behind Abelard.

Carefully sliding his right hand into his overcoat pocket Émile slipped his hand downward until he found the handle of the nine-millimeter semiautomatic Glock he'd been carrying all evening. He located the smooth metal trigger and wrapped his index finger around it.

Then, in a controlled, meticulously rehearsed movement, he withdrew the pistol, raised it, placed the muzzle one inch behind judge Abelard's right ear and pulled the trigger twice in rapid succession. Abelard was dead before his venerable body struck the stone floor.

Émile did not hear the screams of horror that accompanied the deafening explosion of blood and brain matter. He turned and looked vacantly toward the terrified worshippers. They appeared suspended in time, as in a frieze or a religious tableau from a heroic work by Michelangelo.

Slowly, twenty three-year-old Émile Richard François de la Valois, putative scion and pure blood descendant of de Valois and Marechal, sole heir to ten thousand *hectares* of verdant forests and chateaux, last claimant to the titles of Duc and Viscount, prodigal son to doting parents, riddle to friends and lovers, gracefully raised the Glock one last time, and, as if released from some long pent-up torment, shouted out in a primal scream:

"Mon Dieu, pardonnez moi!" placed the barrel deep in his mouth and pulled the trigger.

4

Washington, D.C.

Izzy walked into her small office at the Eisenhower Executive Office building, hung her blue blazer on a coat rack and stowed her Sig Sauer. She noticed that Wanda, her assistant, had placed the usual steaming soy latte and several international publications on the desk. Skimming them was part of Izzy's morning ritual when not on the road with POTUS. She took a quick sip of the latte and regarded the pile. The Financial Times of London, Germany's Die Zeit, France's Le Monde and Israel's Haaretz were among the dozen or so newspapers and periodicals.

Reading French, German or Hebrew was not a problem. Languages had come easily to Izzy. Her late father had mastered several, a passion he'd passed on to Izzy from childhood. That talent had made her a natural choice for a posting to the American

Embassy in Paris as military attaché after graduating from West Point. Though it took time, reading the newspapers and periodicals was useful. They offered valuable perspectives and coverage often absent from American mainstream media and, sometimes, intelligence briefs. *When your boss is globe-trotting it's good to know what's going on outside the security bubble.*

Izzy rummaged through the pile, pulled out *Le Monde* and blanched. The headline left her momentarily stunned. *"LE MAGISTRAT ABELARD MORT – Assassiné par un étudiant de 23 ans"*

Abelard dead? Why? She'd met the distinguished jurist several times during her Paris years as attaché to the American Embassy and had always found him to be a gentle unassuming man who never drew attention to the enormous power he wielded. Izzy couldn't fathom why anyone would want to harm him. She picked up the landline and dialed a contact at the French Embassy in Washington.

"*Oui.*"

"Vincent, it's Izzy Stone."

"Izzy, *bonjour,* how are you?"

"*Très bien, merci,* Vincent." Izzy said. "I just read the Le Monde piece on magistrat Abelard."

"Ah, *oui.* It is unbelievable. You knew him, yes?"

"Yes," said Izzy, "though not well. But enough to know he was not a man who made enemies, much less enemies who would want him dead. And then the young man's suicide. It's baffling. Forgive me for asking, but is it possible there was a personal relationship involved?"

"Abelard? At his age? *Non, mon dieu,* never!" Vincent said, "He was a saint. The law and his family were his life. He was very attached to his dog Pascal, a small yappy terrier - slept all day and barked at everyone who visited. But you know, Izzy, there may have been a political motivation."

"How so?"

"*Alors,* the young man was no ordinary assassin. He was a university student from a prestigious Paris family. Very correct. No criminal record. Nothing.

But it's possible he'd been radicalized by someone and had become a political extremist. At least that is one of the theories."

"Hmmm," said Izzy. "But what did that have to do with Abelard? He wasn't politically active as I remember. So why?"

"*Et voilá!*" said Vincent. "That is the sixty-four dollar question."

"I think you mean the sixty-four thousand dollar question," said Izzy.

"*Non,*" said Vincent, "The sixty-four thousand dollar question is when are we having dinner again?"

Izzy laughed. "Soon, *mon chèr.* I just need to get the state visit to Jordan behind me. Be well. *Salut!*"

Izzy hung up the phone and was quiet for a moment. "*Yes, a big world with lots of moving parts.*"

5

Islamabad, Pakistan -Two a.m.

"I can give you Omar Mohammed al-Azzam." Pakistani Colonel Badar Khan of the powerful Inter-Services Intelligence had the full attention of Bill Powers, CIA Chief of Station, Islamabad. Omar Mohammed al-Azzam was the world's most wanted terrorist, responsible for the gory beheadings of Westerners and a staggering biological attack that had killed twenty-one thousand Americans in the city of Columbia, South Carolina, leaving the nation in stunned mourning and terror.

Powers sank his beefy hands into his pockets, snorted once and jutted out his thickset Irish face like a flinty bartender asking *what'll you have?*

"How?" Powers said. He'd heard similar offers from wealthy Pakistanis, goatherds and everyone in between - all of them delusions or swindles.

But hearing it from Colonel Badar Khan made the offer special. U.S. intelligence officials had long suspected Khan of being one of several high-ranking Pakistani ISI officers who sympathized with Mohammed al-Azzam. So an urgent message from Khan via a third party requesting a late night rendezvous was something Powers couldn't ignore.

Using taxis, switchbacks, slipping in and out of darkened passageways, Powers found his way to a ramshackle apartment building in a run down neighborhood plagued by potholes, broken street lights and decrepit, graffiti-marred shops.

He found Khan in the back room of a barren third floor apartment that appeared abandoned. Kahn was in a corner, leaning against the wall smoking a pungent, hand-rolled cigarette. A dirty, cracked window faced onto a grim airshaft. A lone yellow bulb dangled forlornly from the ceiling, providing the only illumination. Plaster flaked from the ceiling and walls and a small wood chair with peeling green paint, a leg missing, lay on its side.

"I'll be told where he will be," Khan said.

"When?"

"It could be a week or a month from now. We're never informed until the last minute. But I will be told. Mohammed al-Azzam needs money and medication. He has diabetes and heart problems. He also needs information from my unit in the ISI. He never stays anywhere more than a day or two so once I tell you, you will have to act immediately."

"Why are you telling me this?" Powers said. He didn't believe in looking a gift horse in the mouth. But on the other hand he wasn't sure this was a gift horse. The world Powers traveled in was rarely what it appeared. Khan could be setting him up, could be setting the U.S. up. Still, he'd known Kahn for six years. In his experience the man was not given to playing games.

Khan inhaled the cigarette then slowly released through his nostrils.

"Mr. Powers," he said, "We've known each other a long time. I trust you've learned I'm not a timid man. But after many years with ISI, I'm tired. I'm forty-three, yet I feel a hundred. Death is stalking me. I sense my days are numbered."

Powers noticed a slight trembling of hands. He'd never seen Kahn like this before.

Khan continued in a halting voice.

"Fear…was once nothing more than an uninvited guest. I could chase it away with my prayers, my devotion and my hatred of apostates. I was younger, stronger. But…no more."

He took a deep drag. "I have friends who are loyal to me. But I also have powerful enemies in Islamabad. It's only a matter of time until one of them finds a way to disgrace me, betray me, perhaps kill me. Then what will become of my wife, my children?"

Powers studied Khan in the dim light. He'd aged greatly since they'd first met years earlier. His shoulders drooped noticeably and his face bore the haggard look of a man who slept too little.

"I'm listening," Powers said.

"I will tell you where Mohammed al-Azzam will be. Once I do I am a dead man. And, of course, my family will be slaughtered."

Powers took the hint. "Colonel, if your information is correct we'll relocate you and your family to a safe place and provide you with a new identity."

"Yes, I'm sure you can," replied Khan. "But there is the matter of how I will support my family."

"Right, of course. My government understands this involves a great personal sacrifice. Once we've confirmed the information and completed the operation it will honor its pledge of fifty million U.S. dollars, delivered anonymously to a secure account in Switzerland, Hong Kong, or any other place you choose."

Khan nodded in agreement. "Good. I have a specific condition concerning our relocation."

"Yes?"

"There is no place on earth where we can be completely safe. However, no place is safer for us than America."

"That can be arranged."

"I wish to have a house." Khan said, "a real American house with a back yard and grass where my children can play."

"My friend," said Powers, "the United States is a big place. I'm sure we can find a home for you and your family. You would have new names and a legend."

Khan shifted slightly. "It will not be necessary to look for us. I have already a place in mind."

"Really? where?"

"Mr. Powers, we are not a third world nation. Thanks to your American Google and real estate web sites I've looked into this matter. God willing, I wish to have a two-story, three-bedroom, two-bath house with a pool, located in Malibu or Beverly Hills, California, depending on which location is most convenient for the United States government. My children are still young. They've dreamed of going to Disneyland and it would be pleasing if we were close enough to drive there." Khan quickly added, "Of course, my wife is a great admirer of Native American jewelry so we would also consider something in the area of Taos, New Mexico."

Keeping his composure, Powers nodded. "Yes, yes, of course." *JESUS!*

But he was anxious to wrap things up. They'd already been there too long.

"Now," Powers said, "just a couple of details."

"Yes?"

"First, here's a number to call in an emergency. You will be directed to an address. I'll meet you there." Powers gave Kahn a small piece of paper with a phone number on it. "Memorize it and destroy the paper."

Kahn took the slip of paper and studied it for a few moments. Then he pulled a cigarette lighter from his pocket, lit it and burned the paper.

"You need a name we can use for future contacts," Powers said. "Do you have a suggestion?"

"No. I would prefer it if you chose," Kahn said.

"Fine," Powers said. "Then your name is Walt."

"Walt," Kahn said, "Like Walt Disney?"

"Like Walt Disney."

"Walt. Walt," Kahn repeated to himself in a low voice, his head nodding in acknowledgement.

Powers thought he saw a brief smile cross Kahn's face but it quickly faded.

"Before I go," Kahn said, "there's something you should know. I can offer no specifics but I suspect Omar Mohammed al-Azzam has planned the assassination of your president."

6

Amman, Jordan

U.S. President Leyland Childs' twelve-car motorcade roared at high throttle through central Amman in the Hashemite kingdom of Jordan. An elite Jordanian police motorcycle unit had the point. It was mid-afternoon and a hot day had shortened tempers and dried out the city. A wind-whipped choking dust added to the misery as the entourage sped toward the Jordanian King's royal office complex located on the western edge of the city. Throughout the capital an unprecedented number of police, military and security personnel had been deployed at the request of the Secret Service.

On the avenue thousands of spectators lined the roads braving heat, dust and wind, hoping for a glimpse of the charismatic forty-three-year-old

American president. Intermixed with the well-wishers, angry groups of protesters waved placards that shouted, "Satan America," and "Death to U.S. War Criminals."

"WHAM! THUMP!" Large rocks were hitting the cars.

Agent Izzy Stone was in the front seat of the third car in the motorcade. As head of the presidential detail it was her job to protect POTUS and she didn't want anybody screwing it up, especially given the CIA's urgent warning that Mohammed al-Azzam was planning an assassination attempt. She drew some comfort in the knowledge that the Jordanian intelligence services were among the best in the world and Halim, her Jordanian counterpart, was a complete professional. Still...

She touched her communications module.

"Halim, it's your turf. We need to keep the route clear. We've got people throwing everything but grandma at us. I want daylight and a lot of it."

"We're doing everything we can but there are many more trouble-makers today. These people were not on our radar." Halim said.

"Watch it!" Izzy said to the agent at the wheel as larger rocks and chunks of metal struck the side of the car with a jarring clang.

Looking out the back window she saw pieces of concrete, shoes and other debris raining down on the motorcade.

I sure as hell don't like it, but I've seen worse.

"Tighten up," Izzy said. The motorcade accelerated with a roar. Only sixty inches separated the cars.

Three cars behind Izzy's vehicle, president Childs was reading. Relaxed on the plush seat of the presidential limo, known as "the Beast," his long fingers quickly flipped through pages of the CIA work-up on the Jordanian King's inner circle. Speed was a hallmark of Childs. It had been the secret of his meteoric political ascent from young charismatic California governor to *enfant terrible* of the Party establishment, defying conventional wisdom and capturing, against all odds, his party's presidential nomination, going on to win the general election. Tall, over six feet, with a lanky yet athletic body, his wide pearly smile, angular face and mischievous demeanor disarmed even the most wary. And once he'd focused his penetrating blue eyes on a person, he could make the lucky recipient feel they were the only person in the room.

He put down the *Eyes Only* file, turned and looked affectionately at his wife, Meg, seated next to him. The First Lady was wearing an American designed powder-blue suit, lavender blouse and black *Chanel* leather pumps with white heels. A Wellesley-educated, Boston Brahmin with chestnut brown eyes and high cheekbones, Meg Childs' upper-class bearing contrasted with her crowd- pleasing street smarts. With her left hand clutching one of the overhead straps, she'd placed her right hand in his outstretched palm.

"Lee, I'm always amazed how calm you can be when any normal person would be chewing his nails with all this commotion."

"Just not a lot I can do about it, Meg. We're in good shape. These folks know what they're doin'." He gave her hand a reassuring squeeze and resumed skimming the CIA work-up on Jordanian King Obeidat, unaware that Meg Childs had tightened her grip on the strap.

Mid-point between the lead car and the Beast, Izzy was busy coordinating the security detail.

As the speeding motorcade approached Zahran Street, the deep, thrumming sound of a diesel engine filled the avenue.

Izzy looked ahead and to the right.

"Goddammit!"

A large, aging dumpster truck had suddenly lurched out of an alley, broken through a wooden barricade and was moving to the center of the boulevard.

Izzy barked into her module. "Hostiles ahead! Repeat, hostiles!"

The motorcycle escort never had a chance. Cyclists collided violently with the decrepit dumpster throwing the riders against lampposts, steel bollards and trees. From rooftop positions above the boulevard, secret service counter-measures sharpshooters began raining gunfire onto the rogue truck. But the heavy vehicle continued to lurch forward.

In an evasive maneuver the agent in the lead car pulled hard left.

Too late, as the lumbering dumpster truck suddenly detonated with a massive roar, incinerating the lead car in the fireball. Unable to stop, the second car slammed into the flying debris, overturned and exploded.

With Izzy's car now in the lead, the remainder of the motorcade executed a screeching hairpin turn and careened down a dim, narrow, one-way street.

As the vehicles accelerated into the tight passage, automatic weapons opened up from darkened doorways and rooftops. Ahead, a van blocked exit from the street. Behind, a large bus chugged in blocking retreat. The motorcade came to a skidding halt.

"Engage! Engage!" Izzy said, grabbing her Uzi.

Secret Service Counter-Assault Teams in black battle-dress uniforms immediately exited their large SUV's and began laying down fierce suppressing fire with heavy weapons as other agents sprang from vehicles to provide covering fire for the Beast.

Several agents went down as they leaped into the violent fusillade of AK-

47 rounds and rocket-propelled grenades.

"We can't hold this position!" Izzy yelled into the intercom. "Secure Dumbledore and take cover in the buildings. Go!"

She saw two agents dash to the Beast and heave the rear door open for the president. The first agent's head snapped back as a sniper's bullet found its mark. The second agent leaned into the open door but quickly slumped as a burst riddled his back.

"Shit!" Izzy shoved her door open, slid out and dropped to a crouch. An agent lay next to her. His expression one of surprise, a gaping wound on the side of his head.

Get to the Beast before it's too late.

Staying low, Izzy advanced at a quick stride, her right hand clutching the Uzi. Closing the distance, she saw one of the attackers running toward the president's car, assault rifle blazing. She dropped to one knee, took aim and squeezed off a short burst. The attacker fell. Izzy went into a full sprint.

Just a few more yards.

"BOOM!"

A powerful explosion rocked the Beast and threw Izzy to the ground. Her head felt wet.

She wiped her forehead. Blood.

Now more attackers were rushing toward the president. Izzy saw their eyes. Wild, wide, expectant. She knew that look. They were coming in for the kill.

She'd seen it before - as a child the day her dad was murdered.

From deep within Izzy, a volcanic rage erupted. Back on her feet, her hair, face and white blouse soaked with her own blood, she charged head-on at the attackers, firing point blank, screaming:

"No! You bastards, you can't have this one!"

A shooter lunged at her. Izzy sidestepped him, pushed the nozzle of the Uzi into his neck and held the trigger down, decapitating him. A second assailant panicked and dropped to the ground. Izzy shot him between the eyes. Drenched in blood from close combat, she tore into the attackers, a human scythe, a hurtling panjandrum.

The remaining assailants broke off their attack and ran away.

Izzy reached the Beast, now engulfed in flames, the back door open. She saw the president, suit torn, face bloody, trying to pull his wife to safety. Secret service agents lay mortally wounded near the door.

"Sir, let me help you," she said, panting, fighting for air in the acrid smoke. The First Lady appeared to be dazed, a large smudge on her left temple. Izzy shouldered the Uzi and helped the president pull her from the back seat towards a nearby doorway. They were close.

Just a few more steps.

Izzy saw a sudden look of alarm in the president's eyes and turned just in time to see an assailant with an AK-47 step from the shadows. The president and the first lady were both in the direct line of fire.

Izzy threw herself against the president just as the gunman fired. She felt a sudden blow to her right side. Swiveling awkwardly to her left she pulled the Sig Sauer from her shoulder holster and got off two rounds as she fell. The shooter crumpled, half his face gone.

Feeling lightheaded Izzy regained her footing and helped the president half-drag, half-carry his wife through the doorway.

Hold on, Izzy.

The First Lady was heavier now and appeared unconscious.

Hold on, Izzy.

They were in a small shop stocked with colorful *Beirsheba* dolls, traditional embroidered shawls, *Moire* prayer mats and curios.

Hold… on.

They lay the First Lady down on the shop rugs. Izzy noticed a bright red spot spreading across the First Lady's blouse. Izzy tried to stand and speak but staggered, fell against the wall and slumped to the floor, the right side of her uniform soaked with her own blood.

Hold...

She could hear other loud voices in the room. Groggy, she reached for the Uzi and groped her jacket pockets for an ammo clip. The voices drew closer...Then...*English... thank God.*

Now more agents were rushing in. Izzy floated down, down, the din fading. As voices dissolved into an indiscernible buzz, she slipped into a euphoric reverie. She could see her dad, her hero, the one they'd taken from her that terrible day in a long-ago childhood.

7

Annapolis, Maryland

The black Land Rover pulled onto the gravel driveway and came to a crunching stop in front of a tree-shaded, white clapboard two-story home set in a rustic tableau of Maryland countryside. Flowering Soapwort, Pokeweed and wild Columbine embraced a freshly painted white pine fence.

Chester Davis, former vice-president of the United States, heavy-set with a receding hairline and a slight limp stepped from the driver's seat of the Rover onto the gravel and slowly made his way toward the house.

The large cherry wood front door of the house opened. A young woman emerged and rushed down the steps, her long, auburn hair framing vivid green eyes, her broad, toothy smile evoking a youthful Kathryn Hepburn.

"Dad!"

"Hi, Viv."

"Dad, it's great to see you. Where's your secret service escort?"

"They're down the road a bit," Chester Davis said. "I wanted to drive today so they just followed."

"I'm impressed you're driving again after all these years of chauffeurs."

"Sorry it's been so long since my last visit, Viv. It's silly, the capital is only a short drive from this beautiful place, yet when I'm there it's like I'm on a different planet."

"Dad, Washington is a different planet. Besides, you've had your hands full with the grand jury rummaging through your life. They're behaving like a lynch mob. It makes me sick."

"Not to worry, honey, I've got more tricks than Houdini."

Viv laughed. "Come on in and have a cup of tea with me. We can catch up on family gossip until Misha finishes at the office. Then we'll all have dinner *chez* Viv and Misha."

"Sounds wonderful."

Arm in arm they entered a living room tastefully furnished in Early American colonial craftsman. Three large, angled bay windows bathed the room in golden afternoon light.

"Hope you don't mind chatting in the kitchen. I've got a roast on."

"On the contrary, the kitchen brings back happy memories of our old place in Chevy Chase with you, Mom and me..." Davis' voice trailed off.

Viv placed her arms around her dad, hugging him tightly. She turned and looked at him.

"Dad, I know this is a tough time for you, everyone treating you like a criminal." Her voice became bitter. "How can they forget the gutsy things you did as a young senator, fighting for hard-working American families?"?"

"Long time ago, sweetheart. Things change."

"Okay, okay, I'll get off my soapbox. Help me set the table?"

"Great. By the way, where's my granddaughter?" Davis removed four placemats from the cupboard. "I brought a special gift for her. Is it sixth or seventh grade?

"Seventh grade," Viv said, "you really are AWOL, Dad. Rebecca's in Europe. She left last month. She's spending several months in Paris with a wonderful family we've known for years. Misha and I want her to be exposed to other cultures and points of view. Besides, isn't that what you and Mom believed?"

Davis became thoughtful and inclined his head as if recalling something.

"That's Mom more than me. Always a step ahead. Probably her New England pedigree - trying to gentrify a meat-and potatoes Mid-Westerner like me."

"Anyway," Viv said, "Rebecca texted me this morning. She's going to be a sort of teacher's aide at a school located in the fourth arrondissement. That way she gets to learn a bit more French while teaching the kids some colloquial English."

"It does sound great. Still, I miss her."

"If she were here you'd be spoiling her rotten."

Davis smiled. "She's my only grandchild. Nothing's too good for Rebecca."

The sound of a car on gravel broke the conversation.

"That's Misha," Viv said.

8

Bethesda Naval Hospital – Maryland

President Leyland Childs was standing alongside the bed where Izzy Stone lay almost motionless but for the shallow rise and fall of her breathing amid a web of tubes tethered to beeping machines. It wasn't his first visit. He'd been to the hospital several times ever since Izzy had arrived via a specially chartered medical transport. They'd almost lost her during the Amman attack. Miraculously she had held on long enough for other agents to stop the bleeding, stabilize her and Medevac her to Ramstein Air Base in Germany where doctors had performed emergency surgery and then accompanied her back to the U.S. and Bethesda.

"How is she today, doc?" said the president.

"Better, but it's been slow," said Dr. David Brian, the attending physician.

"I'll settle for better. Thanks, Doc. Do appreciate all you're doin' for her.

"We'll do everything we can, Mr. President."

"Good. You do that."

9

Paris

"Émile was a maudlin Royalist xenophobe with his head stuck in the eighteenth century. You know how those Royalists are, Sylvie, they think Marie Antoinette was a saint. That young man always worried me. He was a terrible student, spoiled, unstable, a political extremist. His last essay sounded violent and alarming. Now he's dead and after several months we still don't know why he killed magistrat Abelard."

Sixty-year-old Rene Hachard, professor of politics and philosophy at the prestigious École Supérieure des Arts of Paris, was holding forth at the folding kitchen table of the modest apartment he and his wife shared in the working-class eighteenth arrondissement of Paris.

She sighed. "Rene, calm down. Who knows what was going on in his mind. Children of wealthy families aren't exempt from lunacy. Did you ever speak to monsieur Camus about it? After all, he's the head of the department."

"No, Camus wouldn't have understood. He's a self-important ass who never even visits the classrooms. He's seventy-five and spends half the day in the WC."

"What bothered you so much about Emile?"

"Well, he loathed immigrants, refugees, Muslims, considered them parasites. But most of all he hated Americans. He blamed them for everything that's gone wrong in France."

"He blamed Americans for the smelly Metro?"

Rene threw his hands upward in exasperation.

"Voilà! I wouldn'thave put it beyond him. In his last essay he railed about America's human rights crimes and the Americanizaton of France."

"Americani…what?"

"The fast food chains, the music, the films, the slang, the social media, the clothing, the violence and everything else coming from America."

"Americans aren't forcing us to eat their food or watch their films."

"I agree, but Emile was a young zealot who'd been listening to the wrong people."

"What do you mean?"

"I mean Malevu, the new chief magistrate. Malevu had a strong loyal following among some of the students at the École."

"Oh, that right wing fanatic. He's an awful successor to magistrat Abelard.

But I don't see what hatred of immigrants or Americans has to do with the murder of magistrat Abelard."

"I don't either. But I can't escape the feeling that there's some connection."

10

Paris

Chief Magistrat André Malevu, built close to the ground with a low center of gravity, knobby hands like thick Jerusalem Tubers and an explosive temper, was a man one gave wide berth. Still unmarried at fifty-two, he possessed a brilliant mind, roiling ambition and strident xenophobic views. His extreme social polemics shocked his courtly colleagues but endeared him to ultra-conservative members of the French establishment and a sizeable portion of the great French heartland of small villages, rural farms and simple people suspicious of immigrants, outsiders and a changing world - *la France profonde.*

Malevu knew that as a jurist his colleagues expected him to avoid controversy. Yet he dismissed his critics as old-fashioned.

"I won't tolerate political correctness when the future of France is at stake. We've had enough of weak liberals who've abandoned the working families of France and corrupted our values. It's time for France to be great again."

His impassioned ultra-nationalist, anti-immigrant views though alarming, were as nothing when he turned to the subject of the United States.

"We would have been better off with Hitler," he'd say. "Yes, he had his faults but at least he was a strong leader who, by the way, treated us with more respect than the Americans. My father told me that during the war if you offered a German officer a cigarette he only took one. An American GI took the whole pack. Americans are an uncivilized lot who've debauched our culture for seventy years."

Whatever fountainhead fed Malevu's swamping hatred of the United States remained unexplained to the rest of the world. But those who sympathized with the fiery jurist quietly signaled their approval of his France First belligerence by flexing their political and financial influence. Soon after the death of magistrat Abelard, Malevu had been appointed senior juge d'instruction of the elite and secretive Paris court overseeing terrorism and other sensitive threats to the Republic. In the pecking order of Paris' judicial system Malevu had now become the most powerful jurist in France with authority so broad the average citizen would have been aghast.

11

Bethesda, Maryland

"Agent Stone, good morning."

Izzy heard her name. She blinked and tried to focus.

"I'm doctor Brian. How are you this morning?"

She was coming back, but confused. Tubes, wires, beeping and some type of humming noise...

Where am I?

She squinted and peered out. A stout, balding figure in a white coat was standing at the foot of the bed.

"It's okay," Brian said. "You're at Bethesda Naval Hospital and you're safe."

She fought the mental fog and visually tried to follow the doctor as he moved around the bed, looking at various machines and checking a chart. He took her left wrist, checked her pulse then stepped back with obvious satisfaction.

"You're gonna be just fine," he said. "You've been through a rough patch the last few weeks. Kept us pretty busy, but you look great this morning. It's a beautiful day and… there's someone very special to see you."

Izzy blinked her eyes to sharpen her focus. Bright sunshine. The pleasant fragrance of fresh-cut flowers. Several people in the room and a vague soreness on her right side. The fog was dissipating. Footsteps. Someone approaching.

"Agent Stone, good morning. It's Leyland."

The president smiled as he approached, his voice, deeper and thicker than she remembered.

"You're looking much improved," the president said. "I'm truly gratified."

"Thank you, sir," Izzy said, in a weak, raspy voice. Her throat felt parched making her words sound more like a croak.

She tried to sit up but winced.

"Whoa, there," the president said, reaching towards her. "War's over. Don't go jumping out of bed for me."

She noticed a stitch line above his left eye. Around it a large fading bruise.

"Yes, sir," Izzy said, easing herself back onto the pillows.

"Mind if I pull up a chair?" he said, sliding a small metal seat to her bedside. His six-foot three frame and long legs dwarfed the chair. He leaned towards her, his face resting on folded hands.

"How're you doin', Izzy?" his tone was gentle, heartfelt.

"Little sore."

"Well, knowin' you," he said, "I'll take that as a Texas-sized understatement."

His delivery was lighthearted and disarming. But Izzy had witnessed the mannerism many times when traveling with the president. It usually presaged a more serious moment.

He leaned in, his manner more subdued.

"Izzy, I came this morning because I wanted to see for myself that you're healing. The doctors say you'll be at one hundred percent in no time, and that's just great. Been say'n a prayer for you every night."

She managed a small smile of acknowledgement.

He looked down for a moment, nodded faintly to himself and looked back at her.

"I also came because I wanted to thank you for everything you did in Amman. I probably wouldn't be here but for the raw courage and professionalism you displayed. And I'm so deeply grateful that you're still with us."

"Thank you, sir."

Izzy had a sudden flashback and felt a wave of emotion sweep over her.

The president leaned closer his words just above a whisper.

"Now, Izzy," he said, "I need to say something to you." He seemed to be summoning his thoughts, fighting to control his emotions.

"I know… there will be days when you'll re-live and re-think Amman. It's natural. I... I've been doing it a lot myself. But I'm going to ask you to promise me you'll never regret or second-guess any of your actions that day." He paused.

"Truth is, that in a moment of mortal danger and against all odds you saved lives, brought great honor to your country, your colleagues and yourself. I know that's how I'll remember you on that day. That's how we'll all remember you. And that's how I'd like you to remember it too. Will you do that for me?"

"Yes, Mr. President."

"You get well now, we need you. When you feel up to it come by and we'll have a proper visit. Coffee's on me. Deal?"

"Deal," she said, in a voice so subdued she wasn't sure he'd even heard her.

He smiled again, a poignant smile that seemed to leave something unsaid. He placed his right hand on her left shoulder affectionately tapped it twice, stood up and walked toward the door.

"Sir," Izzy said, her throat tightening. *Could she get the question out?*

The president turned. "Yes, Izzy?"

"Sir, the First Lady?"

A pall descended on the room leaving the question hanging mid-air.

The president returned to her bedside and appeared to float down to a crouch so close to her that she was sure she could hear his heart beat. The color had left his face.

"I'm afraid she didn't make it, Izzy." His voice came from a distant place, had lost its earlier energy. "A bullet severed a major artery, did a lot of other damage. She went pretty fast. At least that was merciful."

He said nothing for a moment then raised himself up slowly, lips pursed, an empty smile on his face, and said. "You come see me when you're up to it. We'll talk." He turned and walked out of the room.

Dr. Brian approached her. "Probably a good idea to rest now."

Izzy ignored the comment. "I noticed some stitches above his eye."

"A bullet graze. Not too bad. But another few centimeters and it would've been fatal."

Brian paused, as though searching for something else to say. After an awkward moment he looked at the two nurses standing nearby then back at Izzy.

"We'll let you rest now."

When they'd left, Izzy fixed her gaze on the closed door, willing it to open, willing the First Lady with her megawatt smile to step into the room light it up and prove it was all a sordid dream.

She lost track of how long she'd been staring at the door, but gradually became aware that the morning sun had shifted its angle in the room.

Izzy lowered her head, placed her hand where the president had touched her shoulder and held it there as her body convulsed with sobs.

12

Islamabad

The burned, mutilated body of Colonel Badar Kahn of the Pakistani ISI was found in a roadside ditch by a truck driver delivering water on the outskirts of the city. The naked body bore evidence of torture and Kahn's tongue had been unceremoniously ripped out. Pakistani police and investigators from the ISI found that Kahn's home had burned to the ground. His wife and children had disappeared. A government official speaking off the record to a prominent journalist made mention of possible gambling debts or a love triangle gone bad adding that Kahn had been a minor, low-level intelligence officer described as a heavy drinker and womanizer by co-workers.

CIA Chief of Station, Bill Powers ginned up his street runners and ISI sources but came up empty-handed. No one was talking and the family was nowhere to be found. A good man was gone and with him the possibility of taking down the world's most wanted terrorist. The grisly murder must have been an inside ISI job.

"Goddammed fuckers!"

He fired off a cable to Langley, went to his favorite watering hole at the Hotel Crown Jewel, sat in a darkened booth and knocked back shots of Jack Daniel's. After a moody hour he took a taxi back to his modest third-floor walk-up apartment, threw up, and drove his fist into the bathroom mirror.

13

Paris

Professor Rene Hachard of the École Supérieure des Arts of Paris had not been sleeping well. The murder-suicide of young Émile had interrupted his sleep night after night. He needed to think things through, clear his mind. What was the connection between Émile's anti-Americanism and the murder of magistrat Abelard?

Why would Émile have chosen the aging Abelard as a target? It was true that unstable people were capable of anything and young fanatics were the most prone to craziness. But something told him this wasn't a simple matter of a spoiled young aristocrat who'd indiscriminately put two bullets into the head of a revered and gentle jurist. And, of course, it didn't escape the professor's notice that Malevu was the one great beneficiary of Abelard's death. Malevu was now immensely powerful. Was that the link? It was a monstrous thought to contemplate. And then there were the police. Detectives had interviewed Hachard about his former student somewhat perfunctorily, it had seemed to him, yet had shared nothing about the investigation, saying only that it was "a matter they could not discuss."

Hachard rose from his chair. His path forward was clear to him now. He knew what he must do.

I can't talk to the same detectives or Dr. Camus or anyone connected to the school. They would simply mark me as a troublemaker and that would be the end of me. Instead I'll try to contact someone at the most senior level of the Préfecture de Police and privately share my concerns about Émile and Malevu. After that, I'll wash my hands of the entire matter.

14

Washington, D.C.

Izzy pushed the polished, brass-frame revolving doors of King's Bar and Grill on 16th Street, NW, not far from the White House and made her way to the wood-beamed Derby Bar where a small group stood drinking at the mahogany counter.

She'd guessed that special agent Will Bergan, her second-in-command, and several of her Secret Service detail would be at their favorite after-work watering hole. They were.

Five weeks at Bethesda Hospital had been just about all the pampering she could take. *I'm ready to get back in the game.*

She took a deep breath, threw her head back and walked up to the group.

"Well, I've never seen a sorrier-looking bunch!" she said.

"Izzy!" Will said, as he and the others turned and saw her.

Shouting *Hooah*s and high-fiving each other Will and the other agents rushed to give her a big hug.

"Easy with the merchandise, boys," Izzy said. "There's a heck of a restocking charge if they send me back to Bethesda."

"Izzy, it's damned good to see you," Will said. "We've been on the road with POTUS and just had a couple of chances to drop in on you at the hospital.

Not that it did any good. You were *non compos mentis*."

"They told me, thanks, guys." She said, "but enough chit chat, boys, is anybody going to buy me a drink?"

The bar erupted as agents scrambled to get the barkeep's attention.

Izzy took in the scene –*It's good to be back.*

They lingered in the Derby Bar, exchanging anecdotes avoiding any further mention of Amman. Platters of Bee's River oysters, Jose Cuervo and Cuban Chicharonnes were downed as Izzy and her team reveled in seeing each other again.

Afterward they commandeered a table in the Senate Room, a snug, mahogany-paneled alcove located on the upper level where they downed large portions of house-smoked New Orleans ribs, mashed potatoes, corn on the cob, Caesar salads, Capitol Pie, and several bottles of Australian merlot.

As the evening wound down and rounds of brandies were ordered izzy looked at her comrades, resting her gaze on each, drawing quiet comfort from their presence and their genuine affection.

Will Bergan had taken note of Izzy's sudden subdued composure.

"Izzy, you haven't said a thing for a while. You okay?'

"I'm good," Izzy said, giving Will a light pat on the back, "let's just say I've been looking forward to this reunion ever since I woke up in Bethesda feeling like I'd been hit by a Peterbilt eighteen-wheeler."

Will and the others looked on in silence.

"I want you to know that I really missed you guys..." Izzy struggled to maintain her composure, "and I really, really miss the ones who didn't make it."

No one spoke for a long moment.

Then Will rose, turned to Izzy and raised his glass.

"To courage...to honor...to the Service."

The others stood, turned to Izzy and lifted their glasses, their expressions a mosaic of emotions.

15

Later that night, Izzy eased herself onto the green velvet Victorian chaise-lounge resting by the large sitting-room windows of her Georgetown townhouse.

Outside, a light rain was falling. The amber glow of the quaint lamps along the leaf-strewn cobblestone street evoked in her mind an earlier Georgetown, a time of horse-drawn carriages, long dresses and mannered society.

Izzy loved the timeless beauty of the scene, when leaves slipped into golden yellows, pinks and russets, creating a lush tapestry of color on the red-brick sidewalks.

She felt emotionally drained. She knew she had not fully healed. The physical injuries from Amman had mended for the most part, but it was the deeper injury, the one tied to the loss of the First Lady that troubled her sleep. She had replayed the final scene countless times, asking herself if she had missed something that could have prevented the death of Meg Childs. She had no final answers. Nor could she ignore the bond that fear, violence and survival had forged that morning and now drew her to the president in a way she'd never contemplated. She felt conflicted, confused, and was struggling with powerful emotions. She needed time to sort it all out.

16

Islamabad

Powers had used every human and technical asset available to him to find out what had happened to Kahn's wife and children. If there were witnesses they were either unable or too frightened to come forward. NSA sigint intercepts of ISI and Foreign Ministry traffic were equally unproductive as were back-channel inquiries. Powers, not easily given to guilt or second-guessing, was nevertheless having a hard time sleeping. He did not want to dwell on the darker possibilities, but could not avoid them. Did the ISI have the family? If so were they being brutally interrogated? And if ISI was responsible for the family's disappearance were they still alive? The only thing he could do at this point was to hope that someone, somewhere would provide answers.

17

Paris

Professor Rene Hachard pulled his overcoat more tightly around him to ward off the night chill. He gripped his briefcase firmly and scuttled down the stairs of the RER B train stop at *Lozere* just south of Paris. It was past eleven at night and he didn't want to miss the last train back to the city.

He'd just left the École Supérieure campus after a long evening reviewing exam papers - always an excruciating experience. *Didn't anyone know how to write an exam anymore?* The essays increasingly resembled error filled text messages and one hundred-forty character tweets. Hachard was anxious to get home to Sylvie where a late dinner and an ample supply of Burgundy awaited.

Tonight there was no one else on the quay - not unusual given the lateness of the hour. One never knew what to expect on the RER, especially on the outskirts of Paris. Some days, it teemed with riders, other days not. Still, he always felt uneasy surveying a platform devoid of trains, gendarmes or passengers.

He drew some comfort from the fact that Paris trains were exceptionally punctual, which meant his train would arrive in less than two minutes.

He was relieved to see two sturdy RER maintenance workers lumbering down the stairs with cleaning equipment. Hachard counted himself lucky not to be in their shoes. The Paris rail system was a wondrous thing, envied round the world. But keeping it safe and clean and running required an army of sweepers, electricians, painters, and masons.

Hachard felt the familiar tremor and rush of air that always preceded the train's imminent arrival.

As the cars emerged from the tunnel and surged toward the quay, Hachard felt himself suddenly lifted on either side by powerful hands, then propelled, legs dangling, feet peddling wildly, toward the edge of the platform and violently sent airborne directly into the path of the engineer's hurtling cabin.

Izzy's secure cell phone was vibrating. She looked at the screen. *White House switchboard.* The call was from her assistant Wanda. She pressed talk.

"Stone."

"Hi, it's Wanda. There's a call for you from Vincent at the French Embassy. I told him you're out of town and really busy but he said you would be interested in what he had to say. Shall I put him through?"

"Sure. Thanks, Wanda." A moment later, Vincent was connected.

"Vincent, it's Izzy."

"*Bonjour,* Izzy."

"Hi. I'm in Chicago with the boss. Good thing you got me at the hotel I have to leave soon for an event here. What's up?"

"Yes, I saw that the president is speaking there today. I won't keep you but I thought you might want to know this. You recall the death of magistrat Abelard?"

"Yes, of course."

"Well, yesterday a respected professor at the university that the young assassin attended was found dead in a metro station. The engineer who was driving the train says he believes the professor was thrown into the path of the train."

"Jesus," said Izzy. Any connection to the student?"

"Perhaps. It seems that the professor, whose name was Hachard, taught the young man and had expressed serious concerns about the student's anti-American attitudes."

"Anti-American attitudes? This gets stranger," said Izzy. "So a powerful jurist who has no enemies is assassinated by a rich university student with anti-American attitudes who then commits suicide, and now the professor who taught him is dead. What do the police make of it?"

"Well, you can imagine. They say they have launched a major investigation but at the moment there are more questions than answers."

"Keep me posted," said Izzy. "Got to run."

"*À bientôt*, Izzy."

"*À bientôt.*"

18

Washington, D.C. Press Club

Former vice president Davis strode heavily down the hallway of the National Press Club on Fourteenth Street. His face was a tight grimace, head skewed forward as though it wanted to arrive first. Ever since the federal indictment had come down naming him as a criminal co-conspirator in a massive arms-dealing corruption case, the Washington press corps, had been eager to direct fire at him as payback for the way he'd treated them during his tenure as vice-president.

He would have been the first to admit he'd treated them with disdain during his all too short four years in the White House. In his mind, when it came to the Washington press corps the First Amendment was greatly overrated and, as far as he'd been concerned, optional. There'd been no second term, something he and the former president had blamed on a sinister left-wing media conspiracy of slander.

"Chester," president Koch had once said to him in his inimitable South Carolina drawl, "why don't you just play along with those fellas. I know they're a no-good bunch o' sunsabitches but show'em a little leg. It'll do us both a world'a good."

As with all the other cornball advice Koch had proffered over the years, Davis ignored it. The former president was a fool. Always had been.

"What kind of a turnout is it?" Davis snapped, turning to his press aide, Ron Tanaka, a five-foot eight, one-hundred-ten-pound workaholic who spoke in a rapid-fire clip.

Davis was agitated. When he spoke, his large restive hands and aggressive body language invaded the personal space of anyone near him. He was a political carnivore who spent his days replaying every indignity, real or imagined, ever suffered, and every score to be settled.

"About eighty print and electronic," Ron said. "GNN, BBN, the Nets, Washington Daily, New York Globe, etc., ...it's a shark swarm. They smell blood."

Davis' anger grew. *It's that goddamn Leyland Childs and his Justice Department who are behind the Grand Jury indictment. But that smart-ass president's pulling the tiger's tail goin' after me.*

"Slow down at bit," Davis said, scowling at Tanaka, whose rapid strides were leaving Davis winded.

At age sixty-six Davis sported a pacemaker and a ragged line of ugly, dull-pink, raised abdominal scars, the result of a quadruple heart-bypass operation.

His corpulent body and stooped posture gave stark evidence of a physically sedentary life.

Four years of boring White House photo ops, mind-ossifying West Wing policy sessions and dreary Potemkin cabinet meetings where he and the President had routinely feigned pretense they actually practiced government by input had almost been too much for his sanity. That, combined with the odious barnstorming trips to the American "heartland," where he obligingly throttled down rhubarb pie, tailgate burgers, short ribs and grits that he considered as inedible as the Polish kielbasa, Russian borscht, Salvadoran pupusas, Ethiopian doro wat and other ethnic foods gleefully thrust upon him day after day – had gradually morphed his body, a once reasonably athletic physique, into a sluggish, trans-fat vestibule.

Still, he had to admit that as much as he had loathed the mindless backslapping rituals, it had been a whole lot better being a sitting vice-president than being an "ex" under federal indictment.

19

Izzy was sitting on a shield-back side chair that was upholstered in a Jacquard floral damask print when the door to the Oval Office opened. She stood as Hannah Wellborn, the president's personal secretary approached.

"The President will see you now, Agent Stone."

Though the two knew each other well, Hanna was always careful to acknowledge Izzy's official position.

"Thank you, Hannah."

Izzy had gotten to know Hannah after becoming head of the presidential detail. An intelligent, laconic New Englander in her fifties, Hannah functioned as gatekeeper of the Oval Office, a simple fact that made her one of the most important staff members in the West Wing. Pity the visitor who thought of her as nothing more than a high paid secretary. Izzy had seen Hannah keep self-important Committee

Chairmen and industry titans cooling their heels while allowing others of lesser stature to step in for a minute or two of the president's time. She could charm effortlessly but would not be charmed.

"Izzy," Hannah once told her. "I don't have the luxury of chatting. It leads to special favors being asked."

But this morning, Hannah broke her usual reserve and turned to Izzy, her eyes misting.

"I just want you to know what an honor it is to know you."

Izzy placed her hand lightly on Hanna's arm.

"Thank you, Hannah, it's good to be back," and strode into the Oval Office.

The room never failed to awe. The historic space gleamed in the splendid mid-day light filtering through the eleven-foot high windows facing the South Lawn. In the center of the room, an oval, ivory-colored starburst rug bearing the presidential seal echoed the oval shape of the office. On a wall to the right of the Resolute, the president's desk, a luminous painting by Childe Hassam added to the subdued elegance.

"Izzy, come on in," the president said, smiling broadly as he stepped away from the desk to shake her hand.

"Good afternoon, Mr. President."

"It's good to see you again, Izzy. You look wonderful. Please sit down."

"Thank you, sir."

He motioned her to one of the two gold fabric divans next to a cherry-wood coffee table bearing a wedge cut crystal bowl filled with crimson apples. A silver coffee pot and two china cups and saucers rested on a small side table next to the president.

Izzy sat down on one of the divans.

The president dropped easily into a high-back colonial wing chair upholstered in striped navy and cream silk. Despite his cheerful tone she noticed fatigue lines framing his eyes, and a new grayness in his temples. She'd heard of sleepless nights and three a.m. walks on the South Lawn.

He leaned forward and cupped his hands under his chin. Izzy noticed the gold wedding band on his ring finger. A sudden pang shot through her.

"About to have my coffee ration," the president said with a wan smile.

"Something I look forward to each day. But the White House physician has drawn the line at two cups. It's a challenge for a serial coffee-drinker from Seattle like me. Won't you please join me? Cream? Sugar?"

"Yes, I mean no, thank you." Izzy said, somewhat flustered.

"Got it," the president said, "It's black, straight up."

Izzy was still unsure as to the purpose of the visit. She hoped it did not involve a transfer to a desk job.

The president poured two steaming cups and handed one to Izzy.

"Thank you, sir."

He took a quick sip from his cup and beamed.

She was amused and charmed by his obvious pleasure. She took a sip. Hot and delicious. His demeanor softened, his tone muted, more intimate.

"Izzy, what happened in Amman dwarfed any personal danger I ever imagined I'd face. We all know there are folks out there who want to harm us. Still, I suppose I'd secretly hoped we'd be spared a truly awful day."

Izzy studied the president's face for clues. His eyes conveyed inner turmoil.

"In one violent moment they took Meg. I don't know that I'll ever recover from the loss and the guilt. Then there are the twelve agents who died protecting me. You almost died. How can I ever repay that debt?"

"Mr. President, I grieve for your loss. I too feel I failed in not keeping the First Lady out of harm's way. It's caused me much pain. But I console myself remembering that those of us who fought, even died on that day would gladly do so again. If you'll forgive me, sir, you're not just a man or a president; you are the symbol of everything our country stands for. To let them take you would've been to let them take away everything we cherish. Those who fell paid a heavy price but it's no less a price than has been paid by so many others before."

Childs was moved by Izzy's words and found it ironic that the person who had risked everything to save him and had been so grievously wounded herself was now doing the comforting.

"Izzy, I can't tell you how much those words mean to me." He paused. "You know, while you were at Bethesda I met with your mother. I know how devastating the tragic loss of your dad was for the two of you. It made me ask myself if I had the right to place you in more danger and risk bringing more pain to your mom. Yet there's no one I'd rather have watching my back. But only you can make that call. Take a few days to think on it. I'll respect your decision."

"Yes sir, I will," Izzy said.

The president stood. Izzy took the cue and stood too. It was time to leave. Then to her surprise he took her hand and gently clasped it between his hands.

He held it for a long moment as if about to say something more then nodded slightly in silence, apparently shaking off a thought, and simply said:

"God bless."

"Thank you, Mr. President," she said, touched by the unexpected display of affection. She turned and walked out of the Oval Office.

20

Driving back to her townhouse Izzy tried to sort out the events of the last few weeks. While greatly relieved that the president had not arranged to have her promoted to some desk job with a fancy title, she wondered what to make of his offer. He'd obviously left the door open. Was he implying that it would be better if she moved on? The remark about watching his back. True? Or, just a polite way of telling her that if she was reassigned, it wouldn't be because he'd developed any reservations about her? Then there was the way he'd held her hand. What was it he wanted to say?

Is there some sort of emotional or psychological pathology at work that makes me more important to him? Could it be something as simple as fear? Fear that he's not safe if I'm not there beside him? Am I his rabbit's foot now? Is it something else?

She recalled how he'd kept his wits about him as he tried to save the first lady's life even as gunmen descended on him. No, the president didn't lack courage. And since Amman, he'd evidenced great concern about her future safety should her identity and actions in saving him from certain death that day become public. She didn't need a target on her back for every crackpot and terrorist out there. As a result the Secret Service and key players in the intelligence community had put a tight lid on the identity of all agents who'd been in the firefight, merely commenting that "courageous agents of the Service had foiled a violent attempt on the president in Amman;" that several had been mortally wounded in the assault, and others were recovering from their injuries.

Her cell phone buzzed. She looked at the number.

It's Greg.

Izzy assumed that Greg Neal, her wonky on-off boyfriend who worked at Global Solutions, a Washington think tank, was calling to apologize for his petulant outburst at dinner two nights earlier. He'd been upset that she hadn't shown more enthusiasm about an op-ed piece he'd been asked to write for the Washington Daily, the Capitol's leading newspaper. But she'd found the subject of European Union monetary policy dry and boring.

I suppose I could have shown a little more enthusiasm. He must have worked hard on the article.

She pressed the talk button.

"Hi, Greg."

"Izzy, I'm so sorry, can you forgive me?"

"You're forgiven. And I'm sorry I didn't show more interest in your piece."

"No worries. Listen, Iz, there's a very cool event in Foggy Bottom on Friday evening. They've invited a couple of us at Global. We can bring a guest."

Izzy felt her stomach tighten.

"There'll be a lot of foreign policy folks from the Hill, from State and the diplomatic corps. It's black-tie. Should be a lot of fun. Won't you please come?" Izzy pulled off to a side street and stopped. She could feel the stress building. But maybe Greg had a point. A social evening might be a welcome break from her constant mental replaying of Amman.

"Izzy? Still there?"

"Okay, Greg, sounds like fun."

"Great," he said. "I'll text you the details. Can we meet up at the embassy? I'll be on a tight schedule."

"No problem. See you there," Izzy said blandly and pressed the "OFF" button.

Jesus, why did I say yes?

She wasn't sure how she felt about Greg anymore. It didn't seem that they were connecting on any level. She realized she'd been pulling away from his attentions and intimacy was no longer a part of their relationship.

So much has changed. Am I even capable of a serious relationship at this point?

Greg just wanted to go back to the way things had been before Amman. Impossible.

21

The White House
Second Floor Living Quarters
3:00 a.m.

Meg, I miss you so much.

It was another sleepless night for Leyland Childs. The president was in the paneled study of the upstairs residence of the White House holding a framed photo of his wife, Meg.

It's hard to believe fifteen years have gone by since Egypt.

In the photo, Meg sat smiling on an eight-foot Bactrian camel, her hazel green eyes focused on some distant point. They were atop the Giza plateau on the west bank of the great Nile. Meg was leaning forward under the noon sun, a safari hat casting a faint shadow across her face, her white linen bush shirt opened wide at the neck where small beads of perspiration had formed. In the distance the Great pyramid of Giza seemed to float on shimmering waves of heat.

Childs, recalled that he'd been wearing a brown khaki shirt, jodhpurs, ammo boots and a cream-colored Woolseley pith helmet.

We were just an ordinary American couple on an adventure. Things were so much simpler then, long before the politics began. If I could turn back the clock I'd return to that perfect moment and never leave.

Childs felt exhausted. For weeks he'd been unable to sleep through the night, often walking in the Rose Garden or the South Lawn until dawn. He had difficulty envisioning a future without Meg. And now, inexplicably there was Izzy. He'd always admired her complete professionalism and dedication to his protection. She was strikingly beautiful and though she was aware of her beauty she neither acknowledged nor denied it. It was just who she was. It allowed her to shoulder the awesome responsibility of protecting the most powerful man on the planet without distraction. But something had changed between them in the months since Amman. And though he tried to push away a gnawing need for her presence he knew he'd never again be able to see her as just his protector.

He made his way from the study to the bedroom, removed his robe, tumbled into bed and turned out the light.

22

Foggy Bottom – Washington, D.C.

Izzy winced.

Dammit, Greg.

Greg had blown up again and stalked out leaving her standing alone in the middle of a chandeliered, cherry-paneled, embassy reception packed with Washington's A-list.

Greg's outburst left her feeling awkward, a half-empty crystal flute of Veuve Cliquot listing precariously in one hand and a tightly held clutch purse in the other as the red satin of her new tube dress amplified the blush spreading across her face. She gave the flute to a passing waiter.

Great, she thought, *I can take down a 240-pound bruiser but I can't handle Greg's childish tantrums.*

People had turned and looked, stared.

Everyone, that is, except the tuxedoed man moving towards her with an open smile and easy gait. He appeared to be in his mid-thirties, tall, wide at the shoulders with an airy confidence that reminded her of the polished, boarding school trust-fund plebes she'd met her first year at West Point.

His urbane manner was in contrast to his hair, an unruly sand-colored mop, that would have been more at home on a wind-blown East Hampton beach, or a rugby field.

"Oh, here you are," he said, as if two friends had drifted apart during the evening and found each other again.

"I'm Liam," he said, *sotto voce* appearing not to notice her flushed cheeks as he inclined his head towards hers in greeting.

"Hi," she said, relieved by the interruption even if it was by a complete stranger. His accent was English. A literate accent. *OxBridge?*

She noticed the room resuming its normal social buzz and turned to him.

"Thanks for the moral support. This room is filled with piranha posing as diplomats."

"I'll take piranha any day," he said. "at least their intentions are unambiguous."

She smiled and extended her hand. "I'm Izzy Stone."

"Liam Cabot." He extended his right hand to hers with a slight, awkward motion.

The movement drew Izzy's attention to his hand, a perfectly constructed five-finger prosthetic hand with a convincing life-like appearance. Hiding her surprise, she took it amiably, struck by the stark contrast between the cold, artificial limb and Liam's otherwise robust physique.

"You're new to Foggy Bottom," Izzy said.

"Correct, do you specialize in faces?" Liam said wryly.

You have no idea, she thought.

"Not really," Izzy said, "just a guess. These soirees are a familiar Merry-Go-Round. Anyone new stands out."

"I see," he said, "although I do believe it was you who was standing out."

"*Touchée,* Mr. Cabot."

"My pleasure, Ms. Stone."

"How long have you been in Washington?" she said.

"Just recently arrived from across the Pond."

Izzy's West Point linguistics caught an inflection, subtle, almost undetectable, something about the way he pronounced the word 'pond' – *Slavic?*

"Liam, Izzy!"

Both turned in the direction of a beaming, attractive blonde walking towards them in a short, skin-tight, low-cut black dress and heels.

Izzy recognized Heather Fields, a well-connected Senate staffer who used her Stanford smarts and stunning looks to maximum effect in the sex obsessed, male-primate habitat known as the U.S. Senate.

"Heather, hi," Izzy said.

Heather gave Izzy a short hug, placed a firm kiss on Liam's cheek and smiled back at Izzy, "I didn't know you two knew each other."

"Actually, we just met," Izzy said.

Heather placed her hand on Liam's back. "Liam's with the British Embassy," she said. "He and I worked closely on a Senate Sub-Committee matter."

"Sadly, only a few meetings," Liam said ironically. He looked at Izzy. "I'll get us a glass of wine, red? white?"

"White and very dry, please," she said.

"Anything for you, Heather?"

"Thanks, no," she said. Liam headed for the bar.

When he was out of earshot, Izzy turned to Heather.

"He's interesting, who is he?"

"Actually, I don't know much about Liam." Heather said. "Something of a puzzle, charming but hard to pin down. The word is that he's from an influential British family with a country manse straight out of Brideshead. He has some junior position with the British Embassy here. Way below his pay grade in my opinion."

"How so?"

"Well, like I said we worked together. A god-awful trade issue. Half the time he didn't show up for the meetings. But when he did the men hated him, way too smart, and the women all wanted to have his baby..."

Heather saw Izzy roll her eyes upward... "sorry, Izzy, and pardon my French, but he's just got that look."

"Aah, and what about you?" Izzy said, with unconvincing indifference.

Heather produced a facetious look. "You mean do I like him? What do you think?" she said, "tried, but I'm not his proverbial cup of tea."

Liam was returning with the drinks.

"Got to go," Heather said. "Just spotted the chairman of the Senate Banking Committee."

"Bye," Izzy said, watching Heather lock and load her hips as she bore down on the Senator.

"Your wine," Liam said, deftly holding his flute with his artificial right hand and giving Izzy hers with his left.

She noticed there was no ring and was relieved.

"Thanks," she said.

Liam took a sip. "Are you with the diplomatic corps?"

"If you mean the piranha, no," Izzy said.

"Feel safer already," he said, "but I imagine you're not here just to see folks fresh off the boat."

"Well," Izzy said, "I did have a date, but he had to rush off to his think tank."

"Hmm," Liam said, taking a quick sip, "If it's a good think tank he'll waste no time rushing back."

Izzy arched her eyebrows as if to say, *who knows?*

"So, we've established that you're not with the Foreign Service." Liam left the statement hanging mid-air.

"I'm in the security business," Izzy said. "Probably no more interesting than your work with the Embassy." She produced a delphic smile.

Liam grinned broadly. "I've a feeling you're very good at chess," he said.

"I do like chess. I especially like the move where queen takes knight."

They clinked glasses and exchanged an assessing gaze.

"Enjoying your assignment here in Washington?" Izzy said.

"I'm afraid it's a bit boring, I'm sort of an errand boy for the keepers of the flame at the Embassy. When they need a body to warm a chair at some dreary meeting they send yours truly to show the flag, laugh at bad jokes and appear sufficiently grave discussing oxtail tariffs. All shamelessly low-level, actually."

"And you're here tonight, because…?" Izzy said.

"Aaah, truth is, I was dreading it. Had no choice. We small people are just told to go fetch."

A small orchestra had begun playing in an adjoining room and couples were drifting to the dance floor. Liam angled his head slightly and looked at her with a thoughtful expression.

"Would you care to dance?" he said, his words tentative.

"I'd like that," Izzy said.

Liam took her glass and placed it on a nearby waiter's trolley. He placed his on the trolley as well and turned to her, extending his left hand. She placed her hand in his, surprised how naturally they fused – like two molecules adhering perfectly.

When the music ended they made their way to a flowered patio through ceiling-high French doors.

Izzy turned to Liam. "Would you excuse me for a moment?"

"Please," Liam said.

She found her way to the guest bathroom. After checking for other people she locked the door, turned on the faucets, took a small, encrypted cell phone from her clutch and pressed speed dial.

"Will Bergan," a voice said.

"It's Izzy. I need you to run a name. Are you close to your computer?"

"Chained is more like it. My boss's name is Torquemada."

"Right. The name is Liam Cabot, British Embassy, here."

"Hold on," Will said.

Izzy could hear Will typing. She knew he was logging into a secure search engine attached to several intelligence databases. Will was a workaholic, a complete professional and a godsend to her detail. Still, the way he looked at her sometimes made her wonder if his dedication might not be tinged with a bit of infatuation.

"Got it," Will said after a couple of minutes.

"Go," Izzy said.

"Well, he's not a serial killer if that's what you want to know."

"Delighted. What else have you got, Einstein?"

"Right. Do you want the short version...rich, single, or the novel?"

"Let's try the Cliff Notes version."

"Okay. Liam Hastings Somerset Cabot, thirty-four, unmarried. Born in London to old money, attended Harrow public School, DPhil, Oxford University, spent several years in the Middle East, mostly academic conferences, some trade missions. Lost a hand while abroad, no details…I didn't know academia could be so hazardous. Posted to D.C. two months ago. Pretty far down the pecking order at the Embassy. I'm shooting a file photo to you right now."

"Great. Anything else?" Izzy said. "Personal problems? Legal run-ins? Intelligence connection?"

"Nope, clean as a whistle. If there is anything he's really good."

"Thanks, Will."

"I only live to serve you, master."

Izzy felt reassured by Will's report yet an intuition told her there was more. It was not an apprehension but rather an aroused curiosity that drew her back to the patio.

"Still here?" she said.

"Amazing, isn't it?" Liam said. Then: "Say, I know it's late but would you like to get a bite?"

Izzy hesitated for a moment. Her professional watchfulness argued against it. Yet her personal instincts told her otherwise.

"Sounds good," she said, "I'm embassy'd out and I'm famished. But not here. The tables at these events are always piled high with mouthwatering food yet I can never bring myself to eat any of it. In fact, I don't think anyone ever does."

Liam grinned. "True. It's difficult to have a serious discussion about nuclear proliferation and regime change when your mouth is full of sushi."

There it was again. A micro-inflection in the word "change".

With Liam trailing behind, Izzy re-entered the crowded embassy and smoothly navigated her way to the front door, taking her leave of familiar faces and their hosts. After getting her evening shawl from the cloakroom the two stepped out to the *porte-cochère.*

"I'm the newcomer," Liam said as they waited for the valet to bring Liam's car around. "Any suggestions as to where we can go?"

"Yes, I do," Izzy said. "I came by cab but if you'll drive, I'll direct."

The valet pulled up in a vintage, silver Alfa Romeo convertible, its engine emitting a low throaty roar, the steering wheel mounted on the right side. Izzy cast Liam a fleeting glance of approval as she got in.

From Embassy Row, she guided Liam to "M" Street crossing Key Bridge. As the Capital receded behind them they angled northward on Canal Road past Chain Bridge to Clara Barton Parkway.

Above them, fleecy clouds moved languidly in the moonlight, creating dappled pools of luminescence among the Flowering Dogwoods, Japanese Stiltgrass and Wineberry thickets that lined the Potomac. Izzy felt a sudden intoxication as the road slipped away and the stress of Greg's outburst subsided.

A half hour later they left the main road and pulled onto the gravel driveway of a small, rustic inn nestled in a stand of trees. A cool, invigorating breeze was off the river.

Entering, they found a cozy leather booth next to a stone fireplace. The restaurant was now almost empty and the burning logs had reduced to glowing embers. Still, the warmth lingered invitingly. They ordered Slane Castle Irish whiskeys and hickory burgers piled high with shoestring fries.

Izzy made no effort to delve further into Liam's background. She would leave that for tomorrow. Besides, she'd be traveling soon, having informed the president of her decision to stay with the detail. With an upcoming trip to Malaysia, and then later in the year a state visit to Nigeria followed by an economic summit in France the president had seemed genuinely happy that she'd decided to stay.

But tonight, she wanted to leave her professional persona at the door and simply enjoy the company of the Englishman who'd awkwardly entered her life.

Liam seemed to be of a similar disposition and the two spent the waning hours of the evening in easy banter comparing favorite films, sports teams, foods and Liam's encyclopedic knowledge of cars.

Afterward, they drove back to Georgetown along the banks of the broad Potomac, the roadster's engine purring, the top down, Verdi answering the wind and the fragrance of the river.

23

Georgetown – Washington, D.C.

Two weeks on the road with POTUS. I'm beat.

Izzy climbed the weathered brick stairs of her stately Georgetown townhouse, swiped the encrypted card across a metal device located beside the large maple front door, turned the ornate brass handle and went in. She passed through the entryway, briefly glanced at the well-organized stack of mail and magazines the housekeeper had left for her on the walnut architect's table, and stepped into her living room.

The beam-ceiling room was eclectically furnished with Persian rugs, cherry-wood furniture and an *art deco* crystal chandelier. An imposing, gold-leaf mirror hung above the marble fireplace adding depth to the room. Photos of Izzy's family, friends and the president, adorned the mantle.

Izzy placed her briefcase on one of the side chairs. It felt good to be home. After a grueling fourteen-hour return flight from Malasia she needed a mental break. The so-called "good will" trip had been unnerving from beginning to end, plagued by death threats and violent protests. 'Situational awareness' exacted a high price from those responsible for protecting the life of the leader of the free world.

In contrast to the trip's frenzied pace, the solid serenity of the Federal period residence was reassuring. The townhouse with its pedigree of former statesmen and wealthy patrons seemed in some inchoate way to say that the pressures and human foibles that daily sought to ensnare her were no more than small, angry brush-strokes on life's larger canvas. The graceful permanence of the structure spoke to Izzy's recurring need for perspective and balance; for reaffirmation of the value of her work, the basic goodness of people, and the transience of evil.

Situated on a corner of tree-shaded R Street NW and Thirty-First, the top floor of the residence with its tall French windows looked out onto the beautiful gardens, terraces and grounds of the historic estate of Dumbarton Oaks. The privacy of her location on the block allowed Izzy the personal luxury of shedding honed wariness at the door, and reconnecting with herself.

She turned on the sound system, toggled her iTunes playlist and selected *A Case of You,* one of her vintage favorites, as she happily shed her bulky purse, two side-arms (a Sig-Sauer and small Derringer), secret service ID, communications gear, field shoes, dark blue suit, white linen blouse and undergarments - until she was finally naked as a newborn... safe, happy, in her private domain.

Later, following a long bath, feeling deliciously relaxed, Izzy wrapped her wet hair in a fresh towel, put on a white floor-length silk robe embroidered with cherry-blossoms, and went downstairs to prepare a pot of Mandarin green tea.

She placed the kettle on the stove and turned on the burner.

"Zinnnng, zinnnng."

The zithered sound of the landline broke Izzy's reverie. She looked at the caller-ID screen.

Mom.

She flinched and turned off the burner. It would be a long conversation after a long, long day.

Loss and tragedy had changed her mother so much over the years that it was hard to talk to her now. The violent murder of Izzy's dad, a wealthy developer, during a street robbery when Izzy was only ten, had left her mom inconsolable, irreparably damaged. Izzy had been with her dad that day shopping for her first bicycle when three men demanded money then attacked without warning as she stood screaming in horror.

The trauma of that day had haunted Izzy all her life. But unlike her mother she"d become a survivor who'd turned the loss, the pain and the anger into a ferocious drive to achieve, to excel, to vanquish all competitors. Her mother had not been so fortunate gradually retreating further and further into herself, unwilling to return to the world of literature, art and music that had once defined her.

Izzy pressed TALK.

"Hi, Mom."

24

Paris

"So, the American president is going to Nigeria then coming to France for a G6 meeting."

Chief Magistrat André Malevu was in chambers. He put down the morning paper with a gesture of disgust, took a short sip of his *infusion*, sat back in his oversized leather chair and considered the news. Though a jurist, he nonetheless possessed the political viscera of a populist and the personal habits of a barroom brawler.

Malevu's mind was in overdrive.

He believed the sacred France of his youth and that of his forebears was dying. There were many reasons of course. First, thanks to hordes of immigrant Turks, Romani, Muslims, Africans and god knew what other overly fertile undesirables, France was in danger of losing its genetic identity. Second, the European Union had given faceless bureaucrats in Brussels indiscriminate power over the citizenry of France. The Franc was long gone, sacrificed to the Euro. Would the next generation even have a French flag?

These influences were bad, and there were others. But in his mind, the greatest threat to France, the once-upon-a-time France of empire, literature, art, science and commerce, was coming from the United States. For decades, no, generations, Americans had been tearing through two thousand years of French traditions and institutions leaving a trail of banality and destruction. Small farmers, boucheries, cremeries and boulangeries were being driven to extinction by American copycat hyper-marches selling cheap mass-produced cheeses, breads and meats. Restaurants, tabacs, bistros were disappearing thanks to souless American fast-food chains. American jeans, sneakers, T-shirts, slang and social media were everywhere. French television and motion picture producers, directors, and film studios owners were being crushed by two-hundred-million-dollar Hollywood blockbusters and warmed-over television re-runs.

France was facing an existential crisis. Yet Malevu was a realist. He knew he could not reverse the powerful American influences driving those changes. But in his own way, on his own terms he would strike a blow for France. He would make a point. He would be remembered as the man who had singlehandedly brought America to its knees, if only for one earth-shaking moment. It was something that Magistrat Georges Abelard would never have grasped. The meddlesome old man wouldn't have understood that whatever benefits Americans had bestowed on France in the twentieth century, they were dwarfed by the collateral damage. Fortunately, Abelard was dead and it was he, magistrat André Malevu who was now France's pre-eminent *juge d'instruction.*

Yes, a blow must be struck. But how? When? Simply attending a G6 meeting is hardly a good enough reason to bring the American President to account. No, that would be seen as lunacy. I will just have to wait for the right opportunity to present itself.

25

Virginia

Former vice-president Chester Davis watched the fading afternoon light and checked his watch again.

Goddammit, Wheeler, where are you?

Davis did not like it when people weren't on time. Exactly on time. Sure, sometimes folks were just late. But in the high-wire act of deception and Potemkin politics that had spanned Davis' life, lateness, like honesty, usually spelled trouble.

"Make sure you're not followed," he'd told Wheeler when he gave him the location deep in the Virginia woods. "Take I-95 then switch to the back roads that I marked on the map. Pull over from time to time to check for cars, cyclists, helos, drones."

Davis wasn't sure it had been a good idea to go ahead with the meet. It had been set in motion by an early morning call to him three days earlier.

"There's an old friend of yours who has information you might be interested in," the caller had said. "Here's the number. Tell him you have a question about sailing."

The caller had not identified himself. He didn't need to. Davis immediately recognized the distinctive bulldog voice of his former chief-of-staff Don Gates.

Using a disposable phone, Davis placed the call.

"Yeah," the voice at the other end said.

"An acquaintance said you could help me with a question about sailing," Davis said.

"Are you on a secure phone?" the voice asked.

"Better. A disposable."

The conversation had been brief, a rendezvous location agreed on. Davis liked what he'd heard so far. But Davis would have to find a way to shake his secret service detail for a day.

It hadn't been that hard.

He'd told the head of his detail that an old female friend had popped up and he needed privacy. "No need to advertise, I'll be ok by myself," he'd said.

"Got it," the agent said, feigning male complicity.

Davis hadn't bought it for a moment. He guessed his minders were indifferent to whether some malcontent shot him dead or some drunk ran him down.

He just figured it was organizational payback for the dismissive way he'd treated Secret Service agents during his White House years. It didn't matter. As far as Davis was concerned, they were merely the hired help.

Still, involving himself directly with Wheeler was dicey. Thirty years in Washington's snake pit had taught him that whether mistress or priest, no one could be trusted. If Wheeler were caught or got cold feet there would be no firewall, no deniability. On the other hand, the more people involved the greater the risk of exposure. Better to keep the circle small. Besides, risk or no, the opportunity Wheeler presented simply could not be passed up.

Davis had been looking for a way to derail president Childs ever since the federal indictment had come down. Now Wheeler had handed him the perfect opportunity on a plate, or to be more exact, in an algorithm. Pulling it off would be sweet revenge.

Childs, you bastard, you'll regret you ever went after me.

Davis peered down the narrow dirt road that led from the small cabin to the thick stand of elms and oaks bordering the approach. The shadows cast by the tall trees had lengthened, obscuring the path.

The distant humming of a motor caught his attention. Then two headlights appeared far down the road. Davis felt his body tense. The headlights grew larger, bobbing as the vehicle traversed the uneven surface. The humming was louder. Davis felt his heart beat faster.

Moments later a red, late-model Crown Vic lumbered onto the gravel driveway with a crunching sound, and stopped. The clearing fell silent except for the hum of unseen cicadas. The car's headlights bathed the front porch of the cabin, illuminating Davis. He'd mentally rehearsed a cover story in case the driver turned out to be someone else.

The headlights extinguished and the driver's door swung open.

In the dim light cast by the porch light, Davis saw Colonel Bud Wheeler, former lead submarine-missile targeting officer at the Pentagon, swivel his large body and drop his left foot onto the gravel driveway with a thud. Even in the weak light, Davis could make out the metal brace Wheeler had limped around on since the First Gulf War. Why he hadn't upgraded to a better, high-tech device remained a mystery to Davis. But there were a lot things Davis didn't understand about Wheeler, though he'd known the man for twenty years.

The one true thing he did know was that Wheeler had an abiding hatred of the individual sitting in the Oval Office. A red-hot, volcanic sentiment they both shared, though for different reasons.

Davis watched as Wheeler extended his other leg onto the gravel and leveraged himself out of the Vic.

At six-foot-five inches, forty-seven-year-old Wheeler towered over the vehicle with his massive body.

"C'mon in." Davis snapped as Wheeler approached the porch.

Wheeler barely acknowledged Davis and made his way to the low-lying stairs, his rigid left leg providing a heavy accent.

The cabin, a small wood frame structure, contained a sparsely furnished living room that opened to a cramped weakly illuminated dining room.

Davis motioned Wheeler to an aging wood chair at the rough-hewn oak table and pulled up a chair for himself.

"Drink?" Davis said reaching for the near-full bottle of Old Grand Dad on the table.

"Sure."

Davis picked up the bottle and filled two heavy glass tumblers. They each took a stiff drink.

Davis leaned forward.

"How confident are you in the intel?" he said.

"Intel's good enough that CIA and DOD are recommending POTUS green light the operation," Wheeler said.

"D'you know anything about the identity of the target or the *humint* source in Islamabad that passed the information to Langley?"

"Can't help you there," Wheeler said, "Lid's on tight. All I know is that it's a high-value target. But there's been a glitch somewhere. A few weeks ago CentCom was all hot and bothered to do the missile strike, probably sub-launched. Predator Hellfire might work to but they wanna make sure he's dead as the Wicked Witch of the West. Something went wrong so now they're in a hurry-up-and-wait mode."

Davis took another swallow. "Okay," he said, "assuming we all get lucky, the human intel holds up and the president authorizes a sub strike, how will it go down?"

"Once the White House gives the green light," Wheeler said, "the commander of a designated sub will be advised of the mission on an eyes only basis. He'll be given target coordinates by Joint Operations Command. The crew won't be informed of the human target or targets until the operation is complete and the White House goes public."

"What's your role in the operation?" Davis said.

"Although I was transferred out of the missile targeting unit when this ass-hole administration came in, I can still hack into it."

"How?" said Davis.

"I built a back door into the system. I can change the targeting coordinates, send that fucking missile anywhere I want. Just has to be at the very last moment, otherwise they'll be on to it."

"How difficult will it be to nudge the solution?" Davis said.

"Not very. We're talking about a slight shift in the point of impact. By the time anyone catches the change it'll be too late."

Davis knew they were at the moment where he had to put the matter directly to Wheeler.

"You realize," Davis said, "that you'll face court martial and worse if you're found out."

"I crossed that bridge when I decided to contact you," Wheeler said. "I'm willing to take the risk if it means that son-of-a-bitch in the Oval Office ends up looking like a horse's ass to the whole frigg'n world." Wheeler tossed back the remaining whisky. "This military investigation he's cranked up is gonna burn a bunch of my buddies. Maybe even yours truly."

Davis unleashed his signature crooked smile, an expression somewhere between a twisted sneer and wicked amusement – it was an ugly smile.

26

Izzy's chance encounter with Liam Cabot at the embassy party had led to brief coffees, spur of the moment bag lunches and two matinee movies. Both were already over-programmed yet made an effort to spend time with each other whenever they could.

Izzy knew that Heather Fields, their mutual friend from the Hill, had filled Liam in on Izzy's sensitive position as head of the presidential detail. Izzy appreciated that after acknowledging the fact, Liam had simply moved on to other topics.

Her own attempts to elicit more detail about his role at the British Embassy occasioned humorous self-effacing anecdotes about his junior as opposed to her senior level of responsibility.

"Izzy," he'd say, "I'm afraid if I gave you chapter and verse of my day, you'd find it dreadfully boring and send me on my way. I'd never recover."

On her own Izzy had vetted Liam through contacts at the State Department and found nothing inconsistent with what she already knew. She suspected there was more, yet she didn't feel that whatever the "more" might be, that it involved a character flaw.

A text message popped up on her private cell phone one afternoon.

"Knight invites queen to dinner and would greatly enjoy a re-match. This Friday okay?"

She smiled to herself and composed a reply.

Would love to. Have weekend off, finally. This time you pick the place. BTW, love Italian :)

Izzy had been spent a lot of time thinking about Liam since the embassy party. There'd been something that had awakened in her that night, something she'd not felt before. A connection she could analyze and quantify...but not fully explain. The more time they spent together, the more she felt her feelings validated. Liam's droll wit, intelligence, physical make-up and gentle mien were an important part of the attraction. But there was something else, ineluctable, a sweet harmony, like a perfect musical motif, that drew her to him– she imagined two orchestral strings in sympathetic vibration, entwining in endless variation.

27

"The restaurant was great," Izzy said, as they walked along the scenic C&O canal in Georgetown, Liam's arm gently wrapped around her shoulders.

It was early evening. A hint of rain was in the air.

"Glad you liked it," Liam said. "It's a bit hard to find, but the food is terrific. Did you enjoy the osso buco?"

"Excellent. And the red Piedmont Nebbiolo was perfect."

They made their way up Wisconsin Avenue passing the small bookstores, cheerful pubs and shops frequented by students from nearby Georgetown University. The soft, golden incandescence from within evoked in Izzy's mind a picturesque Dickensian tableau.

As they walked she nuzzled closer to Liam and wrapped an arm around his waist.

"Liam," she said, her tone playful, "is there anything you haven't told me I should know? I mean, you don't have two or three wives stashed around the place do you?"

"You'll need to be a bit more specific," he said. "Do you mean two or do you mean three?"

Izzy laughed. "Okay, wise guy, I'll take that as a no."

"Make that a great BIG, no," said Liam. He stopped and turned to Izzy.

"You said you're free this weekend. Let's take a cab to Reagan airport and grab a shuttle to New York tonight. We can spend tomorrow in the city."

"Hmmm," she said.

She considered how much she missed Central Park, the Met and the nightlife of the Village. Though she accompanied the president to New York from time to time, the trips were rarely for more than a few hours and never allowed for personal time. A spur-of-the-moment trip felt counter-intuitive to Izzy whose professional life consisted of planning every move in detail.

Yet during those hectic POTUS visits she'd sometimes found herself envying New Yorkers, free to go about their daily lives in anonymity, enjoying the beauty and excitement of one of the world's great cities. She was drawn to the idea of being there with Liam. It would be a big step in their relationship but one she'd been expecting, even looking forward to.

"Okay," Izzy said. "Let's drop by my place first. I'll need ten minutes to get an overnight bag." She looked at Liam. "But won't you need to pack too?"

"My family has an apartment in Manhattan," Liam said, "I keep some of my things there."

"Are we staying there?" Izzy said, surprised.

"Lord, no," Liam said, "too stuffy, full of antiques and questionable post-modern paintings. I'll call ahead and arrange a hotel for us."

Liam stepped to the curb and hailed a cab.

28

It was nine p.m. when the taxi from La Guardia pulled up in front of the Hotel Provence near Fifth Avenue and Sixty-First Street overlooking Central Park. Izzy smiled her approval as they walked into the elegant lobby, valets trailing with her overnight bag and the small piece of leather luggage that had been delivered to the hotel by courier from Liam's Manhattan apartment.

"Do you like it?" Liam said as they walked to Reception.

"It's beautiful," Izzy said, recalling a warp-speed fund-raising visit she'd made to the hotel with the president during the spring.

After they'd been escorted into their suite on the thirtieth floor, Izzy stepped to the tall windows and took in the magnificent view of Central Park below. An earlier rain had left the city glistening. The streets were bustling with cars, pedestrians and horse-drawn carriages.

I'd forgotten how beautiful New York is at night.

She removed her coat and scarf, placed them on a divan next to Liam's, and took a moment to explore the suite. The main room had a wood-burning fireplace that had been lit in anticipation of their arrival. In front of the fireplace two camel-colored divans faced each other on Persian rugs. Behind the divans two gleaming cherry-wood sofa tables sported deep-blue vases decorated with delicate Japanese drawings and filled with fresh-cut flowers. A collection of tasteful, eclectic furnishings and artwork completed the room.

Adjoining the main room was a bedroom elegantly decorated in earth tones. A king-size mahogany bed was matched by a large dresser and two nightstands. Two white-silk chaise longues rested by a broad window that overlooked Central Park.

A door in the bedroom opened to a marble bathroom with two brass-handled sinks, plush Ralph Lauren bathrobes and an elegant lion-paw pedestal tub with duplicate fluted ends.

Soon, a waiter appeared at the hallway door pushing a candle-lit trolley laden with iced platters of Kumamoto oysters, Caesar salads, Cajun fries a chilled bottle of Sancerre and two large Campari and soda. He extended the folding ends of the trolley placed a side chair at either end said "Good night, Sir, Ma'am," and exited.

They sat down and with the appetite that travel, cold weather and anticipation had produced, savored the Sancerre and ate with relish.

Afterward, they slipped off shoes and jackets and stretched out on the thick rug, sipping Campari and soda by the warmth of the fire sharing favorite films, childhood anecdotes and laughing at Liam's over-the top obsession with automobiles.

Izzy fondly recalled her first visit to the great *Louvre* museum at the age of eight. The endless corridors, stairways and maze of galleries had stirred her young imagination.

"And I said to my dad that day, 'Dad, what a great place this would be to hide if I didn't want anyone to find me.'"

They talked past midnight, drawing closer as the fire faded to flickering embers. At last, their bodies touched and the words stopped. They kissed - tentatively at first, then more urgently as they undressed each other.

They were naked, lying face to face on the thick rug. Izzy arched her slender body toward Liam and pressed herself into him. She kissed him long and hard and felt him stiffen against the soft inside of her thigh. She kissed him again, this time slower, moving her long fingers down his right arm until they found the smooth metal fastener.

"Can I help?" she whispered.

Next Morning

Izzy lay naked, long-legged, her mussed red hair spilling like thick caramel onto Liam's warm chest. Morning's gentle light slipped past scattered clothing, satin sheets and spent bodies. She opened her eyes and gazed at Liam. He was still asleep, his left arm wrapped protectively around her slender shoulders.

He shuddered for a moment. Izzy raised her head slightly and took in the whole of his nakedness. She imagined a Kouros sculpture. Large. Serene. Strong. Suppressing an urge to kiss him, she returned her cheek to his broad shoulder and nuzzled closer to the hearth of his body in the coolness of the morning. Cheek and shoulder rose and fell on each gentle breath. Campari and feral scent lingered on them. Izzy pressed closer and felt the stirring in her again.

29

It had been a week since Izzy had seen Liam. The days had gone by quickly, filled with intense planning and advance work for the president's scheduled state visit to Nigeria and the G6 conference in France, due in four months.

A state visit dwarfed all other outings. Planning took months. Every moment of the trip on Air Force One from wheels-up at Andrews Air Force Base to touch down on the return, was painstakingly choreographed. Prior to the visit, every person who would come in contact with POTUS needed to be vetted by CIA, DIA, DHS, FBI, State, Interpol and a slew of other agencies foreign and domestic. Every venue would have to be swept and re-swept for explosives, biological agents, chemical weapons and other potential threats. Intelligence work-ups on all principals involved in meetings with POTUS would have to be generated and analyzed. Potential terrorists or lone wolfs had to be gamed out and contingency plans developed. After Amman, Izzy and the Service had moved to a hyper state of vigilance.

Tonight, Izzy settled for a light supper at home by herself. She watched the ten o'clock news and went to bed. Tomorrow would be another taxing day.

30

White House – Eisenhower Executive Office Building

"Good morning, Larry," Izzy said, rolling down the driver's window of her government-assigned Chrysler sedan as she pulled up to the kiosk of the White House gates. It was seven in the morning, but due to heavy cloud cover, nighttime illumination still bathed the entrance.

The rich aroma of freshly brewed coffee wafted from the White House mess and hung invitingly in the bracing air.

"Good morning, Miss Stone," the Executive Protection Service agent said as he stepped out of the kiosk, dressed in a crisp, white shirt and a blue jacket that matched light blue pants.

"May I see your pass?"

Izzy knew Larry had recognized her right away, but the Executive Protection Service went by the book. She gave him her pass. He stepped into the kiosk and inserted the encrypted credential into a terminal. In the few seconds it took to authenticate the pass, several concealed, high-resolution digital cameras scanned Izzy's face, vehicle and hologram-imbedded license plate. In less than five seconds, the image archive matched her face using an advanced 30-point recognition system. Soon the screen displayed a photo of Izzy with the words: Isabella Baker Stone – United States Secret Service Presidential Protection Division.

Larry handed the pass back to Izzy.

"Thank you, ma'am," he said with a smile.

He stepped back into the booth and activated the heavy gates. Two massive ten-ton blast suppression metal I-beams that had remained unseen behind the elegant black gates silently descended into a housing in the driveway. As the gates swung open, Izzy drove to the small parking area that separated the West Wing of the White House from the Eisenhower Executive Office Building. Sensors scanned the vehicle for traces of radioactive, bio-chemical and explosive materials.

She pulled into one of the prized West Executive Avenue parking spaces and turned off the engine. Thanks to completion of the massive Deep Underground Command Center, the small area between the West Wing entrance and the EEOB was once again in pristine condition.

Dressed in a blue blazer, starched long-sleeve white blouse and dark slacks Izzy quickly checked her hair in the mirror and exited the car. She walked into the EEOB, flashed her ID to the EPS guards and took the elevator to her office in the Secret Service Presidential Protection Division.

Entering her paneled office she closed the door, removed her jacket, and stowed the Sig Sauer and holster on a coat rack next to her desk. A faint fragrance wafted from the jacket. She reached into the right inside pocket and withdrew a white carnation bud and a business card that read: *Liam Cabot – British Embassy, Washington, D.C.* She drew the bud to her face, closed her eyes and inhaled.

There was a knock on the door.

"Come in," Izzy said. The door opened.

Will Bergan, Izzy's second in command, poked his head in. "Morning."

"Hi, Will. Com'on in," she said, wrapping her hand around the card and small flower. "What's up?"

"Brought you the daily Threat Book and a few other Eyes-Only items."

"Thanks, Will. Who've we got visiting the West Wing today?"

"Pretty vanilla," Will said. "Here's the Visitor Schedule."

Izzy took the schedule and did a quick scan. It contained a full but otherwise routine list of individuals arriving to meet with high-level presidential staff or, if they were very lucky, the president.

The list of those scheduled to visit the Oval Office, located in the West Wing, included Ed Valucek, National Security Advisor, two senators, the president's chief-of-staff, the head of the Joint Chiefs of Staff, a celebrity billionaire, a small town mayor from Wyoming, and the new ambassador from Vanuatu, the South Pacific nation whose national anthem Izzy recalled was "Yumi, Yumi, Yumi," one of the quirkier factoids she carried in her head.

She knew that with few exceptions, such as key presidential advisors and senior officials, most individuals ushered into the Oval Office would stay no more than five minutes – long enough for a spirited greeting by the president, a minute of pleasantries - laughter included, two to three minutes of sober-faced conversation and several photos taken by the ubiquitous White House photographer - after which the visitor would be amiably escorted out. Yet, however brief the meeting, the memory and photos would last a lifetime. The general public would have been surprised to learn how rigorously every minute of the president's time was measured and apportioned.

Although relatively small in size, the West Wing consisted of a warren of offices occupied by presidential assistants wielding enormous power in their role as surrogates for POTUS. Access to a member of the president's personal staff meant an opportunity to gain the president's ear. Industry titans were often hard put to contain their glee upon being ushered into the West Wing. If the great edifice of the United States Government could be thought of as a colossal pyramid, the West Wing represented the last stone at the apex.

Short of being invited into the Oval Office, an invitation to lunch at the White House Mess with a staff member was just about the next best thing. A beehive of power, it wouldn't have been unusual for the Director of the CIA, Secretary of Defense or a Hollywood icon to be seen lunching at a nearby table.

"Whaddaya think?" Will said.

"You're right. Pretty vanilla."

"There's just one more thing," Will said. "I don't know what it means, but I picked up a rumor that there's a group in Ed Valucek's shop at the NSC in the West Wing that's been meeting off the books. Guess the prez wants them below the radar. They don't show up anywhere."

"Interesting," Izzy said. "We've got more work to do on the Nigeria trip. But first, can you find out anything about this NSC group? I know NSC staff is very touchy about these things, but we are owed a few favors."

"Oh sure," Will said, his voice hamming it up, "send the lamb to the abattoir, 'cause the boss likes secrets that Ed Valucek doesn't want to share."

"C'mon," Izzy said. "Can't be all that bad."

"All right," Will said, drawing his words out, "but you're buying coffee for a week."

"Hope you like instant. Bye," Izzy said, fluttering her fingers.

"Hi, I'm back."

Izzy looked up and saw Will Bergan poking his head in. She looked at the wall clock. He'd been gone about an hour.

"What did you find?" she said.

"Not sure you'll like it."

"Try me."

"Okay. Sources are usually helpful," Will said, "even when the conversation's off the record. But today they weren't willing to say much."

"Hmm," Izzy said.

"I did, however, pick up a couple of tidbits."

"And?"

"First," Will said, "Valucek's NSC working group is deep into some "need to know" project dealing with the Chechen-Russian pisser. Might even involve a stolen nuke, but no one's confirming. Chechens would love to have one to keep Russians off their backs. Anyway, it's pretty sensitive stuff."

"Okay," Izzy said, "What's the part I won't like?'"

"Here goes," Will said. "The makeup of the group is usual staffing - with the exception of a new player… your buddy, Liam Cabot."

Izzy felt her face flush. *Liam meeting off the books on an eyes-only with the NSC?* She hadn't expected it.

So much for low-level diplomat. Liam, you bastard.

"I went back and checked our intel on Cabot more carefully," Will said. "Everything lined up pretty much with the intel the first time we ran him. But in checking his service chronology I found a two-year gap. No info at all. I completely missed it the first time."

"So," Izzy said, "He disappears for two years and no one knows where he's been…"

"Or what he's been doin'."

"Then bingo," she said, "He's suddenly meeting off the books with the Oz of the NSC."

31

"Izzy, I'm sorry," Liam said.

They were sitting in a car off of Rock Creek Parkway.

"Bullshit, you weren't straight with me. Did you think I wouldn't find out you were in the West Wing?"

"On the contrary, I expected you would. But there's a difference between your getting that information, and my providing it. The meetings were strictly off the books, no exceptions, mum's the word."

"What's going on in Valucek's shop?" Izzy said.

"Can't talk about it."

"Are you MI6?"

"C'mon, Izzy."

"There's a two year gap in your chronology. I assume you weren't just sipping piña coladas in Aruba."

"It was a research sabbatical."

"You have a background in Slavic languages." Izzy took a flyer.

"A failed attempt at Russian."

"What about Chechen Ingush?"

"Where are we going with this, Izzy?"

"Evidently, nowhere. How'd you lose your hand?"

"A hunting accident."

"Hunting bipeds?"

"Look, you deal in sensitive information every day, you should understand."

"What I understand is that I've gotten involved with someone I don't really know and I don't like the feeling. By the way, that first encounter at the embassy, was that a set-up?"

"No, Izzy. I didn't know who you were."

"I think we'd better head back. Maybe we both need a few days to sort things out."

"Might be a bit longer," Liam said, "'afraid I'll be out of pocket for a few weeks."

32

Islamabad

Fifty-three year-old, six-foot four Bill Powers, aka "John Marcus," CIA Chief of Station in Islamabad, was well into his third Glenfiddich, grooming Nasir Malik, a senior member of the Majlis-e-Shoora, Pakistan's Parliament. It was going to be a hefty bar tab, Malik was drinking like a fish.

They were sitting in a dimly lit corner booth at Nick's, a tony bar in the luxurious Hotel Crown Jewel on busy Aga Khan Boulevard. Powers had dressed his face in the feathers and lace of an enthralled listener as Malik delivered pompous accounts of his responsibilities and achievements as an MP – and, in the process, scattered morsels of useful information about rivalries and alliances within the Pakistani government.

Powers privately detested Nasir Malik. He was a set piece. A slick-haired politician on the make, eager to ingratiate himself to the American government in the hope of advancing his career in Pakistan's byzantine world of politics and perhaps, picking up some loose change along the way.

No, Powers didn't think much of Malik. But then Powers wasn't in the business of hanging out with "really nice people." Really nice people weren't willing to betray their own country for personal gain.

A waiter approached their table. "Mr. John Marcus?"

Powers gave the waiter an acknowledging look.

"There's a phone call for you on the house phone, sir."

"Are you sure the call is for me?"

"The gentleman on the phone, sir, he said to look for a tall American with large ears."

Powers stood up, emptied his drink, grimaced and followed the waiter to a small cubicle.

He closed the door and picked up the receiver. "Yes?"

"Good evening, Mr. Marcus."

Powers did not recognize the voice, though its inflection suggested an Urdu speaker.

"I don't think we've met," Powers said. "May I ask who is calling and why?" Powers didn't appreciate the venue or the circumstances of the call. Yet an intuition kept him from hanging up.

"No, Mr. Marcus, we have not met. My name is Zuhar. I was entrusted with a message by a close friend. He asked that I deliver it to you."

"I'm not expecting any messages, Mr. Zuhar, you've made a mistake. If your friend has something to say then I suggest he call. Goodnight."

"Excuse me. There is no mistake. Regrettably my friend is unable to speak with you."

"Who is this friend?"

There was a pause.

"His name is Walt."

Powers' hand violently coiled around the phone pressing it so hard against his ear that he winced. No one, not even his case officer at Langley knew he'd given that moniker to Kahn. But Kahn was dead. How did this caller get the name? Powers reconsidered his approach. His voice became congenial.

"Yes, Yes, I believe I may have met Walt some time ago. His message?"

"That your guests arrived this evening. You will want to make arrangements to welcome them."

"Thank you," Powers said. "By the way, how did you know I was here?"

"We have many relatives in Islamabad, Mr. Marcus. The gentleman you've been drinking with in the bar is a cousin of mine. He told us you would be here. Good night."

The line went dead. Powers put the phone down, walked out of the hotel and hailed a cab. *The fucker can pick up the tab himself.*

That evening, a young boy wearing no shoes, an oversized *Arsenal* soccer t-shirt and a pair of weathered pants barely held up by a tightly knotted strand of rope, maneuvered a wobbly bicycle to the entrance of a modest apartment building in a working class neighborhood of Islamabad. He climbed the cement stairs to the third floor and walked to apartment 301. On the door a small sign read *Granite Trading Co.* The boy withdrew a small manila envelope from under his shirt, dropped it through the narrow mail slot, turned and scampered away. The envelope simply said, "Mr. Marcus."

Powers heard the footfalls and saw the envelope fall through the mail slot onto the aging wood floor. The meager interior of the twenty-square-meter apartment contained a small table with two metal chairs, a lumpy cot, a desk piled with a stack of cheaply printed brochures entitled *Granite Trading Co.* and numerous other non-descript furnishings. A sole unwashed window looked onto the street below. The apartment, rarely used, served as a CIA safe house, one of several maintained by Powers. Powers had told Badar Kahn that mail could be sent to that address care of Granite Trading Co.

After carefully examining the exterior of the envelope he opened it and read the contents. Over the next hour, Powers drafted an encrypted FLASH cable to CIA headquarters in Langley, Virginia.

True to his evasive ways, Mohammed al-Azzam had entered Islamabad earlier than he'd indicated to ISI. He was now in hiding in a heavily reinforced underground bunker in an industrial building on the outskirts of the city.

Powers emphasized that Mohammed al-Azzam was unlikely to remain at the site more than thirty-six hours leaving too little time to mount an extraction operation. It would have to be a missile strike.

"Recommend immediate action."

He did not include mention of the hand-written note at the bottom of the document: *Walt's family is safe and well. When the time is right you will be contacted.*

In Washington the joint chiefs examined satellite images of the building where Omar was hiding and concluded that a Predator strike with Hellfire missiles might be insufficient to ensure the full destruction of the reinforced bunker. Taking out the terrorist would require much heavier ordinance.

The president quickly approved their recommendation and ordered a sub-launched missile strike.

Former vice-president Chester Davis picked up the humming phone and looked at the screen: *Wheeler.* He pressed TALK.

"Yes?" he said.

"It's on. They just green-lighted the operation."

"How soon?"

"Next twenty-four hours."

The phone went dead.

33

Indian Ocean
USS Longstreet
Ohio Class Attack Submarine
Fire Control Center

Submarine Commander Dan Swall was standing behind Senior Fire Control Officer Josh Jimenez, staring intently at a twenty-four inch LED display, his gaze fixed on the small, flashing red image of a basketball hoop. Two green spheres resembling basketballs were moving toward the hoop in an arc-like trajectory.

The spinning spheres represented the two cruise missiles the USS Longstreet had launched fifteen minutes earlier. Commander Swall knew the details of the top-secret mission, and that the order for the missile strike had come directly from the President of the United States. But all he'd said to his crew was, "It's payback for some real bad guys."

The clear, tenor voice of Jimenez broke the silence.

"Sir, missiles have verified final coordinates. We are three minutes from target."

"Very well, seaman, steady as you go," Swall said.

Tension in the control center rose as those in the room realized that somewhere, one or possibly many humans were unknowingly breathing their last moments of life.

Two minutes later Jimenez began calling out the final countdown.

"Sixty seconds to contact, sir."

"Thirty seconds."

Commander Swall watched the two basketballs descend gracefully, towards the hoop.

"Twenty seconds." A somber quiet descended on the Fire Control Center.

"Ten seconds..nine, eight, seven, six, five, four, three, two, one…"

The basketballs silently dropped through the hoop. The hoop momentarily became a bright flash.

"Contact! We have contact! Target destroyed!" Jimenez said.

At that moment two hypersonic Trident III advanced, cruise missiles launched from undersea by the USS Longstreet, were detonating on the outskirts of Islamabad.

Traveling in a sub-orbital path at speeds up to 13,000 miles per hour, the missiles had taken mere minutes to travel from launch in the Indian Ocean to the outskirts of Pakistan's capital. Each missile contained thousands of shards of hardened tungsten metal. As the explosive charge in the missiles detonated, the metal shards were violently hurled outward in a tornadic wind that shredded all concrete, metal, human flesh and bone within a 200-yard radius.

The speed and lethality of the missiles would not have been good news for Omar Mohammed. In the control center of the USS Longstreet, the mood was ebullient.

"SUBMARINERS KICK BUTT!" missile technician Tip Barnes said.

"AHOOAHH!" shouted all the others in the control center.

Commander Swall looked proudly at his elite crew.

"Well done, gentlemen."

Turning to officer Ron Fagan, his Chief of Boat, he said "COB take the Conn."

"Aye, sir."

Fagan stepped forward to assume command of the control room.

Commander Swall proceeded to the radio shack to send a "Flash" message confirming the strike to the White House Situation Room and Strategic Command Headquarters at the Pentagon.

34

Situation Room – West Wing

Vice-President Isaac Stein, Secretary of State Noel Traficante, National Security Council Advisor Ed Valucek, and five other senior government, intelligence and defense officials were gathered in the Situation Room monitoring the strike on Omar Mohammed.

The president was on the South Lawn preparing to welcome the new Chinese Premier with full pomp and circumstance, projecting an air of public normalcy while the military operation unfolded. The president had asked to be immediately informed as soon as the missile strike was confirmed.

Air Force Brigadier General Peter Piper, seated with the others at a conference table in the Sit Room, had been updating the operation on his computer.

As Assistant Commanding General Joint Special Operations Command his task was to coordinate the flow of intelligence and operational information coming into the Sit Room from half a dozen intelligence sources. He turned away from his computer and looked at Vice-President Stein.

"Mr. Vice-President," he said, "U.S. Strategic Command at the Pentagon reports telemetry confirming Trident III detonations on the outskirts of Islamabad."

"What do we have from USS Longstreet?" Stein said.

"The USS Longstreet is just coming in via satellite. We're decrypting."

A moment later, Piper said, "Sir, the USS Longstreet reports ninety percent confidence on destruction of target."

Sitting next to General Piper, Ed Valucek, National Security Advisor, smiled. He was starting to feel really good. He knew the president anxiously awaited the outcome of "Slingshot," the code name for the strike on Omar Mohammed.

But Valucek was a detail man. Although he wanted nothing more than to whisper the words 'Bandito-EKIA' in the president's ear, he wanted everything nailed down before he went trotting up to the president. For Valucek it could mean a major promotion, possibly Defense or CIA.

He turned back to General Piper. "General, what do we have from our Special Ops team on the ground in Islamabad?"

Piper shifted a bit in his ergonomic swivel chair.

"We were expecting our 3-man team to report in about five minutes ago. It's possible they're having difficulty with their satellite uplink."

Valucek didn't like operational hiccups. Especially in a strike as critical as this. On the other hand, he knew that stuff happened. A solar flare, a blown chip, an improperly oriented dish could complicate a transmission. Besides, the Pentagon and the USS Longstreet had pretty much said it was a done deal. No need to panic.

As he mulled this, the relative serenity of the Sit Room was jolted by the gut-wrenching sound of an incoming FLASH CRITIC message. All heads in the room turned to the klaxon beside the senior duty officer. Meanwhile General Piper was reading the incoming message on his computer as his own intelligence sources decrypted the CRITIC.

The duty officer quickly disabled the klaxon. The FLASH CRITIC was from the Special Operations team that had been tasked to monitor Omar Mohammed in the event he began to move from the industrial building. Assured that he'd not left the building, they had called in the missile strike.

General Piper read the message then appeared to read it again.

"General," Valucek said, "what do we have?"

The General looked up from the screen, his expression grim.

"Our Special Ops team in Islamabad is reporting a targeting anomaly."

35

Islamabad, Pakistan

"Mother of God!"

GNN war correspondent Tabatha Bliss screamed as the all-terrain Global News Network vehicle skidded to a jaw-rattling stop.

In front of her lay the bloody carnage of dead and injured men, women and children. Amidst the wailing voices of the victims, Bliss saw rescue workers and emergency vehicles converging on the chaotic scene.

Through the acrid smell of cordite, black smoke, burning automobiles and burning flesh, Bliss saw a child, moving aimlessly in a circle. Grabbing her first-aid kit, water canteen, satellite phone and digital camera she leapt from the passenger side door of the SUV shouting to her film crew.

"Hurry! Goddammit! Hurry!"

Jesus, it's Baghdad all over again.

Bliss was racing through the smoke toward the child. She tripped on something and fell, slamming hard to the ground.

"Shit! Shit!" she yelled at the offending debris until she saw the armless body of what appeared a boy. The scorched remains were dressed in a school uniform. Horrified, Bliss furiously scooted backward on the rubble-covered street, slicing her palms and tearing through the kneepads of her khaki fatigues.

The smoke had become heavier. Back on her feet Bliss continued running in the direction of the child she'd spotted earlier. She saw a crumpled shape on the ground, stopped and knelt.

A girl, perhaps nine or ten years old, lay face down in the debris-strewn street, a red wound on the back of her head. Bliss slid her arm under the body and turned the face upward. The child's expression was one of bewilderment.

She's gone.

36

The White House
Situation Room – West Wing

Ed Valucek motioned everyone toward the wall-sized high-definition display.

"Listen up!" he said.

The monitor was scrolling GNN Breaking News to a background track of rolling timpanies, brass flourishes and crash cymbals.

"I'm Gerald Riddle. We're interrupting our regular programming to bring you breaking news from our GNN correspondent Tabatha Bliss on the phone from Islamabad, Pakistan. Tabatha, can you hear me?" There was a three second delay.

"Yes, I can hear you, Gerry."

A large photo of Bliss, press credentials dangling from her safari shirt, appeared behind Gerry Riddle.

"Tabatha, while we try to establish a video uplink please tell us what you know so far about the explosions that took place on the outskirts of Islamabad approximately twenty-five minutes ago."

"Yes." "At about 1800 hours, Islamabad time, several large explosions rocked a several block area in the southern part of the city."

"For our U.S. viewers," Riddle said, "that would be about six in the afternoon Islamabad time and 9:00 a.m. Eastern is that correct?"

"Correct. My camera crew and I were doing an interview with a candidate for the parliament when we felt and heard the powerful concussion of explosions. They were like explosions we'd heard many times covering Iraq and Afghanistan, but these seemed a lot more powerful."

"Got it, and what were you thinking at that point?" Riddle said, as his program producer motioned that he should draw out the drama until local stations across the country could interrupt regular programming and switch to live GNN coverage.

"Well," Bliss said, "I didn't know quite what to think. Islamabad is not an active war zone. We thought it might be some kind of industrial explosion since that part of the city is a sort of underbelly to Islamabad. But frankly the sound, the sound was distinctively similar to heavy ordinance going off."

"Right," Riddle said, "having heard military ordinance myself when covering the Gulf wars, it is distinctive." He saw his producer giving him a thumbs up.

"So, tell us what happened next."

"We immediately noticed a large smoke plume rising about a mile or two from our location. We cut short our interview and took off as fast as we could towards the source of the smoke."

"Tell us what you witnessed when you arrived?"

"Right, when we got there we observed a scene of total destruction and pandemonium."

"Were there casualties that you saw?" Riddle already knew the answer.

"Yes. Tragically. Many injured, dead or dying children and adults. I can't give you exact numbers; it was just too crazy and devastating. I saw a child…"

Her voice faltered.

"It's okay," Riddle said, giving Bliss time to compose. "I'm sure it's a pretty grim scene."

"… it's the worst civilian carnage I, as a war correspondent, have ever witnessed."

"Tabatha, we're getting reports from Al Jazeera and other news sources saying that missiles were seen impacting. Can you confirm any of this?"

"I've heard similar reports from a number of people who were in the area, but I can't confirm those reports at this time. What I can say is that several persons told us they saw what appeared to be low-flying, very fast-moving rockets or missiles detonate almost simultaneously. One person described them as speeding like a meteor."

"Tabatha, do you have any idea who these children were?"

"I noticed that several of the children were wearing school uniforms but as to who they were or what they were doing in that isolated part of the city, I don't yet have any details."

Vice President Stein turned to National Security Advisor Ed Valucek, his face in turmoil.

"Better activate the Deep Underground Command Center and get the president down here stat. This is going to get ugly fast."

37

Washington, D.C.

Former Vice-President Chester Davis' restricted cell phone rang in the study again, the fifth call in only a short while. Davis looked at the digital clock on the nightstand. Eight p.m.

Still groggy from the sedatives he'd taken mid-afternoon he wasn't in any mood to get out of bed and walk to the study where he'd left his phone. He let it ring.

Earlier that day had been taxing, full of federal investigators, defense attorneys and prying journalists asking questions about the indictment. By one-o-clock in the afternoon he'd been ready to call it a day. To escape the stress, he'd taken several prescription pills, something he'd found himself doing more and more. He wondered if he wasn't developing a dependency problem. In any event, tonight he didn't want to talk to anyone, including those few who had his private number.

The day's only bright spot had been the breaking news from GNN announcing the missile strike in Islamabad. He'd been surprised to hear that there'd been civilian casualties. That meant a hellacious PR disaster for president Childs.

Enjoy, you bastard, Davis thought to himself. *But Wheeler told me he didn't expect civilians to be in that remote part of the city. Did Wheeler nudge the targeting solution too much?*

Davis swiped a sweaty palm across his mouth.

Well, I suppose those are the breaks. It's a dangerous damn world.

Riinng, riinng, riiinng.

Dammit. Who the hell keeps calling?

Davis got out of bed, walked to his study his gait unsteady, picked up the cell phone, sat down in his large leather chair and squinted at the screen. Six missed calls. He pressed the "recent calls" button.

Viv. His daughter.

Davis quickly paged through the other missed calls –

Viv, Viv, Viv, Viv, Viv.

He hit speed dial. A moment later he heard the phone pick up at the other end.

"Viv?"

"Dad, where are you?" He could hear Viv sobbing. "I've been calling and calling."

"I'm sorry, sweetheart. I was napping and didn't hear the phone. What is it?"

"It's horrible, horrible, I can't breathe. I want to die."

Is it Viv's husband, Misha?

"Has something happened to Misha? For God's sake Viv, tell me."

Davis heard Viv's wail at the other end of the line. It was a strange, pain-filled keening he'd never heard his daughter make. A disquieting chill seized him.

"Tell me what's wrong, baby. I know I can help, but you have to talk to me."

"She's dead! My baby's dead! Oh, God, I want to die."

Davis was sure something had violently struck his chest. He slumped forward and leaned his elbows on the large mahogany desk.

"Viv, what…what are you saying? How? When?"

"The school in Paris called me. She was killed in an explosion."

Davis' mind began racing. *An explosion in Paris? No, impossible. I would have heard about it. It's obviously a terrible mix-up. Viv's confused.*

"Viv, listen to me. There was no explosion in Paris. This is a mistake. Someone has just screwed up royally and given you bad information. Believe me, Rebecca is fine. She's fine."

"No. The explosion wasn't in Paris."

"What!" He felt his chest tighten.

"It was in Islamabad. They were on a bus from the airport. All the children were killed by some kind of bomb. They were visiting with their middle-school. They were delivering books and medicine to a children's hospital."

Davis dropped the cell phone onto the desktop, his head pounding, his face on fire.

Islamabad. Dear Jesus. It's not possible. It can't be. This isn't happening. It has to be some vile dream. Wake up! WAKE UP!!

He slammed a coiled fist on the desk's edge again and again. The cracking sound of his radius bone and shooting pains that quickly followed told him he wasn't hallucinating.

"Dad, Dad, talk to me. What's happening?"

Davis picked up the phone.

"Why didn't you tell me she was going to Pakistan? It's a crazy idea. You should have said something! You should have said something, goddamit!"

"I know, Dad, but you've had so much to deal with." Her words were racing. "I didn't want to worry you. The school had done it before, I...I thought it would be okay...BESIDES, WHAT DIFFERENCE WOULD IT HAVE MADE!"

Somewhere within, tendrils of sharp pain began spreading across Davis' abdomen. The tendrils fattened, became thick gnarled roots tightening around ribs, his arms, his throat. He clutched his chest. A giant Oak was pressing down on his sternum, enveloping him, choking the air from his lungs.

"Dad, are you still there? Please say something!"

As he slid to the floor Davis imagined himself falling through the thick brown carpeting and concrete foundation, squeezing downward between molecules of sand and sediment, descending deeper through the earth's crust, inexorably pulled downward by some malevolent, diabolical force.

Then he knew where he was. Hell.

38

PARIS

"*Mon dieu*, this is unbelievable!"

French commandant Joseph Chopin simply could not process what he was witnessing. Before him a turbulent sea of blood-red placards read: *U. S. WAR CRIMINALS - BUTCHERS OF FRENCH CHILDREN - DEATH TO WAR-MONGERING AMERICANS.* The embassy was under assault by a massive, epithet-hurling, stone-throwing mob.

In his twenty-three years of riot control duty Chopin had never encountered anything as menacing as the roiling human sea rising from the Metro stations along the Champs-Élysées and rushing toward the American Embassy on pencil-thin avenue Gabriele.

Ever since the Radio France news bulletin that an American missile strike had killed and injured dozens of French elementary school children in Islamabad, the crowd outside the embassy had ballooned in the cool Paris morning from a few noisy demonstrators to a half-million by midday.

Using texting, e-mail and other social media, a large part of Paris' citizenry had rapidly galvanized. Students from elite universities on the Left Bank, professionals from government bureaus and law offices, Algerians, Moroccans and Arabs from the working-class arrondissements, shopkeepers, bus drivers, retirees and even members of parliament had burst forth like a North Atlantic gale.

On the boulevards, American tourists, or at least those resembling them, were harangued and assaulted. At exclusive Left Bank restaurants, Americans arrived to discover their reservations rudely canceled. At a fast food restaurant on the Champs-Élysées, young toughs violently attacked an American tour group. At the splendid Jardin du Luxembourg, Bartholdi's original bronze model of the Statue of Liberty was toppled and defaced. On the Seine an American couple was thrown overboard from a tourist boat plying the river.

The regular contingent of French riot police guarding the perimeter of the American embassy had been augmented by an additional fifty officers in full riot gear. Inside, embassy personnel and the heavily armed contingent of U.S. Marines had gone on high alert as the size and anger of the protesters grew.

Commandant Chopin nervously pressed the police radio to his mouth and called the Préfecture command center.

"We're being overrun! We need as many gendarmes, security police and military backup as possible. We can't hold the perimeter much longer."

"Acknowledge, commandant," came the reply. "Have already dispatched reinforcements, but streets are now totally impassible without use of deadly force. Do your best. Will try to break through."

Too late. The cataract of humanity surged over the vastly outnumbered French cordon, swamping their lines of defense, hurtling past concrete bollards, toward the elegant, black steel gates of the American Embassy. Within minutes the outer guard kiosk had been destroyed and the reinforced gates bent beyond recognition. As the mob rushed onto the embassy grounds thick cobblestones and Molotov Coctails began raining down on the compound. Trees were toppled and set afire, shrubbery uprooted, heavy plate glass windows smashed. Soon the entire complex was ablaze.

"Embassy breached!" Marine captain Charlie Isaacs said into his communication module. "Hostiles are now on embassy grounds. Marine Embassy Guards, lock and load. Secure all staff."

Throughout the embassy, high-speed shredders began destroying Top Secret cables while the on-duty signals operator dispatched *CRITIC* messages to the White House Situation Room, the State Department and the Pentagon.

Following rehearsed procedures personnel were directed to a concealed corridor leading to a reinforced concrete staircase. The stairs wound down to a secret Panic Room located in a chamber far below the embassy grounds. As they did, blast-proof doors emerged from overhead containment housings and recessed walls to form a hermetically sealed space.

Soon the United States Government would be in full-blown crisis mode.

39

Chicago – next day

The blaze at twenty-five East Oak Street was first reported at four in the morning.

A passing Chicago cabbie saw smoke and flames pouring from the Hèrmes of Paris flagship store where thirteen-thousand-dollar gold bracelets and five-thousand-dollar tote bags lined the counters and shelves of one of France's fashion dynasties.

Within minutes First Alarm fire units arrived on scene. Fifteen minutes later the fire had escalated to an out- of- control Four-Alarm blaze. Four battalion chiefs were coordinating a massive response to the raging inferno. Pushed by volatile accelerants, the flames sped through the structure igniting several floors of the exclusive store.

Three hours later the building was declared a total loss.

Larry Pulaski, Chief Arson Investigator for the city of Chicago wasted no time offering an opinion to the assembled Fire Chief, Mayor and Chief of Police. Standing in the water-filled street packed bumper-to-bumper with ladder trucks and medical emergency units, the stocky, pug-faced arson sleuth glared at the smoldering remains and turned back to them, his voice a low growl.

"It's arson," he said. "Doesn't look like a professional job though, kind of sloppy." Pulaski took a deep drag from the cigarette dangling between his thumb and index finger. He stared at the building.

"More than one perp," he said, cigarette smoke mingling with his words. "Accelerant containers and gloves are layin' all over the frigg'n place. Got shoe prints and a fair amount of forensic DNA crap. Shouldn't be too hard to find the bums... sloppy."

"Sloppy or not," the Fire Chief said, "it's about a twenty-million-dollar loss. They totaled the place."

"Damn sure they did," Pulaski said. He flicked the cigarette butt to the pavement, stepped on it with the toe of his shoe and ground it into the asphalt.

"Just one more thing I'd like to show you."

They followed Pulaski to the back of the building. He pointed to the wall. The words were scrawled in large, awkward graffiti: *Kill French basterds,* and, *Hands off the USA.*

"Great spelling," the mayor said.

"Ya think?"

40

Same day

There was a festive nighttime party underway in the main square of Achoogoville, Alabama, population 1,238. Amid raucous laughter, fried potato jojos, Alabama barbeque and free-flowing beer from fifty-gallon barrels mounted on the back of a dented flatbed pickup, a bonfire in the center of the square leaped higher with each piece of kindling added to the flames. The town's two policemen looked on, amused.

The residents of the tiny, rural community hadn't taken lightly to the news that the American Embassy in Paris had been attacked by a mob.

At the local bar, an Achoogoville, resident fired up the patrons: "Next time we have to take that damn country back from the Krauts, we're just gonna keep it."

As a loud "Ahooah" rose up from the patrons, he added a "By God!" for good measure.

Things quickly escalated. Before long, a boisterous crowd descended on the aging one-story, wood-frame library, emptying its small collection of French novels, language textbooks and picture books. Two old VHS French films and several children's music tapes were found in an alcove and added to the fire.

Next, the town's residents took to their homes, rummaging through meager personal collections of French tourist brochures, yellowing postcards and calendars with pictures of France.

As each article was thrown onto the pyre, the chant rang out,

"What do we want?"

"To nuke France!"

"When do we want it?"

"Now!"

A local teenager captured the revelry on his smart phone and uploaded it to You Tube.

It went viral.

41

Same day

"We're interrupting our continuing GNN coverage of the burning of the American Embassy in Paris to bring you breaking news from here in the United States."

It was almost midnight in Nashville, Tennessee, and veteran GNN anchor Gerald Riddle stood front and center on the newsroom set as the BREAKING NEWS…BREAKING NEWS… chyron trailed at the bottom of the screen. Riddle, fifty-three, stood a mere five-feet-five-inches, a fact he tried to conceal from his global audience by wearing Tony Lama boots when interviewing his subjects.

With thin graying hair, a craggy face and drooping eyelids that suggested chronic insomnia, Riddle had filed news stories from some of the world's most restive places. He'd been everywhere. He thought he'd seen it all. But this thing in Paris was a whole new animal straight out of Twilight Zone.

The U.S. Embassy in Paris sacked…by the French? Unbelievable!

He looked directly into the camera and spoke with the facile combination of cultivated glibness and urgency that were indispensible to the theatre of breaking news.

"As we've been reporting since the U.S. Embassy in Paris came under attack yesterday morning, Americans across the country have begun taking matters into their own hands to express their personal outrage."

Riddle shuffled the notes in his hands for effect but didn't look at them. He didn't need to, he could extemporize for hours.

"As we told you earlier, the FBI has now entered the investigation into the arson fire that destroyed the Hèrmes store in Chicago early this morning. But here at GNN we're being swamped with reports of assaults on French tourists, book burnings, bomb threats against French interests such as airlines, exchange students and French diplomatic personnel in the U.S."

The camera zoomed in for a tight close-up of Riddle's face.

"The White House has just issued the following statement from the president, and I quote: 'Tonight

I call upon all Americans to show restraint and good judgment during this turbulent and tragic period. Violence is not in keeping with the best traditions of our country and must be avoided. Acts of vigilantism only inflame an already dangerous situation and those who choose to take the law into their own hands can expect to face the full force of the law.'"

As the camera pulled away, a GNN staffer could be seen rushing to Riddle, a single piece of paper in his hand.

Off-camera now, Riddle took the sheet and quickly scanned it.

Jesus…is the president nuts?

42

Annapolis, Maryland

It had taken several days for the French government to conduct an autopsy of Rebecca's body and fly it to the United States.

The funeral service at St. Timothy's church was packed with family, friends and dignitaries. Outside, hundreds of print and electronic media were covering the story.

Rebecca's death had thrown the nation into mourning. The cruel irony of an American child on a humanitarian mission being killed by a missile fired by her own country had made her death all the more horrifying.

Following the burning of the Embassy in Paris, the political storm all across Europe had grown to a category five. To millions, the United States had become an international outlaw. European governments were struggling to contain the rising anger. In Medan, Indonesia; Alexandria, Egypt; and Karachi, Pakistan, U.S. consulates were overrun and torched. In Yemen, the American ambassador's motorcade was attacked, the ambassador murdered and dragged through the streets.

In Washington, the president had come under political assault on all sides. At a loss to explain how the mission could have gone so wrong the White House found itself facing calls for investigations and Congressional hearings.

It mattered little that the intended target had been the world's most dangerous terrorist or that collateral damage had not been foreseen.

The only thing that mattered was that Omar Mohammed still walked the earth and that an innocent American girl and twenty-nine French school children and their teachers were dead while ten others fought for their lives in French hospitals. Ironically, with the exception of the bus driver and an interpreter, no Pakistanis had died in the attack.

In only a few days, the world had turned on its axis. Now Leyland Childs, the much-admired American president who'd lost his wife and barely survived an assassination attempt in Amman, had become a monster, a reckless child-killer reviled around the globe.

The graveside ceremony had been brief. Viv, dressed in severe mourning black, her demeanor catatonic, had not said a word, unable to even acknowledge her husband's presence or the condolences of friends and relatives.

Afterward, regaining her composure somewhat, Viv turned to her father, her eyes red from days of inconsolable grief.

"Dad, thank you for being here. I know it's been a terrible day for you too. You don't look well. Would you like to come back to the house for a while?"

Davis looked at his daughter. His face ashen, eyes bloodshot.

"Thanks, sweetheart. I really need to be alone now."

His limp more pronounced, Davis made his way to the Rover. He waved off his secret service detail, got in and drove away. A mile past the cemetery he pulled off the main highway onto a dirt road sheltered by an outgrowth of trees and underbrush. He turned the motor off and leaned forward, resting his forehead on the steering wheel. His mind became clouded and he lost track of time as the afternoon sun descended below the tree line. By the time he roused himself, night had fallen and a cold rain was pelting the roof of the Land Rover.

43

Vice-President Davis looked at the clock. It was almost ten p.m. The funeral the previous day had been mentally and physically draining. He hadn't returned to his townhouse in the Capital until late that night. Exhausted, he'd taken two sleeping pills and slept far into the morning. Since waking, the hours had passed to evening at an achingly slow pace, his mind in a stupefying fog, his stomach churning in a way that made the thought of food repulsive.

Davis was seated at a red-mahogany desk in his study. The elegant desk, large and imposing, had been his first present to himself when, at the unlikely age of twenty-six, he'd achieved partnership at the prestigious Case and Jewel law firm.

His rise had been exceptional. Propelled by a brilliant intellect, a boundless work ethic and exuberant idealism he'd soon become a favorite among the firm's wealthy clientele. However, years later, his entry as a young senator into the toxic world of Beltway politics had started him on the cancerous path of ethical compromise, metastasizing self-interest and terminal corruption.

Davis had spent the last two hours revisiting photos and treasured memorabilia. His most prized memories were those of his wife, Eleanor, his daughter Viv, and his granddaughter, Rebecca. He'd kept every note, card or playful drawing they had ever given him.

Riiinng, Riiinng.

Riiinng, Riiinng.

His private cell phone beckoned again. He picked it up.

"Yes."

"Evenin', Mr. Vice-President. Rick Kelly, *Washington Daily.*"

"Who?"

"Rick Kelly, Washington Daily. Sir, you got a minute or two for a story we're working on tonight?"

"Sorry, Mr. Kelly, it's ten o'clock at night and I'm not giving any interviews. How'd you get my private number?"

"Was given d'me by someone whose name I can't disclose right now. And I'm not calling for an interview, wouldn't be neighborly at this hour." Kelly's Texas drawl was loaded with amiability and portent.

"Then, what?"

"For a comment on a story we'll be running on tomorrow's front page. Jus' wanted to give you a chance to respond 'fore it we put it to bed."

"What story?"

" "bout serious allegations against you made by a former member of the Pentagon's missile targeting unit. All 'bout the U.S. missile strike in Islamabad."

"Have no idea what you're talking about."

"'Source provided our newspaper with copies of text messages and digitally recorded conversations involving the two of you'all, sir."

"Who is this so-called source of yours? Sounds like some crank trying to implicate me in a ridiculous story. I won't take the bait."

"Running the story, Mr. Vice-President. Have a comment?"

There was a long pause.

"Okay, Kelly, what's the story?"

"That to discredit President Childs you'all orchestrated an unlawful covert operation with this individual. That he gave you sensitive details of a missile strike ordered by the White House 'gainst the terrorist Omar Mohammed."

"Not true."

"That under your direction the targeting data was altered so's the missiles would spare Mohammed and strike other buildings. The missiles destroyed empty warehouses but also struck a passn' school bus killing many children… including, sir, your own granddaughter, and I do regret hav'n to say as much, sir."

Davis noticed his fingers had turned white from gripping the phone.*There's no turning back now. Deny, deny, deny. The truth would kill Viv.*

"Your source is lying."

"Sir, we authenticated the voice on the recorded phone calls. No question. It's yours."

"Voice signatures can be manipulated. We did that with psyops when I was vice-president."

"But, sir,…"

"You've been snookered, Mr. Kelly. The story is bogus. Goodnight."

"Got video."

"Bullshit."

"Mr. Vice-President, d' you'all own a disposable phone?"

"What's your point."

"Well, sir, seems you used a disposable phone when you spoke with our source. Had a video feature."

"I don't even know how to turn those damned things on."

"You didn't turn it on, our source did, remotely. Provided us video of you speaking with him 'bout the operation. A bit jerky, poor quality, but in freeze frame it sure is you, sir."

The giant Oak had returned.

"Became so distraught by the death of those little ones he couldn't stay silent."

"Well, I certainly want to talk to him," Davis said.

" 'fraid won't be possible. Jumped off Arlington Memorial Bridge this evening. District police recovered his body less than an hour ago, sorry to say."

Sweat beaded on Davis' forehead. The migraine was back, hammering his brain. Davis felt the angel of death upon him. His throat clogged with words that could not find voice.

"Sir, would you'all like to comment?"

Davis pressed the "OFF" button.

For several moments he sat in penumbral silence, motionless in the dim light - an old man in a daguerreotype.

At last, he rose from his leather chair and crossed the paneled study to his private bar. Selecting a bottle of vintage Laphroaig, Davis filled a large crystal tumbler to the rim and took a long drink. Returning to his chair he picked up the stereo remote, toggled the tracks to Mahler's Sixth symphony and hit *Play*. He took another drink and sank deep into the leather chair. After a few moments he examined the tumbler. Still half full.

It'll do.

Leaning forward, he released a concealed drawer in the desk and removed a brown manila folder. He opened it and took out a letter.

For Viv. He placed it on top of the desk.

Next, he withdrew two plastic vials from the folder. Each vial contained twenty painkillers. He opened the vials and poured the forty pills into a cut glass bowl next to him. He picked up the first four, dropped them into his mouth, took a sip and swallowed.

Satisfied they'd gone down, Davis looked again at the gleaming bowl. Then, with the single-minded resolve that had defined his life, he scooped the remaining pills into the palm of his left hand and fed them into his mouth between gulps of scotch.

44

President Childs was in bed reading briefing papers in the master bedroom of the White House. The room, located on the second floor of the residence, overlooked the South Lawn and had a commanding view of the Washington Monument.

It was after midnight and Childs had almost finished adding comments to the thick stack of intelligence updates, action memos and news stories on the missile strike and its aftermath. His decision to fly to France had struck Washington and the Secret Service like a thunderbolt. He knew he had no choice but to go. To appear afraid or insufficiently horrified by the death of French schoolchildren would only add to the growing international rage.

There was a light tap on the door. It opened a crack and a member of his security detail poked his head in.

"Mr. President," he said, "Your press secretary's here - says it's urgent."

"Send Mike in."

Mike Espinoza, White House Press Secretary and one of Child's closest advisors, almost ran in. He looked winded.

"Sir, sorry to bust in but I got a call at home twenty minutes ago…Rick Kelly of the *Washington Daily.*"

"You made it from Chevy Chase in twenty minutes?"

"Pedal to the metal all the way. Wanted to tell you in person. Kelly's their chief investigative reporter. He's been poking around the Pentagon and the FBI trying to find out how the Islamabad missile strike went so wrong."

"And?"

"He called to give the White House a heads up. Tomorrow's lead story, I mean, this morning's lead story in the *Daily,* implicates former Vice-President Davis in the strike."

Childs sat bolt upright in the bed.

"WHAT!!" The papers tumbled to the floor.

"Mr. President, the *Daily's* got first-hand evidence."

For a moment Childs was too stunned to speak. Then:

"I can't...We've been trying to get to the bottom of it ourselves. One dead end after another. But I know Kelly's reputation. He wouldn't go with a story like that unless he had it nailed down."

"And the *Daily* would never print it if it weren't," Espinoza said. He looked at his watch. "In about six hours the White House Press Corps is going to descend on us like Genghis Khan and the Mongols."

"Mike, get to the White House switchboard right away," Childs said. "I need the Attorney General, White House Counsel, Chief of Staff, SecDef and SecState and NSC in the Roosevelt Room no later than five a.m."

"Yes, sir." He headed for the door.

MMMMM....MMMMM...MMMM...

Espinoza yanked the phone from his pocket. It was on vibrate. He looked at the screen then turned back towards the president.

"It's Kelly again."

"Let's hear," Childs said

Espinoza hit TALK. "Kelly, it's Mike, I'm putting you on speaker." He pressed Speaker.

"You wi' the Prez?"

Espinoza looked at the president.

Childs nodded.

"Yes."

"Hello, Mr. President."

"Good evening, Rick, what do you have?"

"'Bout an hour ago former Vice-President Davis was found unconscious. His security detail rushed'im to GW University Hospital but doctors couldn't revive – he was pronounced dead ten, eleven minutes ago. The boss thought the White House should know what's coming. We're re-doin' the lead story as I speak. This morn'n's headline's gonna' be one for the record books."

45

SPECIAL EDITION
THE WASHINGTON DAILY

FORMER VICE-PRESIDENT CHESTER DAVIS FOUND DEAD - APPARENT SUICIDE - IMPLICATED IN MISSILE STRIKE –FRIENDS - COLLEAGUES EXPRESS DISBELIEF, CRY FOUL – DEMAND APPOINTMENT OF SPECIAL PROSECUTOR – MAJORITY LEADER: "SOMETHING SMELLS"

President Childs read the banner headline for the third time. Obviously, he hadn't been the only one contacted before the story hit the stands. He was sitting in the small get-away study discreetly located next to the Oval Office. Most visitors were unaware it even existed since the narrow access door to the study seemed to disappear into the cream walls of the Oval Office.

It was the President's personal sanctuary, a place he could step into without being seen, listen to music, read, or have a private meeting. He and David Watson, his Chief of Staff, were watching Gerald Riddle, GNN's senior political reporter, interview sallow-faced Walter Miles, a ranking member of the Senate Intelligence Committee, and arch-foe of the president.

"Senator," Riddle said, "Are you suggesting the White House is somehow involved in former Vice-President Davis' death? That's a pretty serious claim. Beyond serious."

"I'm saying I don't believe this suicide claim, and I'll venture to say I don't lack for company in my opinion." Miles pulled at a cuff of his shirtsleeve and snapped his chin upward with conviction.

"Senator, if it wasn't suicide was there foul play here?"

"I'm saying I'm not going to accept the wild claim that Vice-President Davis took his own life just because some newspaper with a political agenda says he did. It's no secret the *Daily* has been conducting a public inquisition of Davis ever since the grand jury indictment came down."

"But, Senator, certainly you're aware of rumors that the vice-president had become despondent over the death of his granddaughter and the corruption indictment."

"In this town, rumors are about as reliable as campaign promises. That indictment was ginned up from whole cloth, not a thing to it. Anybody who knew Chester Davis knew him as the most honest, generous man you'd ever want to meet. A great human being, an optimist every day of his life..."

"But, sir," Riddle said. "Don't you..."

"I'm not finished," Miles said, tilting his head a bit in irritation. "To suggest that he had any involvement in the missile strike that took his granddaughter's life is about as low as you can get in this town and believe you me that's pretty low. He adored that child and would never have done anything to endanger her."

"Sir, one of your Senate colleagues said on camera only moments ago that he suspects a White House conspiracy to blame Davis for the Islamabad fiasco. Would you go that far?"

"I'm saying that a great American patriot is dead under highly suspicious circumstances and that the good people of this country will not be satisfied until the president tells us the full truth about Islamabad, stops obfuscating, stops delaying, and lets the chips fall where they may."

The president hit the MUTE button on the remote.

"It's going to be a hellacious week, Dave," he said. "They're going to do their best to plant Davis' death on our doorstep."

"Mr. President, they'll have a hard time. We had nothing to do with his death."

"True, but in this town perception is reality. If they keep repeating these talking points, people will start to believe any crazy claim that comes down the road. By the time it's all played out, Davis' death will be as chock-full of conspiracy theories as the Kennedy assassination. No one will ever be able to sort the truth out from cockamamie plots, phony eyewitness accounts, lunatic tell-alls and extra-terrestrials."

"Right. I know Mike's been trying to knock down the claim about a White House connection all day, but the press corps loves a who-done-it and this one's tailor made for them."

"Mike'll have to move fast to get ahead of this beast." Childs said, "This cow dung will be hard as concrete in twenty-four hours."

On the TV, Utah congressman Strom Dumpty was speaking. The rotund body and cherubic face of the congressman had earned him the derisive moniker, "Humpty Dumpty". He was standing at the foot of the Capitol steps, his expression agitated, his cheeks flushed. Childs hit the VOLUME button.

"....an extraordinary public servant, a dear friend, a man of great personal warmth and integrity who would never have taken his life. His death is highly suspicious, and I fear there's a shadowy campaign underway by this administration to blame this great American for the tragic loss of life in Pakistan, and it needs to be called out."

He paused for a moment, looked down, shook his head side to side as if making a painful decision then looked directly into the camera.

"With a heavy heart I say to you, Mr. President, that through your own ineptitude the world's greatest terrorist walks free while you attempt to lay the deaths of innocent children on the corpse of one of this country's towering patriots. It's shocking, it's un-American, and it's beneath the dignity of the office of President. Have you no decency, sir? Have you no decency?"

The president turned to Watson. "It's an ironic use of the phrase, but at least he knows about Welch and Joe McCarthy."

46

Air Force One, accompanied by two F-16 fighter planes lifted off from Andrews Air Force Base and soon disappeared into the heavy afternoon overcast just ahead of Hurricane Thomas, a category three Gulf storm bearing down on the nation's capital.

The president's decision to go to Paris on short notice had created an unprecedented security challenge for his protection detail. Due to the epic number of threats following the disastrous U.S. missile strike in Islamabad, fighter escorts, rotating in shifts, had been doubled for the transatlantic flight.

Out of one tempest and into another, thought President Childs, as he reflected on the political storm ahead.

As Air Force One sped through the growing Atlantic darkness, Childs knew he was bound for a turbulent country on the verge of permanently rupturing its historic relationship with the United States.

"You called for me, sir?" Ed Valucek, National Security Advisor to the President, was standing in the doorway of the president's paneled office on Air Force One.

"Come in, Ed," the president said. "Pull up a chair. What's our latest from Paris?"

"Mr. President, the French government is doing all it can to tamp things down but the public mood is pretty ugly. The burning of our Paris embassy really caught President Jardin and the entire Élysées staff off guard. Even they hadn't fully grasped the depth of public anger over Islamabad."

"Jardin's in a bad spot," the president said. "He's got to express public outrage but at the same time find a way to keep things from completely unraveling in the streets. Islamabad was awful and the Pakistan government is in a red-hot rage, but the deadliest attacks on the United States have been carried out by non-state groups. How can we not go after them, regardless of where they are?"

"That's true, Mr. President. To make matters worse, globalization of technology has magnified every action, every misstep. We screwed up in Islamabad and it went globally viral in less than an hour. We were painted as reckless murderers before we had any opportunity to tell our side of the story. Social network platforms are replacing governments as instruments for shaping world opinion and foreign policy. We can negotiate differences with a government but how do we negotiate with a tweet storm?"

Childs sighed and leaned back in his leather chair. "Well, we'll do what we can to calm the waters in Paris."

Air Force One was an hour away from the French coast, approaching landfall just northwest of the beaches of Normandy where the bloody Allied invasion to liberate France from Nazi Germany had taken place on D-Day, June 6, 1944.

Izzy was sitting across from the president reviewing last minute security details of the president's Paris schedule. When they'd finished, Childs put down his pen, leaned back in his chair and looked at her.

"Izzy, I know you preferred I wait before making this trip. No one had more of a right to be heard on this decision than you. I truly appreciate your concern for my safety and I admit I'm troubled by the thought I'll be placing you in harm's way. But I know you're too much of a professional to stay behind."

"Thank you, Mr. President," Izzy said, "I consider it an honor to be at your side."

It was five in the morning and raining hard when Air Force One touched down on French soil. The temperature hovered just above freezing. After a brief tarmac greeting by Francois Rambeau, the French Foreign Minister, President Childs and his entourage sped off towards Paris and the Hôtel Marly, accompanied by a massive Secret Service and French police escort.

47

Magistrat André Malevu, presiding Juge d'Instruction of the elite, all-powerful and secretive Paris court with exclusive jurisdicton over terrorism and other extraordinary crimes, sipped an espresso and took a last bite of his morning croissant as he watched television coverage of the pre-dawn arrival of the U.S. president.

A man who unfailingly rose at four in the morning, Malevu was already dressed in the business suit he'd wear under his judicial robe while on the bench. He downed the last drops, dabbed his narrow-lipped mouth twice with a white linen napkin and took a final look at coverage as the presidential motorcade left the tarmac and disappeared into the mist.

He turned off the TV and smiled to himself. Things were working out even better than he'd planned. The carnage in Islamabad and the national outrage in France were more than he could have hoped for. He picked up his black leather briefcase and walked to the front door. He'd be in his chambers by six a.m.

This will be a busy day, he thought as he turned the handle and walked down the two flights of his sumptuous Parc Monceau townhouse in the eighth arrondissement. Early morning passersby might have noticed an almost playful bounce in his step.

48

French Foreign Minister Francois Rambeau arrived at the Élysée Palace on rue du Faubourg St. Honoré and was promptly ushered into the private offices of French President Amaury Jardin:

"*Monsieur le Président*," he said, "President Childs and his party are now safely at the Hôtel Marly. On the way in from the airport he asked me to convey his best wishes to you and to tell you that he is looking forward to your meeting tomorrow. He also wanted to thank you for dispensing with the usual diplomatic arrival ceremonies."

"*Bon*, I understand how he feels," Jardin said, nodding in agreement, "This is hardly a time for pomp and circumstance. Make sure that he and his people have everything they need."

"Yes, sir," Rambeau said. "He will spend the day meeting with the American ambassador and staff who were at the embassy during the attack. Tomorrow morning our security teams will accompany the president on a brief visit to the site of the former American Embassy before he arrives here at *l'Élysée.* Even though he's undoubtedly seen video of the burned building I believe he'll be shocked by the extent of the destruction."

"No, doubt," said Jardin.

49

Paris – Hôtel Marly

When is an attack on POTUS most likely? At the burned out embassy when he's getting out of the car? If it's first thing in the morning the hit will get blanket coverage – top of the news cycle - worldwide. But that's also the moment of maximum security. Morning's always heads-up. Big time. No one wants to screw up first thing in the morning. "Sorry, they took him down while I was still thinking about the rack on that French waitress."

Then maybe afterward - when he's leaving the Élysée. Or near evening when security can see the end of the schedule and minds might turn to down time.

If it's a gun it will have to be a head shot for sure. Too much body armor these days. But head-shots are tough. People get in the way, or he turns unexpectedly. You miss. Now all hell's fury is on you.

An IED? They're cheap, easy to make. Almost impossible to find. They were the number one killer in Iraq and Afghanistan. But IED'S can go wrong, the route changes or some dufus drives over it, and "'Boom" when you didn't even send a damned signal. Besides, this is Paris. No IED, no way.

A gun, a bomb, an RPG, maybe a drone, maybe even someone in the French security detail. Hell, maybe some Frenchman with a baguette!

Maybe, maybe…

"Fuck!"

Izzy Stone bent over the toilet bowl and threw up whatever remained of last night's dinner. The air in the hotel room felt heavy. She took a slow deep breath and exhaled silently. Again. Once more…better.

No more Ammans. No more Ammans. That was too close.

She flushed and stepped to the bathroom sink, squeezed out a large dollop of toothpaste and vigorously worked away.

The Sig Sauer P229, cleaned, loaded and ready for business, lay within reach on the marble counter.

Beside the pistol was a bright lapel pin, small, hexagonal, embedded with a light-sensitive hologram. The face of the pin bore a gold star insignia.

Emblazoned around the face of the gold star were the words: *United States Secret Service.* On the back of the pin, a series of numbers.

Izzy picked up the pin and attached it to the left lapel of her blue blazer.

There would be a new pin every six hours.

For Izzy Stone, ever since that proud day when she'd been selected to head POTUS' detail, each morning of a presidential outing had involved the same gut- wrenching routine.

First she would run through all the "what if's" of a possible assassination.

And when done, she would step into the bathroom and retch. The entire ritual was nuts, she knew, but it gave her some confidence about preparing for the dangers of the day ahead.

The attack in Amman, Jordan had changed everything. And now, in the aftermath of the missile calamity in Islamabad, things were even more dangerous. Yes, this was Paris, city of lights, a city she loved and knew well. Yet the events of Amman and the tragedy of the dead children in Islamabad had put her on edge. She knew that even in a great city like Paris that functioned with great civility and efficiency, bad things could happen.

Finished brushing, Izzy looked into the large mirror and fixed her grey- green eyes on the reflection. Her gaze was steady, observing and detached. If fear had been present, it was no longer detectable.

Izzy picked up the Sig Sauer and holstered it beneath her jacket. She took a last look in the mirror, checked her make-up, dabbed the back of her ears lightly with Annick Goutal, her favorite, and stepped into the bedroom.

Hoisting a beige calf-leather satchel from a desk by the window she adjusted the strap and pulled it over her shoulder. It contained her purse, a Mini-Uzi, a backup Walther PPK .380 and a briefing book listing the latest intel on threats against Dumbledore. She walked to the front door and placed her hand on the doorknob. Bowing her head she murmured to herself, words she'd heard in a warrior's prayer.

"My sword is by my side. I seek a life of honor. Free from all false pride."

She took a deep breath, closed her eyes and slowly expelled. She re- opened them. "Okay, Izzy. Game on."

50

Paris – Next Day

Hôtel Marly

It was evening now and president Childs had retired to his room at Hôtel Marly. The day had gone fast for Izzy. From a security perspective things had gone well. She was grateful to the French agents who had spared no effort to keep Childs safe despite angry street crowds.

The president had visited the burned out U.S. Embassy, paid an extensive visit to the Élysée palace where he'd met with President Jardin for several hours, and spent the rest of the afternoon meeting with diplomatic and military advisors. He'd suggested to the French president that a personal address and an apology to the French people might help the healing process. Jardin thought it was a risky move given the public fury, yet it was one worth taking. Arrangements were made for Childs to address the nation the following day before returning to Washington.

51

Ten-fifteen p.m.
Paris –rue de Rivoli

Paris Police commandant Jean Poussin couldn't stop his hands from shaking. Thick-necked and sweaty, Poussin was sitting in the front seat of a speeding police car clutching a sheaf of official documents in his right hand. They'd been delivered to him by special courier an hour earlier. The documents carried the signature of André Malevu, Chief Magistrat and juge d'instruction in Paris' most influential court. Following the assassination of magistrat Abelard, Malevu had become the most powerful judge in all France.

As the car raced down rue de Rivoli, Poussin's thumb and index finger nervously worried his left eyebrow as he mentally replayed his earlier frantic phone call to the magistrat.

"*Monsieur le Magistrat,* this is Commandant Poussin," he'd said. "Forgive me for calling you at this late hour."

"Good evening, commandant, I was expecting your call."

"Monsieur, I've just received a sensitive document which carries your signature. I'm informed you sent it. I will not discuss the contents as I'm not calling from a secure phone. Yet what I am being instructed to do is unbelievable."

Poussin was not in the habit of questioning the actions of judges, much less a magistrat with such immense power. But he felt he had no choice.

"If I may say, magistrat, what I am being asked to do will put me and my men in mortal danger, to say nothing of the possibly grave consequences for the Republic of France. It is of the greatest urgency that I be certain of the authenticity of this document."

"What is the number on the document, commandant?"

"The number is zulu, six, nine, four, zulu."

"And the title?"

" 'JurUni,' " Poussin said, "though I am unsure of its meaning."

"The number and title are correct. I assure you it is the document I sent this evening."

"But…is it legal? I mean, please excuse me, Magistrat. I am no expert in legal matters, far from it, but do you have the authority to issue such an order?"

"The document in your hands was lawfully prepared pursuant to the statutes of the Republic of France, judicial rulings and the applicable statutes and treaties of the European Union. As juge d'instruction, I assure you I have complete authority to issue such an order."

Poussin detected a steeliness in the magistrat's voice. "Commandant," the magistrat said, "I fully expect you, as a sworn officer of the government of France to do your duty and carry out the instructions set forth in the order. It is a judicial order, not some layman's whimsy. Now, I have a pressing engagement and I am late. Good evening."

Poussin had heard the phone disconnect.

Now, sitting in the speeding police car, he realized he'd been handed the most dangerous assignment of his life. The fingers of his left hand continued sweeping back and forth across his brow.

I should never have left my village in Normandy. But I was young and naïve then. I thought Paris would be easy. Wrong. It's a jungle. And tonight I'm the endangered one.

Poussin had been ignoring a growing migraine all evening. But it had now become a massive, disorienting headache. He fumbled around in the left pocket of his weathered impermeable and located the ever-present bottle of aspirine du Rhône. He opened it, poured out six pills, threw them in his mouth and swallowed hard.

"May God protect me," he whispered to himself as the high-pitched klaxons of the caravan scattered pedestrians and motorists like autumn leaves before an ill wind.

Ten-twenty p.m.

rue de Rivoli - Police caravan

"Faster, faster,' shouted Poussin to his driver as they barreled down *rue de Rivoli.* The car surged ahead wildly as Poussin inserted a new magazine into his SIG-Sauer.

In front of them, nine black-jacketed motorcycle police moving in a phalanx took the cue and gunned their Kawasakis. Behind Poussin's car, six other Peugeots carrying five gendarmes each, also accelerated.

Bringing up the rear of the convoy, ten unmarked blue vans packed with French GIGN personnel pitched and yawed as the vehicles careened through Paris' nighttime traffic. The Groupe d'Intervention de la Gendarmerie Nationale was France's elite SWAT unit. Inside the vans, team members gripped their Heckler and Koch MP5 automatics while struggling to keep down their hastily eaten dinners.

As the caravan sped west on Rivoli, past the vast Tuilleries gardens and the exclusive Hôtel de Crillon, shopkeepers, normally unfazed by fast-moving police vehicles, were alarmed. The sheer frenzy and size of the motorcade, a wild, roaring juggernaut that refused to break its stride, was uncommon and menacing as the vehicles circled place de la Concord and turned onto the grand avenue des Champs-Élysées.

Heart pounding, Poussin looked out the front window. At last he could make out the discreet façade of his destination, the luxurious Hôtel Marly. Poussin had visited the exclusive hotel on official business many times. It was a jewel. He knew that inside the elegant building the ambience would be subdued, disturbed only by the sound of impeccably dressed hotel staff scurrying to attend to their eminent guest: the President of The United States.

Ten twenty-five p.m.

Avenue des Champs-Élysées - French Secret Service perimeter Young French secret service agent Luc Renard studied the flashing lights and keening sirens of the cars speeding towards him. Posted on the eastern perimeter of the Champs-Élysées no one had told him to expect a contingent of French police vehicles.

On the contrary, the senior agent at the briefing could not have been more emphatic.

"Agent Renard, no one, absolutely no one is to be allowed inside the safe zone where the American president is staying."

And yet, a police group was approaching. Fast.

Renard hesitated. Freshly graduated from the academy he didn't want to look naive by acting too impulsively.

Maybe there's been a change of plan. After all, I'm not told everything about such matters.

Yet the fury of the phalanx closing the distance triggered a visceral alarm too strong to ignore.

He brought the small transmitter to his mouth,

"Command. This is Lion Two. Police vehicles approaching eastern perimeter along *Champs-Élysées* at high rate of speed. Can you confirm authorization to enter perimeter, over?"

There was no reply. Renard's pulse skipped a beat.

"Command come in. This is Lion Two. Do you read? Vehicles approaching from eastern end of Champs-Élysées at a high rate of speed. Confirm authorization, over."

Still no answer. The young agent was now very nervous. He'd never seen a police group move this fast. He judged it would reach his position within fifteen to twenty seconds. Adrenalin began pumping, his breathing grew shallow and rapid.

His headpiece came alive:

"Negative! Lion Two. Negative! Vehicles not authorized. Repeat, vehicles not authorized!"

The ear-splitting klaxons and racing engines were beginning to drown out everything. Heart pounding, Renard yelled into the mouthpiece,

"Urgent! Lion Two requests permission to engage. Repeat, permission to engage!"

The first cyclists were almost on top of him. He was out of time.

No one, absolutely no one is to be allowed...

He released the safety on his HK MP5 automatic, raised the firearm and placed his index finger on the trigger. He aligned the gun sight with his right eye.

Best to take out the lead cyclist first. Has to be a head shot...

Renard took a deep breath. *God have mercy on me.*

Then...

Three hundred yards, two hundred, one hundred...

CRACK!

Renard saw the cyclist go down, body sliding awkwardly across the boulevard as the bike, engine racing, skidded sideways and smashed into a concrete abutment, metal parts flying as the engine detached from the chassis.

Renard swiveled the HK to the next cyclist.

His headpiece barked.

"Lion two. Stand down weapons! Repeat, stand down! Acknowledge."

"Acknowledge," said Renard, "Lion Two standing down."

At that moment the convoy roared past like a runaway train. Only then did the young agent realize that the vehicles had not slowed their mad pace as they sped past the downed cyclist. Nor did it occur to Renard until that very moment, that his entire body was shaking violently.

Ten twenty-seven p.m.
Champs-Élysées - Hôtel Marly
Less than two minutes had elapsed since Renard's first transmission. But already, French and American secret service agents at the Marly were in frenzied movement, taking defensive positions, issuing orders, unlocking safetys on their weapons and moving *Dumbledore*, the president's code name, to a pre-determined secure room.

Meanwhile, signals intelligence specialist Longo Raines, housed in a small makeshift communications room on the top floor of the hotel, was transmitting an encrypted "FLASH CRITIC," message to the White House Situation Room, the CIA and the National Military Command Center in Virginia.

52

Paris: Ten-thirty p.m.
The White House - Situation Room Four-thirty p.m. EST

"Son of a bitch!"

Senior Duty Officer Gus Franks had just broken the strict decorum of the Situation Room.

He had a good reason.

He was reading the incoming FLASH CRITIC.

Message from Chateau3...FLASHCRITIC...Message from Chateau3...FLASHCRITIC

"Unidentified, unauthorized motor group, size unknown, intentions unknown, approaching Hôtel Marly Champs-Élysées at high speed. French and American personnel preparing for possible assault. Dumbledore being secured. Acknowledge STAT! - 2228:03 hours Paris.

Hearing Franks swear, Sit Room Director, Lieutenant Commander Jerry Sweet called to Franks.

"Officer, your language is out of line."

"Sir, you need to look at this!"

Sweet saw the alarm on Franks' face and rushed to the console. He leaned over Frank's shoulder and read.

"Jesus, Mary and Joseph," he said.

He turned and barked, "Activate Emergency Alert System! NOW!"

The three-member Watch Team in the Sit Room immediately activated codes sending a FLASH alert to the vice-president's security detail at the Naval Observatory residence off Massachusetts Avenue and to senior defense, intelligence and political officials. Within minutes, a highly choreographed crisis response would begin deploying from the nation's capital to worldwide U.S. military and diplomatic installations.

53

Ten-thirty p.m.

Avenue Champs-Élysées - Hôtel Marly

Supervising French secret service agent Albert Royal was in an agitated state on the grand esplanade of the Champs-Élysées outside the five-star Hôtel Marly.

"Communications! Contact Préfecture headquarters, DGSE Special Services and the Élysée presidential command center immediately! Find out what the devil is going on! Who are these people? Why haven't we been notified? We're in the red zone here! Go! Now! Now!"

Royal caught his breath then continued, rapid fire.

"Blue, establish a vehicle barrier three hundred meters east of the hotel and seal off entire avenue. Red, deploy anti-personnel ordenance one hundred meters from hotel entrance. Do not engage unless ordered directly by me. Teams Black and White, weaponize and proceed to designated positions, lobby and roof. Go!"

Standing beside agent Royal, Izzy Stone was mentally thanking her testy West Point French professor for having insisted on total fluency.

Her mind was racing, listening to the cascading French secret service transmissions through her headpiece while spitting instructions in English to her own secret service detail inside the hotel.

"Will, personally take charge of Dumbledore. Advise when secure. Green Label, clear all hallways, stairwells, elevators, service doors.

"Pacific, re-sweep for explosives, chemo and bio. Conduct spectrum analysis of air and make ready hazmat gear."

Then, finally.

"Listen up everyone, we have a situation. A number of vehicles appearing to be Paris police are headed our way. We weren't given a heads up so we don't know if these guys are white hats or black hats. This could be the real deal. Remember your rules of engagement. Stay alert. Take no chances. If in doubt, engage. You may not get a second chance. Good hunting. Stone out."

Izzy and agent Royal made eye contact. They both heard it - the high-pitched Eeeyaw, Eeeyaw of police sirens making their way up the avenue towards the second security perimeter.

Izzy knew agent Royal was no novice. He'd been through urban firefights in Bosnia and terrorist bombings in Paris. She'd made her bones blasting out of a presidential ambush in Amman.

Her expression controlled, withdrawing to a private place within herself, Izzy became calm, serene. She was ready.

54

Ten thirty-two p.m.
Paris - l'Élysée Presidential Palace

The young signals specialist raced down the corridor of the presidential palace, his security pass swinging wildly from his neck. Arriving out of breath at the outer offices of the President of France, he approached the startled secret service agent stationed outside the door.

"They said the minister of foreign affairs is meeting here with the president. I am from the DGSE unit downstairs. We've just received an urgent message. I must speak to the foreign minister immediately."

"Why didn't you call?"

"We tried to, but France Telecom must have messed up the lines when they were here earlier."

"*Quelle surprise*, I haven't been able to get my internet fixed for three weeks. The minister said he is not to be disturbed while he is with the president. Take a seat. Perhaps you can speak to him when he is done."

"This can't wait!"

"I said sit down."

"No, I won't. It's about the president of the United States. Something's wrong! I wasn't supposed to tell anyone except the foreign minister, but you won't let me speak with..."

The young specialist was now talking to himself because the agent had already opened the door and rushed in to the meeting room.

55

Ten thirty-four p.m.
Paris – Champs-Élysées
Second Security Perimeter

Lights flashing, sirens howling, Kawasakis, Peugeots and GIGN SWAT vans came to a wild, skidding halt as they abruptly reached the secret service vehicle barrier straddling the Champs-Élysées. Behind the barricade French secret service agents, automatic weapons ready, maintained defensive positions. Amid the dying klaxons and the pungent odor of burning rubber an ominous quiet descended on the avenue.

The door of the lead Peugeot opened. Commandant Poussin, short, rotund with a pudgy-faced pout that someone once likened to Alfred Hitchcock, stepped out stiffly, shoulders stooped. He was wearing a shopworn raincoat over a disheveled suit, in his right hand a clutch of documents. Hands resting on their service revolvers, the motorcycle police escort had already dismounted. The blue GIGN vans brought up the rear and sat, motors idling, doors still closed.

Moving slowly, Poussin approached the first agent he saw.

"I'm Commandant Jean Poussin, of the Préfecture of Police. I wish to speak with the agent in charge," he said, his voice weary.

Emerging from the barricade an athletic, well-dressed French secret service agent in his mid-30's, automatic weapon pointed downward, walked toward Poussin.

"I'm agent Christian Defoe of the Special Services."

Poussin moved closer. "Good evening, agent Defoe. I realize my arrival is unexpected, but my instructions were that no one was to be notified in advance."

"And now you are here," Defoe said, "What is the purpose of your visit, commandant?"

"Regrettably, I'm not at liberty to disclose that. But rest assured I'm here on official business concerning a grave matter. I must ask that you instruct your colleagues to stand aside and allow us to proceed to the Hôtel Marly."

Agent Defoe did a quick mental tally of the firepower the commandant had with him. He guessed approximately forty police. Their weapons appeared to range from FNP9 side arms to Herstal P90 machine guns.

On his side, Defoe had thirty-two heavily armed, highly trained French secret service agents behind the barricade. He knew his men had a tactical and weaponry advantage.

Troubling however, were the ten unmarked vans idling in the background. Looking more closely Defoe was alarmed by the series of numbers on the sides of the vans.

Defoe recognized the numbers. They belonged to the elite GIGN SWAT teams of the Préfecture. They would be heavily armed, most likely Heckler and Koch automatic weapons, SIG-Saur pistols, concussion grenades, even fifty caliber machine guns. If the vans were staffed to capacity that would mean eight to a van, a total of eighty well-trained killers. They were capable of taking out his men. He had to be careful.

"With all due respect, Commandant Poussin, my instructions from Special Agent-in-Charge Royal, are that no one is to enter the secure zone. So I must ask that you and your officers withdraw from the area. Perhaps you have a message I can give to agent Royal."

Poussin dropped his head as if in thought. His stooped shoulders seemed to sink into the folds of his sad raincoat. There was an air of exhausted resignation about his demeanor.

I didn't spend a lifetime working my way up from the bowels of Paris' arrondissements to the highest levels of the Préfecture to be casually dismissed by an agent twenty years my junior

"*Monsieur Defoe*," he said, with barely concealed anger, "on my authority as Commandant of the Préfecture of Police of Paris and on the direct orders of the highest levels of the judicial branch of the French government, I order you and your men to stand aside and allow us to proceed."

Then, on a hand cue almost too subtle for Defoe to notice, the back doors of the vans opened. In moments, eighty heavily armed, powerfully built, Kevlar-vested GIGN SWAT members sprinted out of the blue vans and fanned left and right to form a firing envelope, as the vans moved to create a defensive line.

Defoe realized he would have to de-escalate quickly. He needed time.

"*Monsieur Commandant*," he said, "would you first be kind enough to provide me with identification?"

"Of course, monsieur." Poussin pulled his police identification from his right pocket and handed it to Defoe.

Defoe examined it.

"With your permission, commandant, I will consult briefly with senior agent Royal and determine how we should proceed."

"Very well, but I cannot wait more than a minute or two. After that, things will get very complicated."

"I understand," Defoe said.

Defoe walked briskly to the rear of the barricade. Out of earshot he spoke into his communications module.

"Did you hear it all?"

Agent Royal and Izzy Stone had been listening in on the conversation through Defoe's open mike.

"Yes," Royal said. "And the ID?"

"It's Commandant Poussin, I recognized him instantly."

"Threat assessment?" Izzy said.

"Real, approximately eighty GIGN SWAT and forty police - and they don't look like they're in a mood to please."

"Did he say he's under orders from a magistrat?" Izzy said.

"Correct, but not at liberty to divulge the purpose of his mission. However, he had official looking documents in his hands."

"Were you able to see what they were about?" Royal said."Yes, the top one appeared to be an arrest warrant."

56

10: 37 p.m.
l'Élysée Presidential Palace

President Amaury Jardin was standing at the open door of his office shouting at his executive secretary.

"Giselle! Place urgent calls to the Prefect of Police, the Minister of Defense and the security detail guarding president Childs. Use a cell phone if the land lines are still down."

Jardin had just been briefed on the looming crisis at the Hôtel Marly by the young courier from the downstairs DGSE. President Jardin turned to Rambeau.

"This is utter madness. How could the Préfecture do something this reckless? Could this be a renegade police official? Francois, you hear everything in your circles, has there been even the slightest rumor about such an action?"

"Mr. President, I've heard nothing. This is astonishing. If we cannot recall this police unit immediately, we will find ourselves in a diplomatic, even a military crisis, with the government of the United States."

The outer door opened. It was Jardin's secretary.

"Yes, Giselle," Jardin said.

"Mr. President, your national security advisor has just arrived. The American ambassador is on the phone and wants to talk to you urgently. France Telecom found the problem and the phones are all working again."

"Send in my national security advisor. Tell the American ambassador I will talk to him shortly. What about my calls?"

"Yes sir, the head of the Préfecture and the Minister of Defense are now on the line waiting for you. We're still trying to get in touch with the secret service at the Marly. Things are very chaotic there at the moment."

"Put the Préfecture through first and tell the Minister of Defense to stay on the line, and keep trying the Marly."

"Yes sir."

The phone rang. President Jardin pushed the speaker button.

"*Monsieur le Prêfet.* What in creation is happening at the Préfecture? We have alarming reports that a contingent of your police has descended on the Marly where the American president is staying. Are they from your department and if so on whose authority have they taken such reckless action?"

"Mr. President, I am only now hearing this horror story from my own sources. I am told that Commandant Poussin organized a large assault group and left the Préfecture headquarters around ten-fifteen this evening. It is now almost ten forty so his operation has been underway for twenty-five minutes."

"Did he explain why?"

"No, Mr. President. He refused to tell anyone what he intended to do, other than to say it involved a grave matter pertaining to a judicial order issued by juge d'instruction, André Malevu. We assumed that Poussin was conducting a late night terrorist dragnet but that was only a guess. I have tried several times to establish contact but either he is refusing to take my calls or there is some problem with the communications."

"You must find a way to immediately recall Poussin. Use whatever manpower you need and get to the Marly. Take personal command and lead your men. Use whatever force is necessary to stop Poussin."

"Does that include lethal force?"

"If necessary, yes. Stay in constant contact with my national security advisor, Monsieur Desplaines who is here with me. Goodbye. "

As the president replaced the receiver, the door burst open and Giselle rushed in.

"Mr. President, a Ms. Stone is being routed to you from the signals unit downstairs. She says she is the lead agent in charge of President Childs."

President Jardin looked at his Foreign Minister and national security advisor. Their expressions mirrored his feeling of dark foreboding.

"Put her through." The phone rang. Jardin picked it up.

"*Monsieur le Président, je m'appelle Isabelle Stone. Je suis résponsable de la sécurité du Président Childs.*"

President Jardin breathed a sigh of relief on hearing the American agent speak French.

"Yes, Agent Stone. This is President Jardin. I'm listening. Please tell me what you know."

"Mr. President, I am calling because agent Albert Royal is busy preparing for an expected assault. A group of police are attempting to reach the Hôtel Marly where President Childs is staying."

"Yes, we're trying to recall them this very moment."

"The situation has deteriorated. We have just learned that a Commandant Poussin of the Préfecture claims to have a judicial order to enter the hotel. We believe he may be attempting to arrest the president of the United States. There will surely be bloodshed if the commandant does not withdraw. I implore you to use your authority to defuse this deadly standoff without delay."

"My God, can this be true? Has the world gone completely mad?"

"Miss Stone, I must take further steps instantly. Meanwhile, I am putting Monsieur Rambeau, my Foreign Minister, on the phone. Please keep your line open. We must know exactly what is happening as it happens. Can you do this?"

"I will try, Mr. President, but we don't have much time."

"Thank you. Our prayers are with you, Agent Stone. Here is Monsieur Rambeau."

As President Jardin passed the phone to Rambeau, a muffled popping sound emanated from the receiver.

57

Paris - 10:42 p.m.
The White House - Situation Room
Washington D.C. - 4:42 p.m.EST

The arrival of the FLASHCRITIC had transformed the Situation Room from one of professional restraint to an adrenalin-charged bunker on a war-footing. Efforts to communicate further with the president's detail had failed. National Security Council staff, Sit Room Watch Teams, senior military personnel and the Vice-President huddled, exchanging information with the National Military Command and intelligence agencies, as they weighed options.

Emotions were running high. Paul Lyles, the vice-president's chief of staff, was butting heads with David Watson, Chief-of-Staff to President Childs.

"Look Dave, face it, the Vice-President is in charge now. We can't reach the president or his security detail and we don't even know if he is free to act as Commander-in-Chief. That means the Vice-President has to take command. What don't you get about that?"

"What I don't get about it is that it's not in the fucking Constitution, Paul. Do your homework. Article 2, Section 1.6, Clause 6, states, and I quote, 'death, resignation or inability,' are the grounds for having the vice-president assume the office of president."

Watson wasn't going to let the VP do an end run.

"We have no evidence that the president is dead, has resigned, or is unable to discharge the powers and duties of the office, and until we do the VP needs to back off."

"You mean you want the vice-president to just sit on his hands and wait for news? That's absurd. We're in the middle of a crisis."

"No, goddammit, that's not what I am saying. Obviously the vice-president has to be involved in coordinating our response. That is what the president would want. But it would be a big mistake for the VP to create the impression he is assuming the duties of president. Alexander Haig tried that when Reagan was shot. They treated him like a lunatic and Haig wasn't even VP!"

"Fair enough," Paul said, "But the moment things really go south for the president in Paris we are going to run the full table, we're not going to just sit here with our dicks in our hands while the world goes to Hell."

58

Paris 10:50 p.m.
l'Élysée Presidential Palace
Office of French President, Amaury Jardin

"*Monsieur le Président,*" said Francois Rambeau, the president's Foreign Minister. "I finally reached Magistrat André Malevu, the judge who issued the judicial order. He's on the line."

"Put him through," said President Jardin. The judge's voice came on.

"Bonsoir, Monsieur le Président," said Malevu. His tone was jocular.

"Monsieur," President Jardin said tersely, "There has been a dangerous misunderstanding tonight. A commandant of the police Préfecture claims to have a judicial order from you directing him to enter Hôtel Marly where the American president is staying. Our French security detail at the hotel fears Commandant Poussin may be attempting to arrest President Childs. This would be madness and surely lead to bloodshed. Please assure me that no such action was ordered by you."

"On the contrary, there is no mistake." Malevu sounded gleeful. "I have issued a valid arrest warrant for the President of the United States."

"My god, man! Do you realize what you've done?"

"I know exactly what I've done."

"No, you clearly don't. Do you want France to be at war with the United States? As president of the Republic I order you to rescind to this absurd warrant. Contact Commandant Poussin immediately and withdraw the order."

"No, Mr. President, I will not. And I wish to remind you, sir, that this is France, not some banana republic. France's constitution is clear that the judiciary shall be independent of the executive branch. You cannot just wave your presidential wand and make the French constitution disappear."

Jardin placed his hand against his forehead and realized it was wet with perspiration. His pulse had accelerated.

"I will have you arrested for treason! Recall Poussin now!"

"There is no treason. The order I issued as juge d'insruction was prepared in strict accordance with the statutes of France and the European Union. I have invoked the well-established doctrine of universal jurisdiction. It gives a magistrat such as myself the judicial authority to order the arrest of a foreign official for the commission of war crimes and crimes against humanity - even if he is a head of state. The American slaughter of innocent French citizens was clearly such a crime. So, with all due respect, sir, even as president of the Republic you cannot undo the warrant. President Childs will be arrested tonight."

Jardin shut off the speakerphone and turned to his Foreign Minister.

"Francois. Can he do this?"

"Mr. President, we've seen this notion of universal jurisdiction employed several times over the last few years."

"Yes, of course, but…."

"Excuse me for interrupting, Mr. President, I know you need to make critical decisions soon, so I will get to the point."

"Continue."

"Over the last twenty years, European judges have applied the notion of universal jurisdiction several times to bring officials of other countries to account, even when the alleged crimes were committed outside the territorial boundaries of the country of the issuing judge. Universal jurisdiction holds that some crimes are so terrible that they are, in effect, Erga Omnes, or Jus Cogens, that is, crimes against all humanity, and as such should not be limited by territorial or sovereign boundaries. It's a notion that dates back to Roman law."

"Yes, yes, fine. But this is the President of the United States. As French president it is inconceivable that I would simply stand by and permit this reckless magistrat to push us into an abyss."

"It's true the magistra*t* may be pushing the doctrine to an extreme. But if you unilaterally annul the court order, you're inviting a constitutional crisis and an explosive backlash from the public, possibly even the military. The nation is still enraged over the killing of the school children. As self-destructive to France as the arrest of the American president might be, the public might take great satisfaction in seeing him arrested."

Jardin had all but stopped listening. He could see disaster no matter which path he took. The only thing he knew to a certainty was that he was out of time. Soon, things would be completely beyond his control. French police would be killing French and American secret service agents and then an apocalypse would descend on his presidency and his countrymen.

I will not be a bystander to history.

"Giselle, get General de Plessy on the line, immediately!"

59

Ten fifty-five p.m.
Champs-Élysées – Hôtel Marly

"Will, come in - it's Stone. I'm on my way up. Have Dumbledore ready to move *stat,* and tell the team I'm coming up the stairwell."

"Roger that," Will said.

Izzy Stone took the steps two at a time. The elevators had been disabled on her instructions.

Reaching the tenth floor, Izzy found the stairwell exit door ajar as she had ordered. She bent forward, panting hard. Two pistols, an HK MP5 machine gun, ammo and communications gear had been a heavy lift.

One hundred ten...one hundred nine...

She cracked the door and shouted into the hallway,

"Stone!"

"All clear," came the reply. Izzy entered the hallway and rushed past a series of makeshift barricades hastily assembled by agents guarding the hallway.

Outside the hotel, the sound of gunfire had become more intense

Not long until they breach the hotel perimeter. After that they'll head for the upper floors.

Out of breath, racing down the corridor, Izzy was mentally counting down, second by second.

Ninety-nine… ninety-eight…ninety- seven...

She was marking off each second, creating a deadline for herself - just as she had done all her life - as a scholar, an athlete, a West Point Cadet.

Except this time the president's life hinged on those seconds.

Only two minutes – three max, to get POTUS out of the hotel.

Reaching the room she saw Will holding the door open with his left hand while cradling a Remington 870 shotgun in his right arm.

Good for close quarter combat.

Will jerked the door open to let Izzy in then quickly re-closed and double-locked it.

Eighty-two… eighty-one…

"Will, is he ready?"

"All set. He's in the next room. His military aide is with him."

"Good," she said, relieved to hear that the president's military aide, the individual responsible for carrying the "Football," the suitcase containing the nuclear codes was there. "Let's move," she said.

Izzy rapped smartly on the bedroom door.

"Mr. President, Izzy Stone."

"We're coming," the aide said.

Seventy-eight... seventy-seven...

BOOM!

The side of the building shook violently, knocking Izzy to the floor.

"RPG !" Izzy said.

Dust and smoke filled the room. She scrambled back up and grabbed the bedroom door handle. It wouldn't rotate.

Jammed.

Izzy heard coughing in the bedroom.

Seventy-one... seventy...

"Will, give me a hand!" She looked back. Will was on the floor, motionless.

Izzy turned to the door, removed her Sig Sauer pistol and yelled,

"Mr. President, stand away from the door, now!"

Sixty... fifty-nine...

She fired several rounds downward into the door armature, shattering it. She spun and delivered a hard backwards kick. The door gave.

The president was on the floor. He appeared dazed. Blood oozed from his right shoulder. Beside him the military aide lay mortally wounded. The Football appeared undamaged. The rifle-propelled grenade had struck the alley-side of the building near the bedroom and collapsed part of the bedroom ceiling, starting a small fire.

Another three feet and no one would have survived.

Izzy touched her com module.

"Green Label, we have incoming RPGS, re-secure alley."

"Acknowledge, Green Label out."

Izzy was relieved to see Will and four agents at the door. She was alarmed to see small trickles of blood were coming from Will's nose and left ear.

"Will," Izzy said, "how bad is it, and don't shit me."

"I'm good, nothing broken. Eyes, ears still working. Was just the concussion of the blast."

"Good," Izzy said, patting him on the shoulder. "Now let's move!"

Together they managed to get Childs to his feet. One of the agents damped a wash towel and worked feverishly to clean and bandage the president's shoulder. A second agent took possession of the Football. Izzy grabbed a grenade from a small pile of munitions in the room.

Twenty-four...twenty-three...

Izzy's headpiece came alive.

"Stone, come in – you have hostiles in the stairwell. Green Label out."

"Acknowledge, Stone out." Izzy could hear shouts and heavy bursts of automatic weapons in the stairwell.

Thirteen...twelve...

Finger on the trigger of the automatic, she dashed to the hallway door and cracked it slightly. The hallway was still clear. Will and the other agents followed, half-carrying the president. Izzy sprinted down the hall towards what appeared to be a dead end. A tall soda and snack-vending machine were the only things visible at the foot of the hallway.

Izzy saw alarm in Will's eyes, as if to say: *It's a dead end.*

"It's okay, Will, stay with me."

Reaching the seven-foot tall vending machine, Izzy shouldered the automatic, placed her right foot against the wall and, with a mighty tug, pulled the machine away. As the vending machine swung loose it exposed a metal door about five feet high and four feet wide. In the center was a thin silver keypad.

Izzy entered six numbers into the keypad and the metal door disappeared into the wall exposing a mid-sized elevator. Dropping their heads low, the group followed Izzy in. As the elevator door closed a spring loaded mechanism pulled the vending machine back to its original position.

Will could not conceal his surprise.

"Did my homework," Izzy said. "This elevator was installed nine months ago to help celebrities avoid the paparazzi. Only the hotel manager knows the code. I got it from him."

"But won't this just take us down into the middle of the fire-fight?" Will said, as the elevator descended, picking up speed.

"Not if my idea works."

Five…four…three…

60

Paris - 11:00 p.m.

Sigint Specialist Longo Raines was midway through the FLASHCRITIC he was transmitting to the Situation Room from his perch in the small room located near the top of Hôtel Marly when the RPG blasted him into kingdom come.

The White House - Situation Room 5:10 p.m. EST - 11:10 p.m. Paris

U.S. Vice-President Stein was reading the incomplete message from Raines in disbelief.

"Situation Critical...Marly under attack... Casualties...Attempting to move Dumbledore...assailants unk.............."

Stein turned to Ed Valucek, National Security Advisor who had joined him in the SitRoom.

"Ed, get with Sec State Traficante and set up a conference call immediately with President Jardin. We need to know what in Hell's Bells is going on at the hotel. And get SecDef and CentCom down here now."

61

The elevator quickly descended fifteen floors and came to a jarring stop.

The door opened and the group exited. They were in a dim, rectangular chamber weakly illuminated by a small light next to the elevator. The walls appeared to have a newer cement surface but the floor was composed of weathered stone.

The elevator anchored the narrow end of the rectangle. Most of the chamber lay in heavy shadow. The air smelled like freshly turned earth.

A grey metal door near the elevator was the only other discernable feature of the chamber.

"Where are we, Izzy?" the president said, holding a hand against his injured shoulder.

"Sir, we're about sixty feet below street level," Izzy said.

"What are our options?"

"Mr. president. See that door by the elevator? It opens onto a stairway that leads to the ground floor of a restaurant next to this hotel. We could exit onto the avenue from there, but the area is probably controlled by hostiles. It would be a long shot." She paused. "There's another way. But it's also high risk."

"Let's hear it," the president said.

"Yes sir. This way." Izzy said, jogging toward the darkest part of the chamber. The group fell in behind her but soon lost her in the gloom.

"Over here," Izzy said.

They moved toward her voice. They found Izzy kneeling on the stone floor, pulling on a large, bronze ring attached to a cast-iron manhole cover.

"I need some hands."

Two agents put their automatic weapons down and helped muscle the heavy cover away from its emplacement as Will and the other agents stood guard.

A rush of pungent air erupted from the opening.

"You may not like it," Izzy said, "but it's our best chance. It's the Paris sewer system. It covers hundreds of miles of subterranean tunnels and catacombs. I think I can get us past the bad guys above. It's your call, sir."

"Let's do it," the president said.

"We'll have to stay close," Izzy said. "The channels have some lighting but many sections are dark and slippery. Cell phones need to be turned off now, and batteries removed. If we don't, they'll find us with GPS triangulation."

They descended into the dimness. Reaching the bottom of the ladder, they found themselves on a wide concrete walkway that paralleled the fast-moving water. Using a small flashlight for illumination, Izzy guided the others along the concrete embankment.

The three-story, high-vaulted ceiling of the channel was enormous.

"It's huge," said Will.

"Has to be," Izzy said. "The volume of water that travels through the system is gigantic. We're underneath the avenue des Champs-Élysées one of the widest boulevards in the world. Every channel parallels the street above it. If the street is narrow, the channel below is narrow. If it's big, like the Champs-Élysées, then the canal channel has to be large."

"Good thing you know where we are," Will said.

"You can thank an old *egoutier,* named Jerome I got to know when I was posted to the Paris embassy."

"Egoutier?" said the president.

"A workier in the underground channels and sewers." Izzy said. "Jerome worked in the system all his life and taught me everything I know about the channels and the catacombs," Izzy said.

Within a few minutes they had covered four hundred yards. Izzy knew the president would need to rest periodically. It was obvious he was in pain. The agents were alternating by twos to help him move forward.

She spotted a small alcove.

"Let's take two minutes," Izzy said.

The group leaned up against the wall catching their breath. Izzy wanted to dial down the tension. She knew they would soon require total concentration. Navigating the labyrinth of tunnels would be dangerous enough. Worse, it was just a matter of minutes until their pursuers guessed the escape route she'd taken.

Soon there was muffled shouting.

"They're in!" Izzy said. "We'll have to move faster."

They broke into a half-sprint, the president half-limping, half-carried by the agents. Izzy's mind was racing.

I need a plan fast. Remember what Jerome taught me.

The sound of heavy footfalls and yelling were louder now. A ripple of fear swept the back of her neck.

There!

Izzy saw it. A small, grime-covered sign with the words, "*rue de Berri.*" She knew exactly where they were now.

It triggered old Jerome's advice.

"Mademoiselle Stone, all the channels have the same signage below as the streets above so that those of us who work in the system will always know where we are. Remember that. It can save your life."

Old Jerome, gnome-like, with leathery hands, protuberant nose and small, intelligent dark eyes, had leaned closer and whispered conspiratorially:

But there are other passages in the catacombs that have no name, no signage. Old, forgotten passages dating back to the Romans that few know. I'll show them to you.

Izzy had quickly accepted his offer. His knowledge of the serpentine web of tunnels, routes and shafts had astonished her.

Pow!... ping!

The report and impact of a round striking a wall made Izzy and the others duck. She heard heavy boots running along the channel embankment. They were closer.

"A wild shot," Izzy said, "They haven't spotted us yet. Keep moving."

Pow!...ping!

Another round ricocheted.

Izzy was intently focused on the wall of the channel.

Then... a familiar feature! What she'd been looking for. Got it!

Barely visible in the shadows, was a small indentation in the wall.

Jerome, bless you!

Izzy felt along the indentation until she found the metal pressure plate.

She pushed it hard with the palm of her hand. A small door gave way.

"This way!"

Bending low, the group entered a tight passageway pitch-black but for the thin beam cast by Izzy's small flashlight. Izzy hit another pressure plate and the door closed behind them, leaving no trace.

The passage was humid and smelled of stagnant water. Unseen things scurried in the darkness.

"Izzy?" the president whispered, question in his voice.

"It's an ancient excavation, sir, probably a thousand years old, dug long before the main channel was built. It's not on any map of the system."

Izzy noticed the president holding his hand over his bandaged right shoulder. It had a faint red sheen in the dim light. Blood.

62

They had been in the passageway about ten minutes. Every few yards Izzy paused and swept the wall with her light searching for something in the gloom. She was quietly counting each footstep the way that old Jerome had instructed her.

The limited illumination of the small flashlight provided some help but not enough. She raised her arms in the darkness, spread out her fingers and began sweeping them from side to side. When she was sure there was nothing hanging from the ceiling or protruding from either wall, she took another step forward and repeated the maneuver.

Has to be here.

She continued her strange ballet in the dim light as the others watched. Izzy's hand brushed against something hard, rough and cold. She threw the light on it. It was the bottom metal rung of a ladder.

"Got it!"

"What?" Will said.

"A way for us to get out of this tunnel. It should lead to a storage area in the basement of the Hôtel Louis Cinq where they store furniture and miscellaneous items they rarely use. We should be able to find our way out to the streets through a stairwell. From there we might make it to the British Embassy a few blocks away."

BOOM!

An explosion filled the passage. Dust and debris engulfed the group, momentarily blinding and disorienting them.

"They're in!" Izzy said. "Move!"

The sound of yelling and heavy boots reverberated in the passage. Through the dust and the cordite smoke, Izzy could make out halogen lamps, arcing wildly as their pursuers closed the distance.

"We need covering fire!" Izzy said.

Two of the secret service agents dropped spread-eagle onto the passage. hugging the tunnel floor, their Heckler and Koch MP5 machine guns pointed toward the on-coming lights.

Izzy shouted to Will, "Go, Go!"

Will and agents Evans and Oberlin strained to push and pull the president and the Football up the metal rungs of the ladder.

"*Ping, Ping, Ping.*"

Fire from their pursuers became a fusillade.

"Engage!" Izzy said.

The two agents on the floor of the passage opened up with a furious volley. Several hostiles went down as their halogen lights faltered and went down.

Will was now at the top of the ladder, pushing open a heavy metal cover.

Izzy chambered her MP5 and let loose several bursts in the direction of the attackers. When she was sure the president had made it to the top, she grabbed the rungs of the ladder and scrambled upward while providing firing cover for the two agents below.

"Disengage!" Izzy yelled at the two agents who were still firing.

One of the two agents jumped up, still firing and moved toward the ladder.

POW!

He slumped as a round caught him.

The second agent moved to help him but also went down in a burst of gunfire.

Heart pounding, Izzy dropped to the floor and opened up on full automatic. Two of the assailants dropped only yards away. Izzy moved from one agent to the other.

Both gone.

Other attackers were close. Izzy took the MK3A2 concussion grenade she had, pulled the pin, pitched it in their direction and hit the deck. In the enclosed passage the grenade exploded with violent multiplying force. Izzy hugged the floor as shrapnel pinged around her and wild screams of pain came from the darkened tunnel.

She scrambled back to the ladder climbing fast. Reaching the top, she slammed the metal cover shut. Will, Evans and Oberlin managed to push a large piece of equipment that was close by, onto the metal cover.

Bent over, panting heavily, Izzy looked around the cavernous space.

"Shit!"

The basement had been completely altered. Instead of the underground storage space she'd expected, the space had been transformed into a slick parking garage filled with stretch limos, Ferraris and other signature cars.

We don't have more than a minute or two until they blow the metal cover.

"Quick," Izzy said to the others, "See if any of these cars are unlocked."

All five were now going from car to car, pulling on doors.

"This Bentley's open!" Will yelled. "Keys in the ignition!"

"The president goes in the back seat," Izzy said. "Evans, Oberlin on either side. Keep him low. Will, you're riding shotgun. Go!"

She slid into the driver's seat and turned the ignition. The others piled in as the Bentley roared to life.

"They'll have units surrounding the hotel...it's going to be a bumpy ride," she said.

She revved the engine to four thousand *rpms* and looked at the tachometer.

This engine can do eight thousand. I'll need it.

Izzy maneuvered the Bentley to the foot of the exit ramp. There would be a security kiosk and a barrier gate. She positioned the Bentley carefully.

Whoomp!

An explosion shook the garage violently.

In front, Izzy saw attendants and hotel security rushing down the ramp toward her. In the rear view mirror men were emerging from the blown manhole.

It's now or never.

She pushed down hard on the brake with her left foot and held firmly as she threw the car into first gear. Revving the engine's huge power plant she popped her foot off the brake.

The Bentley catapulted forward, motor bellowing, tires screaming, acrid smoke rising from the burning rubber. With a thunderous roar it shot up the ramp, splintering the wood barrier gate and emerging onto narrow rue Quentin Bauchart, a howling beast streaking from its lair.

As the Bentley sailed onto the *rue*, pedestrians, hotel valets, taxis and limos jockeyed wildly to avoid being hit by the oncoming vehicle.

"It's a one way street!" Will shouted, as Izzy barreled directly into oncoming traffic.

"I know. Hang on!"

Jaws clenched, body steeled for impact, Izzy accelerated the charging Bentley towards vehicles that were zigzagging wildly to avoid being struck.

"WHAM!"

The Bentley T-boned a taxi attempting a u-turn in the narrow street. The taxi spun out of control, rolled and crashed through the glass windows of a Lebanese restaurant. Flying debris from the damaged front end of the Bentley rained down on the roof and trunk.

Ahead, Izzy could see the flashing blue lights of police vehicles and a makeshift perimeter. The rue, now stacked bumper-to-bumper with cars, left no room to maneuver.

She yanked the wheel to the right, climbed the curb and tore through the black metal bollards separating the street from the sidewalk. The Bentley was speeding down the sidewalk with no clearance on either side. Izzy fought for control as the car scraped the walls of the buildings shooting off sparks and masonry. Pedestrians leaped into doorways.

I've got five seconds before they seal the street completely.

The accelerator was almost flush with the floorboard, the engine bellowing. Bodies, vehicles and sounds became a blur as the six-thousand-pound, dual-turbocharged, six-point-seven five-liter engine bore down full-throated, toward the gendarmes.

The speedometer was approaching one hundred forty kilometers per hour.

Three...two...one...

CRAAASH!

She'd aimed perfectly. The Bentley struck the police van's rear bumper in a forty-five degree pit maneuver. The van spun like a top, smashing into the makeshift line of police vehicles. Car windows exploded from the impact as bumpers, traffic cones and wooden barriers went flying while gendarmes scrambled for their lives.

Izzy braked hard and hung a wild left, crazily fishtailing onto busy avenue Marceau, a broad, one-way street flowing in the same direction. She floored the car picking up momentum as she wove in and out of traffic.

As the Bentley raced toward the intersection of avenue Pierre 1re de la Serbie, she saw a procession emerging from the historic church of St. Pierre de Chaillot at the far end of the block.

"Jesus, a nighttime wedding!" Izzy said.

A priest dressed in an amaranth cassock, carrying a large gold cross aloft, was leading a bridal party in tuxes and satin dresses. The bride's white flowing gown gleamed brightly in the street lights. The wedding party was headed for the crosswalk.

"Damn!" Izzy said.

She sat on the horn but the sounds of wailing police sirens drowned out the Bentley.

"Will!" Izzy shouted.

Will pulled out his pistol, rolled down his window and fired several shots above the crowd.

Floral bouquets, rosaries and open bibles scattered as the party panicked, rushing back toward the church.

The Bentley tore through the intersection as boutonnieres, programs and flowers fluttered and swirled around the speeding car, catching on the grill and bumpers. The bridal veil had entangled around the car's antenna, the long silk tulle trailing the vehicle like a racing banner.

Speeding through the intersection, the traffic thinned and Izzy gunned the engine harder, hurtling down avenue Marceau past rue Goethe, banking left as Marceau became Pont de l'Alma. The bridge loomed ahead.

"They're gaining," Will said, as the pursuing sirens grew louder.

"I know, but if I can get us across the bridge to the Left Bank we have a chance."

Moments later they reached the Pont de l'Alma bridge spanning the Seine.

"Listen up!" Izzy shouted, "As soon as we cross the bridge I'm going to pull a tight one-hundred-eighty-degree. It's going to be a hard stop so hold on. After that we bail."

She accelerated the Bentley until the engine groaned. As they neared the far end of the bridge,

Izzy pulled the steering wheel sharply to the right with one hand, stomped both feet down on the brakes, and pulled the hand brake as hard as she could with the other. The rear end of the Bentley bounced over the small sidewalk curb and whip-sawed violently as the stabilization system fought to keep the car from tipping. A squealing of tires and the thick smell of burning rubber rose from the side-walk as the rear of the car skidded across the broad pavement and slammed violently against a four-foot high metal cage protruding from the sidewalk. Izzy threw the car into neutral as the Bentley came to a jarring stop. The engine, now super-heated, was en-gulfed in a dark cloud of smoke, small tongues of flame quickly appeared.

"Go! Go!" Izzy said, opening her door and roll-ing out, her right hand clutching the Uzi. She jerk-ed open the rear passenger door. Will, Evans and Oberlin scrambled to help the president out.

Before them lay the tangled remains of the metal cage that only moments earlier had securely enclosed a staircase that wound downward and disappeared beneath the sidewalk. The force of the car's impact had pushed the cage to the side, exposing the stair-way. Crouching low, Izzy and the others scampered toward the opening and descended.

63

They followed the stairway downward in a corkscrew pattern until they arrived at a metal gate enclosing a large, vaulted stone and earthen room. Izzy pushed at the gate. Locked.

Backing everyone up the stairway she fired a volley into the gate's armature, disabling it. She pushed the gate open and they entered the huge chamber. The floor and walls of the room smelled of wet earth and cement.

Izzy turned to the president and the others.

"We're in a part of the égouts located on the Left Bank," she said.

Will pointed to an immense twelve-foot high metal sphere resting in a gigantic cream-colored stone alcove.

"What the hell is that?" he said.

"It's one of the giant boules used by the égoutiers to clean the channels," Izzy said. "They drop them into the waterway and the spheres roll along the channel floor pushed by the strong current. They weigh thousands of pounds. As they tumble along they scrape the floor and sides of the channel, cleaning it."

"Let's move," she said, quick-stepping into the dimly-lit tunnel.

The path bordered a long, rectangular wire pen that hung over over the swift channel below. As they moved from one chamber to the next they could hear the water rushing alongside them.

In plexiglass displays along the route, ancient dredging machines and old égoutier's tools told the story of the world's most elaborate sewer system. Giant black and white photographs of hollow-eyed, mud-covered workers dressed in drab nineteenth century work clothes lined the curving walls of the vaulted space, along with swords, scabbards, large coins and other artifacts from a much earlier Paris.

64

They'd been following the channel at a fast pace for ten minutes, staying on the *quai.* The channel was now fully exposed, no longer covered by wire mesh. Izzy knew they were paralleling the Left Bank of the Seine, moving east toward her destination - the Louvre médiéval, an ancient structure buried under the great Louvre museum.

The Louvre médiéval was a mysterious, tenth-century fortress whose massive foundations and ramparts had been unearthed during renovation of the modern Louvre in the nineteen-eighties.

The original fortress, once an imposing fortification and home to early French kings had gradually disappeared as succeeding monarchs demolished more and more of the castle.

Izzy heard a low sound. She looked back. In the shadows behind them a faint light bobbed on the water. She instantly recognized the sound of the small motor craft sometimes used to patrol the channels.

She turned to the group.

"They're in a boat. Stay as close to me as you can."

She broke into a sprint and disappeared into the gloom. As she ran she swept her flashlight along the earthen wall, searching

I know there's one here.

The sound grew until it became a high-pitched whine.

She moved faster. More blank wall.

It's got to be here. But where, dammit?

The rising sound of the motor was now accompanied by indistinct shouts.

Izzy's heart was pounding.

Finally...she spotted the two-foot-square grey metal switching box she'd been looking for. Above the box in large red letters were the words:

DANGER! HAUTE TENSION!

The box was bolted to the wall, its door secured with a steel lock. Peering through the thick mud-stained pane of glass she could make out the hefty black handle inside. She struck the glass repeatedly with the butt of her pistol until it shattered, leaving a small, jagged opening.

She reached through the tight opening, grabbed the handle, and pulled.

It wouldn't budge. She pulled harder.

Stuck! C'mon, C'MON!

The engine of the pursuing motorboat, amplified by the solid walls, grew to an insistent roar.

Izzy pulled again, mightily.

Aaaagh!

A glass shard sliced into her left hand. Blood spurted out.

Damn, damn, damn!

She raised the pistol and smashed the glass again and again. The hole got larger.

She could hear their pursuers shouting: *Allez-y! Arrêtez! Stop!*

The searchlight of the advancing motorboat illuminated Will and the others as they ran to catch up with her. The boat was about three hundred yards away.

It's now or never. The president's a sitting duck!

Izzy shoved the gun into her holster then jammed both hands through the jagged opening. Rivulets of blood appeared and sped down her wrists soaking her watch as the glass cut deeper into her hands.

Still stuck, Goddammit!

She placed her right foot against the wall and violently pulled the handle.

SCREEEEECH!

With a heavy grating noise, the switch reluctantly gave.

A moment later a loud splashing sound emanated from somewhere far in the gloom and Izzy felt a sudden "whoosh" as a bolt of air shot through the vaulted tunnel. The distant splashing soon became a malevolent, low-pitched grinding noise rattling the channel walls.

In the reflection of the boat's approaching searchlight, Izzy saw the water begin to shimmer. The motorboat began to pitch as the water in the channel became more agitated. She could see the crew fighting to keep their balance.

The grinding sound grew louder, its deafening "thump, thump," rapidly approaching like a gargantuan beast.

Plus rapidement! Faster!" Someone shouted from the boat.

Suddenly, the gigantic boule emerged from the darkness with terrifying speed, its towering shape dwarfing the small craft.

"Merde! Non, Non!"

Shrieks of terror rose as the gigantic boule struck the craft's stern, crushing boat and riders under its massive weight. The bow searchlight rotated crazily then disappeared as heaving water roiled forward onto the *quai* and the giant boule continued its turbulent journey.

Izzy instinctively made a sign of the cross as she and the others scurried away from the sloshing water.

"This way!" she said, dashing toward a chain-link gate beyond the switchbox.

"Will, give me a hand."

He rushed to her side.

"On my count," Izzy said,

"One, two, three..."

They crashed their bodies into the gate. It buckled and sent them tumbling to the ground. In front of them, a stairway led down into darkness. They scrambled to their feet.

"Let's go," Izzy said, descending into the void.

Will and the others followed.

Breathless, they reached the bottom of the stairs.

Izzy saw the president half bent over. He was panting heavily.

"Sir, we'll take five."

"No, Izzy," he said. "That was close. We need to keep moving. Don't worry about me. Do you know this route?"

"Yes, sir. It's one of the utility tunnels that the égoutiers use to access the main channel," Izzy said. "We won't be able to stay in it very long because others can enter it from the street above. Then we'll be trapped."

"Ideas?" the president said.

"Look." She moved her light along the wall in a slow arc and stopped.

"See the small opening with the chain across it in the tunnel wall?"

She was pointing at an uneven-shaped hole in the earthen wall. It appeared to be no more than three feet in diameter.

"What is it?" the president said.

"A crude entry to an abandoned passage. They're everywhere in the tunnel system. Some of them lead to limestone quarries dug by the Romans two thousand years ago. Most of them are hundreds of years old, part of a dizzying maze of excavations. The égoutiers are afraid of them. It's easy to get lost and never get out."

"Should we chance it?" Will said.

"If we do, it will be a gamble." Izzy said, "It would be a lot safer if we could stay in this utility tunnel, because farther up it connects with a much larger tunnel at rue de Constantine. I've been in it. If we can make it there our odds will improve."

Will tapped Izzy's shoulder.

"Listen," he said.

Somewhere in the utility tunnel came the sound of muffled voices and running.

Izzy turned to them. "We just ran out of options." She raised the small chain, "Quick, everyone in."

One by one they crawled through the tiny opening into the pitch black passage. Izzy took a last look over her shoulder as she entered.

We may never find our way out.

65

"Where are they?"

Commandant Poussin was perspiring heavily, his stubby fingers worrying his left eyebrow as he angrily questioned the lieutenant. Poussin was sitting in a makeshift command post located on the third floor of a dilapidated office building in the fifteenth arrondissement. There was no number or name on the door. It was one of several safe houses Poussin had stashed away over the years. The last thing he needed right now was for the Préfecture to know where he was.

"Commandant," the lieutenant said, "They're somewhere in the underground tunnels, possibly on the Left Bank, but we're not sure, it might be the Right Bank. We lost them in the Pont de l'Alma channel. Something went wrong. Several of our men are missing. We're looking for them now but all we've come up with is some debris from the boat they were using."

Poussin leaped from his chair, the veins of his temples bulging, his crimson bull neck spilling over the extra-large shirt collar. He pressed his meaty knuckles into the top of the desk. It groaned under the weight.

"Save the excuses," he said. "we're not looking for a simple pickpocket. This is the President of the United States! We don't have much time. It's been two hours already. Soon the entire French government will be down our throats."

"Yes, Commandant Poussin," the officer said, visibly shaken as he turned and left.

Poussin slumped deeper into the creaky desk chair, an old chair upholstered in cheap vinyl, discolored and peeling, nearing the end of its useful life. The irony did not escape him. He too felt old, used up, in a world that had become unrecognizable. Exhausted, his mind in turmoil, he struggled to make sense of the stupefying events that had overtaken him in the last few hours. Without warning his life had been swept up and blown into an alternative universe where everything he'd believed now mocked him.

Throughout his life there'd never been any question about the moral duality of life nor the side he belonged on. It was a simple matter. There were those who were the malefactors and those who were the righteous. In a world of good and evil there was no middle ground. One's personal preferences or station in life were of no consequence. Either a person stood within the law or outside it. As a police commandant he'd always believed that it was his sacred duty to bring to justice those who chose to ignore the rule of law. No civilized society could survive otherwise.

If I hadn't insisted on serving the arrest warrant, violence could have been avoided and those men would still be alive. But the decision whether to serve the warrant or not was not mine to make. I cannot pick and choose which judicial orders to carry out and which to ignore. It would make a lie of my oath.

Besides, if the powerful are exempted from the same laws that punish the weak, then the idea of justice is nothing more than a cynical balance sheet. Good men are dead. It's regrettable. But when the law is tested it must be defended, no matter the cost. I won't abandon my convictions for the sake of political convenience. If it's within my power, the president will be arrested.

66

National Security Council – West Wing

"Whaddya you mean, you don't know where they are?"

Ed Valucek, National Security Advisor to the President, was hurling a volcanic glare at Jerry Graham, Director, National Intelligence. Valucek's Ivy League "Princetonese" had somehow morphed into the vernacular of a Bowery pugilist. But for his lofty West Wing title, it would have been hard to guess Valucek had graduated summa cum laude with a Ph.D in strategic international studies and linguistics. Valucheck knew he was strong-arming Graham, a high ranking, but weak presidential advisor.

"Jerry, you've got the most advanced intel systems in the world available to you and you can't tell us where the frigg'n President of the United States is? You son-of-a-bitch, you're not fuckin' paid to say, 'sorry, I don't know, and now may I have a cookie,' goddammit! We've got the entire national command staff down in the Situation Room waiting for some hard intel!"

Valucek was on one of his bone-rattling rants, usually performed for the simple theatre of it, having learned long ago that going nuclear in a conversation almost always got him what he wanted. The fact that he'd been named 175- pound Outstanding Boxer, Heavyweight Division while at Princeton, didn't hurt.

But not today. This was the real deal and Valucek knew it, knew it could, no, in fact had, set the entire planet on edge. And when the big dogs were on edge, anything could happen, and did – usually for the worse. FLASH messages throughout the intelligence community had already reported rising Defcon levels in China, Russia, the U.K and France. India and Pakistan wouldn't be far behind.

"What's Langley telling us?" Valucek said.

"CIA says there was a firefight at the hotel a couple of hours ago, there were casualties," Graham said, his voice calm, "but Langley lost contact with the president's detail. There's no further."

"NSA, DIA, NGA, NRO? Whadda they got?"

"Zip, They say POTUS is off the grid. Nothing's working. Same for State, Interpol, French Intelligence and MI6."

"Where's the fuck'n Football?" Valucek said.

"Unknown," said Graham.

"Christ," said Valucek, "You've talked to the uber-brains at Rand, what's their game theory coming up with?"

"No consensus. Unlikely the Élysée Palace is in on it. French president Jardin is in a complete panic. It's just mass confusion at this point. No one at the Élysée is really on top of it. Could be a false flag operation – terrorists dressed like cops. Could be a rogue group within the Préfecture, there are some there who may have radical Islamist sympathies – but, could also be French political extremists looking to capitalize on the missile strike. With all those dead children, the French public is sounding like the Paris Commune. They want blood."

"Shit," Valucek said.

He was a hard-ass realist when it came to international bloodletting; it was a dangerous damn world, no place for tree-huggers – *but Jesus, all those kids.*

67

Paris catacombs

Where are we?

Apart from the illumination from Izzy's small light, they were in impenetrable darkness. She was trying to maintain some sense of direction as she and the others made their way through the tight serpentine passage, heads bent down to avoid hitting the low limestone ceiling.

At times they found themselves sloshing through foul-smelling water dripping from sweating walls and ceilings. Other times the air inexplicably changed from stifling heaviness to cool, spring-like freshness emanating from unseen sources in the tunnel. Seashells and other marine fossils protruded from the rough-hewn surfaces, evidence of a rich geologic history.

As the illumination from the light swept back and forth on tunnel walls, odd markings appeared without explanation. Large arrows painted in bright colors seemed to point in every direction; initials and unfamiliar acronyms clustered without rhyme or reason. Izzy took some comfort in the knowledge that even if they were lost, others had at least passed through.

She'd cautioned everyone to remain in physical contact with each other..

"This passage is full of intersecting pathways. One moment of inattention and you can find yourself alone. Stay close."

68

The scene on the grand avenue des Champs-Élysées in front of the Hôtel Marly was apocalyptic. Amidst scores of smoldering vehicles, shattered glass, pools of blood, shell casings and heavy smoke rising from the bullet-pocked Hôtel Marly, hundreds of heavily armed French Special Forces personnel with grim expressions were directing scores of arriving emergency vehicles while guarding medical teams conducting triage on the wounded.

The suddenness, lateness and brutality of the firefight had caught the government and citizenry of Paris completely off guard. On social networks rumors abounded. A Hollywood blockbuster was being filmed. An anti-terrorism exercise was being conducted. ISIS had invaded. The Eiffel Tower had also been attacked. As the rumors spread across social media they were picked up by news organizations.

Soon, even reputable journalists were caught up in the frenzy as they streamed conflicting eyewitness accounts some of them fake and struggled to get hard facts from the Élysée. But the Élysée was releasing few details as it struggled feverishly to comprehend dizzying developments, contain the violence and locate the American president. It was a familiar pattern of chaos and confusion that seemed to have become the new normal in the age of mind-bending urban slaughter.

Incroyable! C'est horrifiant.

French president Amaury Jardin was aghast. In less than three hours Paris had been catapulted from a calm, though tense city, to one of staggering violence and unthinkable peril. Standing next to his presidential limousine, surrounded by a visibly nervous security detail, Jardin could hardly believe the chaos and carnage that lay before him on one of the world's great boulevards.

His decision to abruptly declare a national state of emergency and invoke martial law had empowered him to order the French military to deploy in great strength at breakneck speed to the Hôtel Marly. The arrival of several-hundred stone-faced French Special Forces accompanied by the thundering approach of six AMX56 Leclerc battle tanks and five Tigre attack helicopters settled the matter.

President Jardin saw General de Plessy, expression taciturn, approach, his stride long and assertive.

When he got to Jardin he offered a smart salute that the president returned.

"General, what can you tell me?" Jardin said.

"Sir, I regret to say that thus far we've not been able to make contact with President Childs or the agents in charge of his detail. To be brutally honest, sir, we don't know if Childs is alive or dead. It's possible they escaped, though how they could have done so is still unclear. I've also received unconfirmed reports that an undetermined number of GIGN personnel led by a commandant of the Préfecture named Poussin, are thought to be in pursuit. We're conducting an intensive search for the president and Poussin. Within the hour the entire city of Paris will be on full lock-down."

President Jardin absorbed the words then looked out on the scene once more.

"I can only imagine what it must have been like," he said.

"Sir, it was urban warfare. Close quarters, violent and intense. Thus far, we've counted twenty-two dead and more than thirty wounded - some more seriously than others. We're doing a room-to-room search of the hotel to see if there are other casualties."

"Do we know how it started?" said the president.

"No, sir," said de Plessy. "It could have been anything, a backfire a nervous gendarme or agent. We may never know."

69

Situation Room

"Mr. Vice President, we should have French President Jardin on the line any moment," Ed Valucek said.

"About time." Stein said. For several hours all attempts to contact the French President had been unsuccessful, his staff telling the White House that the president was too busy trying to get control of the situation.

Vice President Isaac Stein looked around the crowded room and did a mental inventory. The head of the Joint Chiefs of Staff, the Director of the CIA, the National Security Advisor, the Secretaries of State and Defense, and representatives of other intelligence and military services were all present. Off to the side, Dave Watson, the president's Chief of Staff, stood glowering, arms folded.

Given the intelligence briefing he'd just received, Stein doubted President Childs had survived. He was conflicted. He'd tried to warn the president that the France trip was too dangerous. If the president was indeed dead, the nation would be thrown into a period of deep shock and mourning. The assassination of President John Kennedy had dramatically demonstrated that. On the other hand, once the national trauma had subsided, the death of the president though horrific, would create a climate of national unity. Stein would inherit a mandate to set national priorities. Ironically, the president's demise might make possible long-sought, sweeping initiatives that had been stymied by political gridlock. But that was for later. For now he needed to focus on the president's safety.

"Sir, it's President Jardin."

The vice-president picked up the phone. He checked his watch: Almost nine p.m.

"Good morning, *Monsieur le Président*," Stein said

"Good evening, Mr. Vice President," Jardin said, in heavily accented but correct English.

"Monsieur," Stein said, "We're gravely concerned about the safety of President Childs. What can you tell us? Is he safe? Has he been injured?"

"Unfortunately, I am unable to say. There was much gunfire and confusion at the hotel. The shooting has now stopped and we've secured the area but the situation is still unclear. "

"What do you mean by unclear?" Stein said.

"At this moment we do not know President Childs' whereabouts or his physical condition. There are conflicting accounts of what really happened at the hotel. This all happened so fast."

"Mr. President," Stein said, "I've directed our intelligence and military services to provide whatever assistance you may need. But the American public will not understand how the President of the United States could just disappear in Paris, one of the best-policed cities in the world. To be blunt, sir, a number of senior congressional leaders are have said within the last hour, that the assault on President Childs is tantamount to an act of war, and could not have happened without the knowledge or consent of the French government."

"I sympathize completely with your point, Mr. Vice President. The assault on the Hôtel Marly came as much of a shock to me as it did to you. We do believe that some ugly plot is behind this. There are several theories but none confirmed. It is even possible that your government's killing of French school children in Pakistan played a part in precipitating this terrible attack."

"Islamabad was a tragic accident," Stein said.

"No doubt, but that explanation is weak tea to the French families who lost a beloved child."

Stein said, "It's our understanding that the gunfire began when gendarmes from the Préfecture attempted to arrest President Childs. If true, then an unprecedented breach of international law and diplomatic immunity occurred."

"You are partly correct." Jardin said. "There was a warrant, but not necessarily improper. My counsel has seen it. It appears to be a validly issued judicial order for the arrest of the American president on the grounds of war crimes and crimes against humanity."

"Then, sir," Stein said, "*you*, as President of the Republic, must void the warrant."

"That will be difficult. Under French law, the president of the Republic is barred from usurping or negating the constitutionally protected authority of the judicial branch. You will recall that we had a revolution to strip tyrants of such power. In this case, the most senior magistrat in Paris issued an arrest warrant, which, under our system, cannot be simply vacated or voided by the executive branch of government, not even by the President of the Republic."

"That is absurd, sir." Stein said. "You're saying that the President of the United States is to be hunted down like some common criminal?"

"On the contrary." Jardin said. "I've taken the unprecedented step of ordering Special Forces of our military to intercept the police units that are pursuing President Childs. But the gravity of my actions is such that I cannot say whether all the senior commanders of the military will carry out my orders."

"I must tell you, sir," said Stein, "that if President Childs is not found immediately and returned to the safety of the United States, the American government will take whatever steps are required to make it so."

"I understand the anxiety and anger," Jardin said, "but if you are implying military intervention, the presence of American troops on French soil would be an unthinkable affront to the people, the government, and the sovereignty of France."

"Sir," Stein said, "the French people did not find the notion so unthinkable when thousands of young American soldiers were spilling their blood on the beaches and hedgerows of France."

Silence. Then Jardin spoke.

"And so, we shall see what the next hours bring. As we say, *les jeux sont faits*. Good night, Mr. Vice-President."

Vice President Stein put the phone on the receiver and turned to the Secretary of State. "Translation?""

"*Les jeux sont faits*," Traficante said, " 'the hand's been dealt,' or, 'bet's are down.' But given the current context, I think he just said, 'fuck off.'"

70

We're lost.

For the first time in her life, Izzy could not see a way forward. Not in Amman, not at the Hôtel Marly and countless other places had she ever been without a backup plan, however risky. But she now found herself moving from one forbidding subterranean passage to next with no clue as to direction or destination.

During her tour as military attaché to the American embassy in Paris, years before joining the Secret Service, she'd spent weeks exploring the catacombs and tunnel system of the city as a defensive exercise, reasoning that terrorists might choose to strike from below. She'd been aided by Jerome, the old égoutier, as well as experts from the French government. Her knowledge of the known as well as the more secretive unknown world of underground

Paris was extensive – but not absolute. There were hundreds of kilometers of tunneling, many still unexplored and treacherous after centuries of neglect and anonymity. Had she unwittingly led them into one of those forgotten digs? Soon she'd have to level with the others. But first, she would have to level with the president.

"Sir, I need a minute with you," she said. They moved a short distance away from the others.

"Talk to me," he said.

"We're lost."

The president was silent for a moment as he absorbed the news. "Can we backtrack?"

"Would be very difficult, sir." She said. "So many twists and forks behind us, just don't think I could remember every one. And with so little light it might even make matters worse. There are open pits in some of these passages. I feel I've let you down, sir."

The president placed a hand on her shoulder with great tenderness. "Hold on a minute, Izzy. It's your turn to take a deep breath. You've been going nonstop. You're the most resourceful, tenacious and fearless person I've ever known and I've known a few. I don't know how you've managed to keep us all alive, but you have. Lead the way. I'm with you, win lose or draw."

"Thank you, sir. That means a lot to me." she said. They walked back to the others.

"Let's step up the pace," she said.

Izzy took the point, moving fast in a half-crouch, head inclined forward.

Every muscle and joint in her body ached from the stooped posture they'd had to employ in the narrow, low-ceiling passages.

In the dimness her right foot struck something, sending her headlong onto the floor of the tunnel.

"*Merde! Qu'est-ce qui ce passe*!" said an angry voice from somewhere.

"Jesus!" Izzy said, stunned by the hard fall and the jarring sound of an unfamiliar voice. On her stomach, she grabbed her pistol, spun around and directed the flashlight with her other hand toward the voice.

"Don't move or you're dead!" she said. Then remembering the words had been French she added: "*Bougez pas, je suis armé d'un pistol!*"

In the beam of her light, two eyes, wide with curious alarm, stared back. Gradually Izzy discerned a human shape, legs awkwardly stretched across the floor of the passage, torso angled upward against the wall.

"Don't shoot, I speak English." The voice was clear but carried a heavy- throated accent.

Izzy came closer, pistol at the ready. Will and the others were soon by her side. She shined the light directly on the gaunt, smudge-faced stranger. An extinguished spelunker's headlamp was strapped to his forehead. The man appeared to be in his sixties or seventies, thin, frail. Yet his eyes were alert and inquiring.

"Who are you?" Izzy said.

The stranger looked at Izzy then lazily swept his gaze upward at the others.

"My name is Victor." He rubbed a palm across his grizzled cheek as if ruminating. "You must be lost," he said. "Not surprising, these tunnels will play with your mi..."

He stopped abruptly and squinted hard into the dimness. He was staring at the president as if trying to make sense of an apparition.

"You… look…familiar."

Izzy took a small step forward, unsure what might happen next.

"Incroyable! I must be losing my mind," Victor said. You cannot possibly be the American president." "

Izzy decided to chance the truth. "You're not crazy. This is President Childs. We need your help. The police are after us and if they find us, there will be bloodshed."

"You mean the Préfecture is after the President of the United States?" said Victor. He seemed incredulous, yet strangely amused, moving his gaze back and forth from Izzy to the president. He smiled broadly as though relishing the irony of the situation.

Izzy took it all in.

He may look like a down-and-out vagrant but there's more to him.

"Yes." Izzy said. "We have to get the president to a safe place. His life's in great danger."

"You've found the right man," Victor said, slapping his thigh, "The enemy of my enemy is my friend."

"You'll help us?" Izzy said.

"Of course," Victor said.

"Good. Now. Where are we?" Izzy said.

"You're in one of the great cataphile galleries of the world," he said.

"Cataphile?" the president said.

"We're trespassers who sneak into the uncharted tunnels and catacombs that are forbidden to the public by the government," Victor said. "We call ourselves cataphiles. Some of us are social outcasts, some homeless or undocumented, some are even criminals on the run. But others are painters, writers, composers, young people, political activists, anarchists, who come from all over the world. We enter through manholes in the streets, descend into these tunnels and secretly paint murals, have meetings, read poetry, build small theatres, restaurants, communications systems. It's an underground city."

"Don't you get caught?" Will said.

"Hah!" Victor said. "We've been doing this since the nineteen-seventies. By the time the cataflics, the police, arrive, we're already gone."

"Victor," Izzy said, "you told us we're at one of the galleries. I don't see anything."

"*Très simple,* just follow me. I was on my way there but I suddenly felt light-headed and had to sit for a moment. I turned off my lamp. Not a good idea to broadcast your location." He switched on his headlamp.

After so much time in near darkness the intensity of the halogen light was blinding. As they adjusted to the sharp light they were able to make out every detail of the passage. They were astonished at the coppery hue of the walls and the true narrowness of the tunnel.

Victor led the way, then made a hairpin turn in the passage. Izzy and the others followed. As they turned into the passageway they stopped in their tracks, astonished at what they were seeing.

71

"*Voilà!*" Victor said.

He was pointing at a vast, illuminated limestone chamber so broad and high that its full dimensions could not be determined. On the immense walls gigantic murals reproducing classic Renaissance artworks had been painted in exquisite detail and color. On other walls, contemporary artworks competed with political statements, irreverent obscenities and cryptic graffiti.

In the foreground, several large stones had been sculpted and arranged to serve as tables. Lighted candles shone from carved niches in the walls. A gigantic rusted metal candelabra hung suspended by a long chain in the center of the expansive cavity, candles flickering,

Knapsacks, futons, books, magazines, clothing, paint cans, brushes, spray-paints, open beer containers, half-empty water bottles, a kerosene stove, and what appeared to be electrical cables were scattered throughout the chamber.

"Incredible."

"Awesome."

Izzy heard the president, and the others remarking on the surreal tableau as she and Victor moved away from them.

"Victor, where are the people?" Izzy said.

"They'll arrive soon, but I wouldn't recommend that you be here. I don't know how some of them might react. This is their sanctuary, their escape from the world above. They'll be very upset that you might be the cause of the cataflics, the tunnel police, following you here. No one from the government has ever found this chamber. It's a miracle you got this close."

"Believe me, Victor, It wasn't by design."

Victor signed. "Life rarely is. I was a successful architect and engineer at one time. I worked on some of Paris' greatest projects. My life was good. But I was strong-willed, something French bureaucrats do not tolerate. Eventually I became disillusioned, withdrew from the world above and became a cataphile. I've lived in these tunnels for almost ten years."

"It must be a strange world," Izzy said.

"On the contrary," he said, "I've never felt more free. It's the world above that has become an Orwellian madhouse run by prying bureaucrats and cynical politicians. I eventually tired of living in a surveillance society where the moment I stepped outside my door I'd already run afoul of countless regulations, ordinances and laws I'd never even heard of. Down here we're free and closer to our natural state."

"Victor," Izzy said, "we're grateful for your help."

"Don't worry about me. I hold no grudge against your president. I do read and listen to the radio you know. He's a good man in a demented world. Sometimes we're caught up in a mistral, a devil wind, and no one is spared. You'll need food and water," he said. "There's not much here but you can take it.

"Thank you." Izzy said. "There's just one more favor I need."

72

"Welcome to France, Mr. Robbins."

"Thanks," Liam Cabot said, with a quick half-smile, as the expressionless passport control officer at Paris' Charles de Gaulle airport examined his British passport. The name read: "Christopher Robbins." Liam possessed several passports courtesy of Her Majesty's Government.

His flight on Turkish Airways had touched down in Paris a little after three a.m. He hadn't planned on being in France. Tradecraft frowned on unscripted changes but events in Paris and the Hôtel Marly had quickly changed all that. He'd been lucky to be staying in a hotel near Istanbul's Ataturk airport when the news bulletin about the attack on the president broke. A quick call to a contact at the British Consulate in Istanbul had allowed him to race through ticketing and boarding onto the Paris-bound flight. He'd avoided telling anyone about the true purpose of his changed itinerary. They would know soon enough for good or bad.

"The purpose of your visit, Mr. Robbins?" the passport control officer said.

"Seeing an old friend at the Sorbonne."

"Hmmm," he said, studying Liam and examining the passport photo.

"Did you enjoy your stay in Istanbul?"

"Afraid I didn't have much chance to," Liam said, "just transiting from a God awful sales trip to Tbilisi."

Liam suspected that the immigration official knew he'd been in Tbilisi,

Georgia; his computer screen had likely told him that. But what the official probably did not know was that "Mr. Robbins" had quietly absented himself from Tbilisi and spent two weeks in rugged mountain passes above Grozny,

Chechnya, negotiating with tribal Chechen leaders about recovering a stolen nuke.

"What were you selling in Tbilisi?"

"Frozen foods," Liam said. "My company develops new markets."

Liam's voice became animated as he warmed to his subject. It was the salesman's default - glib, earnest, one never knew where the next sale might pop up.

"Was trying to interest Tbilisi merchants in stocking frozen Bangers and Mash, Shepherd's Pie, Cumberland Sausage, Lancashire Hotpot, and Toad-in-the-Hole. Some of our favorite UK dishes. But they wouldn't have it. Wasted trip, sad to say."

The officer stamped the passport with a solid "thump" and handed it back, clearly eager to end a conversation about inedible British food.

"You'll want to be careful in the streets, Mr. Robbins," he said in a terse voice. "Paris is not in a good mood."

"Thanks for the advice, old boy." Liam smiled, took the passport, and moved quickly toward baggage claim and the taxi stand.

73

Izzy checked her watch. Three thirty a.m. It was almost impossible to wrap her head around everything that had happened in the mere five hours since the attack at Hôtel Marly. Every gut-churning minute since then had seemed an eternity with death and disaster barely held at bay from moment to moment. Time had somehow stretched into some parallel universe where a lifetime could collapse into the fleeting sweep of the clock.

Victor had been a godsend to Izzy, sharing cataphile secrets with irascible humor and telling her how to decipher the cryptic markings lining the passages.

Now, confidently weaving from one subterranean passage to the next, she paused from time to time to examine arrows and graffiti. Her destination was the tunnel that led to the Louvre médiéval. The one she'd been heading toward when they'd been forced to abandon their route.

They moved deeper underground until the rumble of the number eight Paris metro, once faint and distant, became a thunderous companion as it plunged, rattling, twisting and snaking under the Seine from Invalides station on the Left Bank to Concorde on the Right.

74

"*Monsieur le Préfet,*" Jardin said, "As President of the French Republic I'm ordering you to have Commandant Poussin and his men stand down."

President Jardin gripped the phone tighter, barely restraining his fury. "I asked you earlier to stop Poussin, yet you've done nothing."

"With due respect, Mr. President," Pierre Boucher, the director of the Préfecture de la Police said, "when I spoke with you I did not know the seriousness of Poussin's mission. I've now been advised by Magistrat Malevu that Commandant Poussin was carrying out a lawfully issued warrant for the arrest of President Childs."

"I don't care who ordered the warrant for the American president. This lunacy must stop now."

"*Monsieur le Président,* I was told to expect this call. The magistrat insists that the Élysée Palace does not have the legal authority to set aside a judicial order."

"I do not have the legal authority?" The president thundered. "Then you may tell the magistrat that he will find that line of argument unpersuasive with the French commandos I am about to dispatch to the Préfecture and the magistrat's home."

The president slammed the phone down and turned to his assistant.

"Giselle, get General de Plessy on the line!"

75

Over the next half hour Izzy and her little group made a gradual ascent. They'd reached the lowest point of the tunnels while still under the river. Now each step brought them closer to the surface. As they moved, the dimensions of the passages grew larger until at last they entered a vaulted room with a ceiling high enough to let them stand.

Izzy turned and whispered, "Let's take a short break." Fatigued, they slumped to the earthen floor.

The president had stretched out on the floor, his back resting against the wall. He looked drained.

"Sir, how're you holding up?"

"I'm okay, Izzy. You've got enough to worry about right now."

"Right now, I'm worried about you," Izzy said, sliding down down next to him.

"Let me take a look." she said as she gently shifted his coat to examine the injured shoulder. In the illumination of her light she could see that the blood pattern on the shirt had grown and his shoulder drooped. The physical exertion of the last few hours was clearly pushing him to the limit. He shuddered as a cold draft coursed the tunnel. The president was chilled and shaking.

"You're freezing," she said.

Without asking, Izzy pressed herself against Childs to warm him. As she melded herself into him she sensed his relief at the welcome body heat. In the dim silence the president took her hand and held it. Though Izzy knew he was in great pain, still his hand felt strong, reassuring. And in that gesture she also sensed more. The emotion was unexpected, and Izzy hadn't been ready for it. For a long moment she didn't move, wanting to say how much it meant to her that he was still alive, was still with her, and much more. But he needed rest, and as the heat from her body abated his shivering he nodded into a deep slumber. After about an hour she gently withdrew her hand. She stood, collected herself, and surveyed the scene.

Will came up to her. "Where are we?"

"About one hundred feet beneath the Louvre," she said. "When we entered the Pont de l'Alma we were on the Left Bank of the river. By going under the Seine we crossed to the Right Bank."

"Have you been here before?" he said.

"Yes. When I was stationed in Paris. I know this chamber well."

She panned her flashlight across the walls until the light fell on a waist-high oblong boulder resting against the wall. Lighter in color than the surrounding material, it seemed out of place. Its smooth, almost polished surface contrasted with the darker earthen walls. It was what she had been looking for. Izzy directed the light towards the oblong boulder.

"Okay, Will," she said. "See that boulder? That's our way out of these tunnels. Let's wake everyone and move it."

As Will waked the others, Izzy made her way to the sleeping president, carefully placed her hand on his wrist and whispered, "Sir, it's time."

He opened his eyes and, with her help raised himself up and stood.

Then Izzy, Will and the other two agents took positions on one side of the boulder.

"On my three," she said.

"One…two…three…"

They threw their weight into it. Dust, hardened mud and small rock fragments fell away as the boulder began to move, first grudgingly and then with greater ease until at last an opening bathed in suffused light appeared. Izzy turned to the president.

"Sir, this way," Izzy said.

One by one the group stepped into a circular enclosure composed of perfectly aligned stones that rose steeply. Soft beams of light filtered down from above. The space appeared to be roughly eight feet in diameter and thirty feet high. The stones, though ancient, appeared pristine. In the faint light, they could see that the sides of the cistern were dry, the smooth, grey casement walls remarkably well preserved.

"How did you know about the entrance?" Will said.

"My friend, Jerome, the égoutier, once told me a secret underground entrance to the Louvre médiéval had been used in a siege. I found the story apocryphal. After all, Paris is two thousand years old and there are many strange stories. But I became fascinated by medieval sieges. One day in the archives of the Bibliothèque nationale I ran across an obscure reference to an underground assault on this fortress that took place in the fifteenth century. Jerome had been right. After that it took some serious spelunking to locate the exact location of the entrance."

"What's the plan?" Will said.

"We're going to climb to the top of the cistern," Izzy said. "Once we're there we'll be in the old fortress, or at least what's left of it. Over the centuries it was gradually demolished. What remained of the original fortress eventually got buried by landfill and the new Louvre was built on top of it."

"We'll need a ladder," Will said, assessing the steep wall.

"Look more closely," Izzy said. "The masons who built this cistern, knew they'd have to climb down to clean it."

Will examined the well more carefully. There, along the walls, small stone footholds protruded in two parallel spiral patterns winding upward to the top.

"We'll have to climb slowly," Izzy said, "but the stones are wide enough to stand on."

She looked at her blood-stained watch and cleaned off the face.

"It's five-fifteen a.m.," she said. "Most of the security staff are still gone and we'll have a better shot at making it."

"What about surveillance cameras?" Will said.

"Can't avoid them. Once we climb this cistern and enter the old fortress we'll be spotted. It's just a question of how far we can get before they're onto us."

Izzy had been matter-of-fact, almost casual, but even as she spoke she felt her stomach churn.

Those cameras are everywhere; our chances of making it out undetected are slim.

She looked back at the president in the dim light. He looked feverish.

I've got to get him help soon.

76

Commandant Poussin looked up as Gaston, his senior GIGN special weapons officer, entered the room. It was already after five in the morning and Gaston, like Poussin, looked exhausted.

"Sir," Gaston said, his voice filled with fatigue, "All fighting at the Hôtel Marly stopped. French Special Forces have taken control of the area. General de Plessy has ordered all Préfecture personnel to return to their stations and surrender weapons."

"Ignore de Plessy," Poussin said. "Until I receive a direct order from Magistrat Malevu we will continue to pursue and arrest the American president. General de Plessy is merely doing president Jardin's bidding. It's nothing more than cynical politics. I won't be a part of it."

Poussin gave the officer a forceful look.

"Gaston," he said, "you and I and the rest of our unit have worked side by side for years. We're like brothers, and we'd gladly lay our lives down for each other. Let the politicians do and say what they want. They're a different tribe. We will do our duty and arrest this criminal. Can I count on you and the others?"

"Yes, commandant. We will follow to a man, as we always have."

77

Izzy checked her watch. The'd been on the run more than six hours. Her body ached from arduous running, stooping, crawling and dodging bullets. She'd rested, but not slept. Her red hair, once carefully groomed and lustrous, was now a matted, tangled web. Her mud-stained clothes reeked of stale tunnel water and other things she preferred not to think about. A growling stomach and aching thirst added to the misery. The few snacks that Victor the cataphile had given them were gone.

So far they'd been able to stay one step ahead of their pursuers. But Izzy admitted to herself that eventually she'd run out of time or ideas and make a fatal mistake. Somehow she'd have to deliver them to safety before that moment came.

"It's time," she whispered to the group. "I'm going to climb to the top and look."

"Will," she said, "the president will need help. Make sure you're right behind him. And make sure everyone checks shoes for mud. The stones are slippery."

"Roger."

Izzy stepped into the base of the enclosure and took one last look at the parallel spirals of ascending stones. It was intimidating. But so long as she could keep her footing on the lower spiral of steps while using her hands to grasp the parallel spiral just above her she should be okay. She checked the soles of her muddy boots and scraped them against the stone floor. *One slip and we're finished.*

Izzy placed her right foot on the first stone so that her ankle was flush with the wall. Pushing herself off the stone, she extended her left arm upward, chest turned to the wall until the left hand found purchase on the parallel stone above.

Gripping the stone firmly she placed her left foot on the step in front of her right foot and considered her next move.

If stonemasons could do this seven hundred years ago...

Keeping her grip on the stone above, she pushed away with her left foot until her right hand reached the next stone.

Success. Izzy exhaled a sigh of relief.

Just twenty-eight feet to go.

Repeating the maneuver in a circular pattern she gradually wound her way to the top of the cistern.

Listening for any sound in the corridor, Izzy raised her head just enough to see over the mouth of the cistern and looked out on the ancient remains of the Louvre médiéval. Even through her exhaustion, she found the sight awe-inspiring. The stone floor of the great fortress built in the twelfth century by king Philip Augustus was broad and immaculate, its color a delicate ivory. The stone path wound in a graceful curve along the base of the imposing battlements. As the tower walls rose higher into the dimness, they sloped away, revealing a perfection of masonry so precise that it seemed not even a sword or sharp knife could have found a point of entry between the immense stones.

Peering upward into the near-darkness she saw the concrete ceiling where the remains of the old fortress ended and the Louvre museum began.

She slid her body over the lip and crawled toward the battlement walls, pausing every few feet to minimize detection. Her destination, a thick retaining rope that separated the fortress walls from the pathway used by the public.

Reaching the rope, Izzy took a Swiss utility knife from her pant pocket and cut a section of rope about forty feet in length. Pulling the heavy length behind her, she made her way back to the cistern.

She peered down and saw Evans near the top. Will, the president and Oberlin were still at the bottom.

"Help me pass the rope down to Will," Izzy said to Evans, "and let's get everyone up, stat."

Ten minutes later they had all scaled the cistern.

78

Izzy took in the reaction of the president and the others as they looked upon the old fortress. She knew that in the eerie luminescence the sepulchral power of the fortress had asserted itself, leaving her group awestruck by its raw beauty and size. Buried for centuries, the Louvre médiéval, still retained the mystique and magnificence of the royal fortress and residence it had once been.

"Let's keep moving," Izzy said.

She took the point, watching for any sign of museum guards.

I don't get it. They should have spotted us by now.

She reached into her shoulder holster and removed her Sig Sauer pistol. She checked the clip and chamber. Only a few rounds remained. But at least the weapon looked clean and serviceable.

She turned to Will.

"I'm going to check something out. Try to keep up with me as much as you can."

She sprinted ahead and disappeared around one of the curving tower walls.

Will, the president, Evans and Oberlin traced Izzy's steps. Circling the battlements they found Izzy standing in front of an immense wall tapestry suspended from the ceiling. The elegant textile covered a large area of the wall and depicted a hunting party in splendid attire on horseback. The scene suggested a foxhunt.

Izzy was examining a section of the tapestry. In the center of the artwork, a stately figure sat ramrod straight astride a great white-chested steed, its large ears pointed and alert. A richly embroidered royal-blue sash descended along the horse's flank from the rider's saddle-pommel. Her hands were on the tapestry and she was sliding her long fingers downward. "Got it!" Izzy said. *Thank you, Victor!*

On the sash, a line of gold-thread fleur-de-lis led down to the end of the sash. Beginning with the first fleur-de-lis at the bottom of the sash, Izzy mentally counted upward.

Nine...ten... eleven...twelve.

She placed her fingers on the tapestry and pushed deep into the twelfth iris. A moment later a low, grinding sound accompanied by a gentle rush of air billowed the artwork away from the wall.

"Let's go," Izzy said.

They all slipped behind the tapestry and found themselves standing before a small opening in the wall that led to a narrow stone corridor. Once they were in the corridor, Izzy located the brick sized rock protruding from the wall, pushed it and the stone door behind them returned to its original position with a dull Thump!

"How did you know about that passage?" the president said.

"I didn't. Victor told me. Remember he said he'd worked on important projects as an engineer? When we were alone, he told me he'd been chief engineer during the dig to unearth the Louvre médiéval. Several months into the excavation they discovered a concealed passage in one of the old walls. It wasn't a complete surprise, since clandestine passages were typical of royal dwellings of the time. They enabled unseen access to other quarters of the palace, sometimes for romantic trysts, sometimes for escape. Victor restored the passage, and covered the entrance with the huge hunting party tapestry."

"Where does it go?" the president said.

"Underground from the Sully wing of the Louvre museum where we are now to a small nook under the Denon wing. That's where we're headed."

They followed the corridor as it wound its way beneath the great Louvre museum, passing what appeared to have been other access doors until they arrived at a small stone room. A narrow, chest-high air vent covered by a metal grill was located at one end of the enclosure. Izzy rushed to the opening and looked. Outside, a flagstone courtyard lay bathed in pale light.

"Will, over here," she said just above a whisper. "Take a look."

Will joined her and peered through the metal grill.

"What do you think?" Izzy said.

"Pretty quiet," Will said. "I don't see any movement. Looks like a courtyard."

"It's the courtyard of the Denon wing of the Louvre museum." Izzy said. "It's called the Cour Lefuel."

"Looks neglected, like a place that hasn't been used in a long time."

"You're right," Izzy said. "but it was once a grand staircase that greeted royal visitors at the entrance of the Denon wing of the Louvre."

"Staircase?"

"Yes. An architect named Lefuel designed it for Napoleon III. We can't see it from where we are because we're right under it. It leads to a section of the Denon where Napoleon maintained an equestrian center."

"An equestrian center in the Louvre? You're kidding."

"Not kidding, Napoleon III built it for his show horses. You'll see it when we make our move."

She noticed a look of concern cross Will's face. She guessed what he was probably thinking. She was having similar thoughts.

When we're out in the open, all hell's going to break loose.

Her thoughts were interrupted by the gentle whinny of horses. She pressed her face against the grill and peered out to the courtyard. Off to the left she could just make out the hindquarters of two horses. They appeared to be wearing red and black ceremonial raiment.

"La Garde républicaine?" Izzy said to no one in particular.

"Who?" Will said.

"The Republican Guard. It's an elite mounted unit of the French military. Their horses are highly trained. The guard accompanies visiting heads of state and other dignitaries. But I have no idea what they're doing here at this hour, though it's possible they were brought here from the barracks at Caserne de Celestin for some early morning ceremony."

Izzy looked at the courtyard again. Her line of sight was partially obstructed. She could see horses moving in a manner suggesting they were tethered. She saw no sign of riders.

Surveillance cameras but no alarm raised? Tacked up horses at this early hour but no riders? It's crazy.

Izzy turned to the president.

"Sir, we're about to leave the safety of the tunnels. We'll have to move fast because security will be on us."

She turned to the others. "Check your weapons, make sure you're ready. Do not engage unless I give the order."

The group nodded its agreement.

"Okay, let's pull this grill away from the wall. The casement should give. It probably hasn't been touched in a hundred years."

Will and Evans pulled at the grill. It fell away with surprising ease. The opening was just large enough to allow a person to squeeze through.

Izzy went first, slipping into the dark shadow of the staircase wall. The others followed in a low crouch. The cool breeze off the nearby Seine caught Izzy by surprise. It was a welcome change from the stifling tunnels. The air was rich with the aroma of bakers pre-dawn baguettes, Gauloises cigarettes and tones of leather and musk coming from the purebred horses standing serenely at rest in the Cour Lefuel. The welcoming balm of early-morning Paris gave Izzy a renewed sense of energy and hope.

"Wait here," she whispered.

Staying low she made her way to the horses. Ten or twelve mounts in full tack and imperial rigging stood alongside the magnificent Lefuel horseshoe staircase. They were calm and didn't appear to have been worked for some time. Izzy moved forward with great care, not wanting to spook them. She was now only a few feet away....

In the gloom a figure was moving toward her.

Izzy rolled to the side, landed on one knee, clasped the pistol firmly in both hands while releasing the safety. She raised her pistol, framed the heart and placed her finger on the trigger. A man's face gradually became discernible.

Izzy gasped.

"Liam? Jesus Christ! Is it you? How...? What are you doing here?"

"Well, we could say I just wanted to visit the Mona Lisa."

"No time for jokes. Half the damned Paris police are trying to find us. And if they haven't been able to, then how...I mean, the last time I saw you, you were on your way out of Washington with no explanation."

"Change of plans. When I heard about Islamabad and learned that the president was coming to Paris, I knew it would be dangerous. By the time I got here all hell had broken loose and the president was missing. I pretty much knew you'd be with him. I played a hunch from something you said to me in New York about visiting the Louvre when you were a child."

"My favorite hiding place," Izzy said.

"I'm just so damned glad you're okay, Izzy."

"That makes two of us," Izzy said. "Now let's get the president out of here. I don't know why security hasn't already spotted us."

"A well-paid hacker who strings for MI6 hacked into their video control system last night," Liam said. "Left quite a mess for them, but it won't last."

EEEYAAW, EEEYAAW!

The shrill klaxon of the museum alarms pierced the quiet of the courtyard. Izzy saw lights go on in the windows lining the upper gallery of the Sully wing. Several men in uniform were rushing in their direction.

"Vite, vite, allez-y! C'est le président des États-Unis!"

The commander of la Garde républicaine was shouting to his men. An hour earlier, he'd received a garbled, incomplete account of the events at the Hôtel Marly. It appeared French police officers had been killed and the American president might be on the run. At first the commander had dismissed the call as a ridiculous prank until the distant sound of gunfire made him reconsider. Now, the commander realized that the group in the courtyard below must be the American president and his security staff. He'd been told to stop the president if he encountered him. But what did that mean? Arrest him? Shoot him? Protect him? He'd hardly expected to find the President of the United States in the small Cour Lefuel. There was no time to get better guidance. Yes, the president would have to be stopped but there was no way in heaven the commander was going to assume the personal responsibility of shooting the president of the United States.

"The Republican Guard," Izzy said to Liam. "We can't outrun them. The president's too weak."

Her mind was racing. She looked at Liam. They were both thinking the same thing. Without a word they were running to the horses, Will, the president and the others right behind.

Shouting, accompanied by the clatter of heavy boots stabbed the silence of the courtyard as the Republican Guard rushed down the marble spiral staircase toward the courtyard doors.

"Go, go!" Izzy said, pointing to the horses. Dashing to the nearest mount, she quickly dropped the irons, slipped the reins over the horses' neck, grabbed the withers with her left hand, placed her left foot in the stirrup and her right hand on the back of the saddle. Bouncing twice on her right leg she pushed herself upward, swinging her leg over the saddle of the tall mount.

Thank God for West Point equestrian training.

"Will… Liam," Izzy said, "Help the president get on behind me."

The two practically air-lifted the president onto the hindquarters of Izzy's horse.

"Sir, wrap your arms around my waist and hold tight."

Will and the two agents awkwardly mounted their horses. The horses began shying, jerking violently from side to side, bobbing heads and whinnying.

"Liam!" Izzy said, "They're going to bolt."

Liam was now astride his horse. She saw him expertly maneuver the mount alongside Will and the two agents. It calmed the stallions.

"Don't hold the reins too tight," Izzy said to the others. "Just give them their head, they'll follow my horse."

"Arrêt! Arrêtez vous!"

Izzy saw their pursuers rushing at them through doors of the courtyard, red jackets flying, swords clanging against metal buckles, boots falling heavily on the cobblestones. She wheeled her horse about, and quick-stepped to the foot of the horseshoe staircase.

Taking their cue from Izzy's mount, the other horses raised their heads smartly and advanced.

"Now!" Izzy said, spurring hard.

Her horse lunged ahead. The metal-clad hooves gained purchase on the stairs in a loud staccato.

The other four horses leaped forward to follow. The stone walls of the Cour Lefuel echoed and magnified the crescendo of equine hooves striking stone.

Nearing the top of the staircase, Izzy prepared to dismount and open the heavy wooden doors leading into the *Denon.*

To her great relief, both the twelve-foot doors were wide open.

Liam! You genius!

Izzy charged through the massive portals and into the Salle du Manège on the ground floor of the great Denon wing, where the looming sculptures of Jupiter and Juno framed the towering entry way. The exquisite, high-vaulted Salle du Manège, once home to imperial horses, was now a showcase of rare Etruscan, Roman and Greek sculpture.

As the other horses charged up the stairs and into the Salle, past le Vieux Pecheur and the massive corinthian-styled columns, the ear-splitting hammering of thousand-pound horses, raining steel-clad hooves like giant hailstones on the outer staircase abruptly morphed into a tympanic thunder that rose from the Salle's floor of Lutetian limestone.

Arrêtez! Vous ne pouvez pas s'échapper!"

"Stop! You can't escape!" shouted the Republican Guards.

The Guards, who'd easily mounted the remaining horses, were gaining fast, their stallions responding to the superb horsemanship of their riders. Soon the Salle du Manége was a howling tempest of pounding hooves, angry shouts and snorting horses; past seated Minerva, standing Osiris and Venus. In the bedlam Greek and Roman statuary began to tremble precariously as the seismic chase rattled and shook the hall.

"Heads up!" Izzy heard someone shout.

She looked over her shoulder just in time to see a statue of the Satyrs d'Atlante succumb to the violent vibration, tip from its pedestal, and tumble downward.

CRASH!

One of the Republican Guards tried to avoid the scattering debris by attempting a jump. The mount refused and reared. Izzy winced as she saw the rider topple onto the heavy basalt sculpture of a lion, its massive paw resting on a large marble sphere. Squeezing her legs into her horse's flanks, she leaned into a full gallop, weaving in and out of the statuary. Izzy could feel the president pressing tightly against her back. A foamy lather began gathering on the withers of her mount as it labored under the weight of two riders. Behind her, horses panted loudly as they sought to keep up with her wild, zigzag pattern.

Reaching the end of the Salle du Manége, Izzy slowed her pace, negotiated the seven steps, and swung right onto the diamond-shaped marble of Galerie Daru. Careening through the vast room of antiquities, Izzy pulled the horse's nose hard, just in time to miss the famed Borghese Gladiator, its left arm raised upward in perpetual defiance.

CRASH!

Above the howling bedlam, Izzy heard the gut-wrenching sound of yet another antiquity shattering. She tried not to think which irreplaceable work was now lying in pieces.

Liam's voice called from behind. "They're gaining!"

Izzy spurred harder. The horse tapped into an extra reservoir of energy and lunged ahead with greater urgency. The statuary, marble columns and tall windows became a blur as Izzy raced past Julius Caesar, Germanicus, Tiberius and Trajan.

The ornate gallery led to Lefuel's majestic marble staircase, and one of the Louvre's greatest treasures, the heroic Victoire de Samothrace. The image of the Greek goddess Nike, wings outstretched in triumph at the prow of a ship, exhorted Izzy onward.

"We're going up," Izzy called over her shoulder. She gauged her final strides and slowed her horse to allow it to ascend the broad stairs on its own terms.

Halfway up the glass-smooth steps, the forward leg of the powerful steed slipped and lost its hold. Izzy felt the horse frantically trying to regain its footing. The president began sliding off the saddle pulling her with him and shifting her center of gravity. By sheer brute force she threw her upper body in the opposite direction, wrenching the president towards her and easing the reins so that the horse could fight for balance. Somehow the superb stallion regained its equilibrium, and continued its climb.

Reaching the third set of steps, Izzy urged her horse ninety degrees to the right onto a staircase of the Galerie Daru. She looked back. Will and the other riders were unsteadily starting their climb up the slippery stairs, the Republican Guards close behind.

Izzy turned and spurred her horse deeper into Daru where immense masterworks by David, Ingres and Girodet-Trioson hung in eternal, heroic splendor. Crossing the threshold of the immense room, where the floor changed from smooth marble to Hungarian pointe parquet floor, the powerful horse's hooves struck again and again thundering like giant kettledrums.

Ahead, just beyond the Galerie Daru and to the left was the most sacrosanct room of the Louvre, the Salle de la Joconde, named after its most priceless possession, Leonardo Da Vinci's Mona Lisa.

Opposite Da Vinci's Joconde, Veronese's epic Noces de Cana, the largest painting in the Louvre, loomed immense as Izzy sped into the gallery and across the intricate parquet floor.

"Arrêtez!"

Izzy shuddered. She knew the Guards were gaining on Will and the others. Unless she did something, it would all be over in moments. With a ferocious effort she jerked her horse's nose downward and dug her heels deep into the stirrups in an effort to rein in the powerful animal. Instead, the muscular equestrian chomped down on the snaffle bit and charged onward. Izzy began desperately sawing the reins back and forth to break the steed's momentum.

Finally succumbing to the intense pressure of the bit, the horse came to a jarring halt. Izzy wheeled the mount and called to her companions as they raced toward her.

"Keep going!" she said. "We'll be right behind you."

They thundered past, traversing the room and exiting the Salle de la Joconde toward the Grande Galerie. Izzy quickly advanced her horse to one of the metal stanchions used to rope off the paintings from the public. She reached down. The stanchion was heavy and Izzy strained to lift it upward and across the front of her saddle. With a squeeze of her legs she urged her mount forward toward the priceless Mona Lisa. The masterpeice was housed in a specially built, bullet-proof glass-enclosure resting in a free-standing wall in the middle of the gallery. In front of the Mona Lisa a large, semi-circular wood railing served to keep the public several feet away from the painting.

The Republican Guards were almost in the room.

Izzy considered the unthinkable. *I've got no choice. It's this or the president.* She deftly executed a dressage half-pass and sidled the horse along the wood railing. She was now only about seven feet from the painting. Grabbing the stanchion with both hands she stood straight up in the stirrups and raised the heavy post as high above her head as she could. The president had to strain to hold on to her.

"Non, je vous en prie!" she heard a Guard shout, *"Stop, c'est la Joconde!"*

Summoning all the muscle strength she had remaining, Izzy violently hurled the stanchion, sending it crazily cartwheeling end-over-end, toward the painting. CRAAAAACK!

79

Élysée Presidential Palace

"Monsieur le Président. They're in the Louvre!"

The senior signals intelligence officer was breathless, as he was ushered into the president's private quarters.

"Are you sure?"

"Yes, sir. We just received confirmation from security at the Louvre. They were spotted making their way through the Denon."

"Why in the devil weren't they stopped?"

"They were on horseback, Mr. President."

"On…what?"

"Horseback, sir. Somehow they were able to get to the horses of the Republican Guard."

The president leaped from his chair.

Incroyable!

"Get me the director of the Préfecture and the head of security at the Louvre," he said. "The president of the United States must not be harmed, or heaven help France."

80

"Commandant, they've been spotted in the Louvre."

"Bon!" said Commandant Poussin, as he worried his left eyebrow between left thumb and fingers. He spun away from the lieutenant and stabbed a beefy finger into the center of a large Paris map hastily taped to the wall of his makeshift command center.

Under the tip of his left index finger was the outline of an immense, three-sided building with the word Louvre next to it. Poussin knew the museum as well as he knew his prized vegetable garden in working-class Bobigny. After all, he'd spent four long years as a young security guard in the great museum.

"Where in the Louvre?" Poussin said.

"Denon."

"Yes, yes, but where in the Denon?"

"They were in the Salle de la Joconde," the lieutenant said, noticing that a small patch of hair was missing from Poussin's left eyebrow.

"There are only three exits." Poussin said. "The Pei, the Sully, and the Grande Galerie. Order the museum guards to seal them off immediately."

"Yes, commandant."

Poussin's head was pounding again. He reached for the large bottle of aspirine du Rhône purchased only two days earlier. It was already half empty. As he placed the container back on the desk, he noticed that the thumb and fingers of his left hand were tinged with blood.

81

Situation Room

Vice-President Stein and National Security Advisor Ed Valucek looked up as the Sit Room Director approached them.

"SIGINT is reporting an intercept from the Élysée Palace. They're being told that President Childs is in the Louvre museum, accompanied by several armed individuals. We're assuming it's the president's detail."

Valucek looked at the street map of Paris displayed on the large LED screen in the Situation Room. *Thank God they're still alive.*

"Louvre museum, satellite view," he said.

The voice-activated software instantly morphed from a street map view of Paris to a close overhead still shot of the Louvre.

"Do we know where, in the museum?" Valucek said.

"There was a reference to 'Denon'."

"Denon, Louvre museum," Valucek said.

The image zoomed and stopped at an immense rectangular structure bordering the Seine. The word "Denon" began flashing over the image.

82

Louvre – Salle de la Joconde

CRAAACK!

As Izzy had expected, the violent blow from the stanchion cracked, but did not shatter the layer of thick glass protecting the Mona Lisa.

In that instant, ear-splitting sirens, accompanied by flashing red lights, began wailing in the room.

Izzy wheeled her horse toward the exit that Will, Liam, Evans and Oberlin had taken. As she did, 3,000-pound metal gates began smoothly descending from the top of the broad doorways of the Salle with a low humming sound. She spurred harder and the horse leaped forward. Suddenly her left shoulder was seized from behind by a powerful grip. She winced and looked back.

One of the Republican Guards was on her left flank, his horse in full stride. His expression was intense, malevolent. She spurred her horse harder, but so did he. As their horses thundered in tandem toward the narrowing doorway, Izzy struggled to control her horse while desperately trying to shake herself loose. She felt the crushing grip tighten. She was slipping.

We're not going to make it!

Izzy felt a sudden movement behind her.

"NO!"

The president's voice!

Izzy looked back. The Republican Guard was flying off his horse, releasing his grip. She saw the president's leg half-extended, as if waiting to deliver a second blow.

She hurtled toward the ever-narrowing exit.

Just a few more feet.

The gate was now almost upon the horse. Izzy sensed the fear of the proud mount as it quivered and pulsed feverishly against her thighs, its chest heaving, taut neck thrusting.

Just a few more inches.

"Duck!" she said to the president, dropping her head to the horses' crest at the last moment.

Barely clearing the plummeting steel, they sped through the portal into the next gallery as the massive gates rushed past the horse's hindquarters and struck the gallery floor with a loud THUD.

Aaagh…Merde…Putain!

Behind her, Izzy heard pursuing riders and horses brutally collide with steel.

83

Ten p.m. in Washington. The seventh floor of the U. S. Department of State, fully illuminated, pulsed with feverish activity. It was no ordinary night. With few exceptions, the buttoned-down diplomatic arm of the government preferred to massage world affairs at evening soirees along Massachusetts Avenue's Embassy Row, or at intimate, off-the-record dinners in elegant Georgetown townhouses. Unless, of course, a diplomatic squall kicked up. And by any consular measure, this one was the Nor'easter from Hell.

Inside her C Street, DOS suite of offices - some of the most coveted political real estate in a status-obsessed town - Noel Traficante, the flinty, fifty-six-year-old, "take no prisoners" Secretary of State, was in crisis-management mode, working international diplomatic channels, as she had been doing round- the-clock since the attack on the U.S. Embassy in Paris.

But the jaw-dropping news that the president had come under assault in Paris and was now unaccounted for had escalated the crisis to a diplomatic Defcon One.

"After the Foreign Minister of India gets on the line queue up Germany and China," Traficante said to Peter Kelly, her Undersecretary for Global Affairs.

"Do you want Strauss from Germany first?" Kelly said.

A graduate of the Fletcher School of Law and Diplomacy and twenty-year veteran of the Foreign Service, Kelly knew that the pecking order of calls was symbolic and important to the diplomats at the other end of the line. But between Berlin and Beijing it was always a close call. Big countries, big egos.

"Berlin first, then Beijing," Traficante said. "China's Minister Woo likes to impress me with his command of English. Won't shut up. Man's all mouth and hands."

"Got it," Kelly said without further comment.

"And Peter, any luck with the French Foreign Minister?"

"No go. We've tried twice. They're stalling

"Best guess?" Traficante said.

"Best guess…it's a turf war amidst panic and confusion with no consensus on what to tell us."

Traficante picked up the half-empty crystal tumbler of ten-year-old Talisker scotch from her oak desk. She leaned back in the burgundy leather chair and considered the drink.

"French panic and confusion be damned," she said. "They're sure as hell running out the clock. White House is ready to pull the trigger. If they don't act in the next two hours, all bets are off on the consequences." She drew the tumbler to her lips and tossed the scotch back.

84

The jarring sounds of heavy gates striking the floor of the Salle de la Joconde accompanied by the shouts of pain from Republican Guards colliding against steel were still ringing in Izzy's head as she and the president thundered out of the Salle and into the Grande Galerie, the longest museum gallery in the world, lined with priceless artworks amassed by French kings and emperors over four hundred years,

Izzy took the point again, racing westward on the polished parquet floors of the immense room. Gericault's Raft of the Medusa and the heroic works of Raphael, Michelangelo, Delacroix and Ingres looked on, silent testaments to fleeting mortality.

Nearing the western end of the gallery she heard new cries.

"Arrêtez! C'est la Police."

Ahead, Izzy saw about half a dozen uniformed men rushing towards them on foot. They appeared to be museum security.

"Weapons!" Izzy said, over her shoulder. Removing her pistol, she bore down on the guards at a furious gallop. One of the guards produced a long gun and raised it toward them. Izzy prepared to fire.

A side door flew open and a man burst into the corridor. He was running toward the guards shouting, waving his arms wildly. Then, as if obeying an order, they stepped aside offering no resistance as the Americans sped past toward the western exit of the Grande Galerie.

85

Commandant Poussin was apoplectic.

"What do you mean, the museum guards allowed them to escape?"

"Sir," the lieutenant said. "They told me they had been ordered directly by the Élysée Palace to allow the Americans to pass."

Poussin noticed the officer was sweating. *Poor bastard has to be the one to deliver the bad news.*

The officer continued. "They were also told to disregard any further orders from you. I had to persuade them not to detain me."

Poussin resumed his tirade. His face flushed with anger.

"Is the Élysée insane?" Poussin said. "These Americans are responsible for the deaths of several of my officers. They've conducted themselves like common criminals. As far as I'm concerned, this is now solely a police matter, not for bureaucrats or priggish Élysée officials."

Poussin wasn't done. His expression was volcanic as he pounded his desk with his burly right fist, punctuating syllables with each blow. "Those po-li-ti-ci-ans are al-ways cow-ards when the dir-ty work needs to be done!"

"Yes, sir."

"Do we have any of our own people near the Louvre?"

"Six of our special operations personnel are about to arrive there. They're the only members of the unit who chose to remain. The others have returned to the Préfecture."

"Then tell them I'm personally ordering them to apprehend the American president by whatever means. Shoot them if you have to."

86

White House

"He's still the president and until he says otherwise in writing that's how it's going to stay."

David Watson, thirty-seven, the president's chief-of-staff, gripped the phone tighter. Rail thin, intense, and referred to in the West Wing as "EC" for "early Childs," meaning one of the first to have joined the president's campaign staff - and therefore untouchable, Watson wasn't going to take any crap from Paul Lyles, the vice-president's senior political aide.

"Whoa, calm down, Dave," Lyles said. "You'd better check section four of the twenty-fifth amendment. We don't have to wait on a fucking piece of paper from the president. We can go to directly to Congress and declare that the president is unable to discharge the duties of his office. For chrissake, Dave, you don't even know if he's alive. Sure, there's an unsubstantiated report that he was seen in the Louvre, but even if he is alive, he's apparently unable to exercise the powers of his office, because no one knows where the living hell he is now. It's a de facto inability to discharge duties, and as far as we're concerned, that's enough."

"De facto, my ass," Watson said. "You have no evidence that he is dead or unable to discharge his duties, as much as you and the vice-president would like to make it so. Besides, you'd still need agreement from a majority of the executive officers of the departments before you could go to the Congress with that request, and that ain't happening, my friend." Watson dragged out the words "my friend" with as much sarcasm as he could muster while nervously moving his finger down the list of cabinet officers... still two commitments shy of the number he needed to block the vice-president's move. As for those who had deserted, one word: *payback.*

"Look, Dave." Lyle's voice had softened to a confessional tone, intimate, commiserating. "We're on the same page. You want to protect the president. I understand that, and I respect it, I really do. You're a good guy. And you want to do what's right for the country. So does the vice-president. There's no daylight between us. But the nation is in a very precarious position at the moment. Action is required and someone has to take it. God knows if the president showed up this moment I'd be the first to say Hallelujah, as would the vice-president. But we've got to be realistic. What do you say, Dave?"

"I say fuck you."

87

Their horses gingerly clattering down the exit stairs of the Grande Galerie, Izzy's beleaguered group reached the bottom landing and pushed open the tall doors.

Before them in the crepuscular dawn lay the Jardin des Tuileries, a vast, tree filled garden created by Catherine de Medici. The early morning cloud cover and periodic cloudbursts had lent a diaphanous quality to the sculptured hedges, immense fountains and timeless statuary. Beyond the Tuileries the towering Obélisque of place de la Concorde, and the Arc de Triomphe rose like ghostly Carnacian menhirs above the stately Champs-Élysées.

Izzy saw that amidst the trees, an immense farmers' pavilion of white canvas had been set up, one of those larger-than-life expositions that periodically materialized without notice in the Tuileries. Though the hour was early, the pavilion already bustled with scores of merchants setting up stands brimming with fresh organic vegetables and fruits, exotic flowers, fragrant cheeses, lamb, duck, olives, spices, poultry and countless delicacies. A vast unpaved promenade ran the length of the Tuileries dividing the gardens. A brief shower had dampened the clay-like earth that had once been used to make tuiles – tiles – for the buildings of Paris.

Will and the others brought their horses alongside Izzy.

"They'll be after us again," she said. "We need to keep moving."

"Where to?" Liam said.

"We could head north through the Palais Royal," Izzy said, "and try to commandeer some transportation. But they're likely to have every street..." The jarring sound of vehicles braking interrupted Izzy mid-sentence. Two large blue vans, tires smoldering, had come to a skidding stop on the rue de Rivoli which paralleled the fenced-in *Tuileries.*

The doors of the vans burst open and heavily armored men with automatic weapons poured out of the vehicles.

"It's the GIGN swat team," Izzy said. "Move!"

Izzy spurred her horse forward onto the gravel pathway. The horse responded with a canter that soon became a full gallop as the president struggled to hold on.

Izzy looked over her shoulder and saw the SWAT team trying to open the metal gates to the gardens. A short burst of automatic fire was followed by the crashing sound of the fence as the GIGN team rushed into the gardens.

Izzy saw one of the men raise his gun and take aim.

"Hang on, sir."

She forcefully reined her mount off the open gravel path and charged through the thick stand of poplars, oaks, elms and alders toward the market stalls.

Pak! Pak! Wizz! Their pursuers were shooting to kill.

Weaving through the low-hanging branches, past Giacometti and Rodin sculptures, past the small children's playground with its silent carousel and empty swings, Izzy charged headlong into the picturesque market stalls, as merchants, food stands and carts were violently upended and sent flying in pandemonium and tumult.

The gunfire had stopped, but behind she heard the loud roar of engines and guessed that the SWAT team would try to intercept them at the foot of the gardens where Rivoli met place de la Concorde.

Izzy saw Liam pull alongside her as they raced on.

"They'll try to get to the northwest end of the gardens before we do," Izzy said.

"Even if we get their first," he said, "it looks like the gates are closed."

"We won't need the gates," Izzy said. "Just stay with me."

Izzy signaled the others to follow as she bolted away. Ahead on the left the Orangerie, home to Monet's Water Lilies, and on the right, the terminus of the sixty-six acre Jardin desTuileries. Enclosing the gardens, a high steel fence. Will was directly behind Izzy and Liam, the Football awkwardly strapped to his back, secured with a makeshift harness of belts taken from the others.

Reining her horse hard, Izzy came to an abrupt halt next to a small concrete structure by the fence. Clumps of mud flung into the air as the other horses came to a wheezing, snorting stop.

Izzy was already off her mount, helping the president down. She could hear the GIGN vans approaching the intersection of Rivoli and Concorde.

"Okay," Izzy said to them. "We're going into the subway system. This small building has a narrow passageway that leads to the Metro station. We'll have to force the door, but once we're in we can access the Metro entrance."

Slam! Slam!

The jarring sound of van doors banging accompanied by adrenalin-charged voices rose from Rivoli.

Izzy looked at the president. "Sir, it's our only chance."

"Let's do it," he said.

They ran down the passageway and reached the door.

"Liam, Will," Izzy said.

Liam and Will kicked in the door. It gave quickly.

"Follow me," Izzy said.

She ran through the doorway and down the underground corridor until they arrived at the stairs that led to the Metro platform. She checked her watch.

"The number one line runs an empty train with just a driver to check the tracks each morning," she said. "It stops at Concorde at 5:30. We've got less than a minute."

Bang ! Slam! "Vite! Vite!"

Izzy heard pounding and shouting coming from the *Concorde* entrance.

They're in.

Eeee! Eeeee!

Izzy heard the whistle of the approaching train and the sound of wheels braking.

"Now!" she said.

They rushed to the edge of the platform as the train slowed to a stop and the doors opened.

"Will, Liam, take the president into the second car."

She rushed into the first car and then to the engineer's cabin where the conductor reared back in disbelief. Izzy's clothes were mud-covered, her hair disheveled and her hands cut in several places.

"Non! C'est interdit!" he said, jumping from his seat.

"Calmez-vous," Izzy said, "calm down." She pushed him back into his seat and pointed to the control panel with her pistol.

"Continuez," she said firmly.

Terrified, the conductor placed his hands on the throttle and pushed. The train slipped away from the station, gained speed and quickly disappeared into the subway tunnel. Behind them the platform reverberated with shouts and epithets.

88

Once again, Poussin found himself careening down Paris streets, guts churning, shirt drenched in sweat, right hand gripping a Sig Pro pistol sunk deep in the pocket of his threadbare impermeable.

He was unaware that his left hand, buried in his other pocket, had crushed a pack of Gauloises into an unrecognizable lump of tobacco leaves and rolling paper, or that his driver had been alarmed at the sight of the bright-red patch of hairless skin that had once been an eyebrow. On the other hand, Poussin *was* keenly aware that his feet hurt and that the soles of his scuffed regulation shoes were now so shopworn he could feel the roughness of the synthetic carpeting on the car's footboard.

He looked out the window. The streets were empty. Paris was not yet awake, and in the early light the city resembled a dreamy Monet.

His eye caught a small terrier off-leash, dashing across the road, safely out of the path of the car.

He sighed.

A small dog like that, loose at this hour? Where's the owner?

He made a mental note to remind Emilie, his wife of thirty-seven years, to keep the garden gate firmly closed. Asterix, their aging terrier, could go astray.

It added to an undefined fear, a baleful premonition that had been gnawing at him since he'd first placed his hands on the arrest warrant. Not a fear of physical harm to himself, he'd learned to deal with violence in his work. But an inchoate, evil presence.

His mind drifted back to a walk he'd taken through a shabby, sunless apartment years earlier in the crime-plagued nineteenth arrondissement. An entire family had been murdered. A week had passed, and the apartment had been emptied of bodies, evidence and furnishings. And yet, as he'd walked in the silence of the bare chilled rooms, he'd found himself uneasily turning to look over his shoulder, unable to shake the eerie sensation that something fiendish was there in the room with him, behind him, menacing, malevolent. He wasn't a superstitious man, but it had raised the hair on the back of his neck. That feeling was back.

Poussin looked out the window of the speeding car again. Clouds hung low over the city, threatening rain. The somberness of the weather echoed his dark mindset, made all the worse by the call he'd just received. The conversation still running through his head. He'd hesitated even taking the call, knowing it could be traced.

"Commandant Poussin, this is Boucher of the Préfecture. I've been trying to reach you for hours. I've just received a call from an official at the Élysée Palace. Thanks to the clumsy manner in which you handled matters at the hotel, we may soon have Special Forces Commandos descending on the Préfecture."

"Sir," Poussin had said, "I was merely carrying out the instructions of the Chief Magistrat. I did my duty, sir, as I have for thirty-five years."

"You're mistaken," Boucher said. "You've mishandled everything. You've disgraced yourself and the Préfecture. I'm relieving you of command as of this moment. You're to discontinue your pursuit of the American president and return to the Préfecture with your unit."

"Has Magistrat Malevu rescinded the warrant?" Poussin said.

"He's refused so far, but it's beside the point. You're to return to the Préfecture with your men immediately. You will be stripped of weapons and badge."

The line had gone dead.

Poussin had put down the phone, his expression a mixture of bitterness and grim amusement.

Aahh, I see. So I'm to be the goat. This has become a fiasco and someone must be blamed. No matter the law. To hell with duty and the devil take the warrant and the magistrat. Yes, Director Boucher, I understand the game well.

Poussin looked out the car window. A light drizzle had begun falling.

Now, they'll say it was Poussin, the clumsy one as they run like field mice for the nearest hole. Director Boucher is just another weak bureaucrat trying to curry favor. But they've misjudged me.

He turned to Antoine, the young GIGN officer at the wheel.

"Take the side streets to place de la Concorde and avoid checkpoints.

You know where they are likely to be."

"Yes, sir."

"And don't spare the petrol."

"Yes, sir."

"And stop saying, yes, sir."

"Yes, si..." The young driver said, nervously.

Congratulations, Poussin, you oaf, you now have this gendarme terrified.

Poussin shifted his weight so that his substantial back rested against the door and turned toward Antoine.

"Do you know why I became a policeman?" Poussin said with such unexpected vehemence that he surprised himself and, apparently, the officer, who winced as if expecting a blow.

Poussin didn't wait for a reply.

"Because I believed in the law. To me, it was a noble instrument for justice, a way to hold even the most powerful accountable."

"Yes, sir."

Poussin pulled the Gauloises from his pocket, looked forlornly at the crumpled pack then shoved the lump back into his coat, trying to avoid the hole in the lining.

"You see, Antoine, I thought I could protect good but simple people from being crushed by unscrupulous predators, as I'd seen my own father crushed. Do you understand?"

"Not exactly, sir."

"How old are you Antoine?"

"Twenty-two, sir."

"Hah, you're still a child, no offense intended. What I mean is that I thought the law is something pure and inviolate. In a way it became my religion. It's why I chose to be a policeman."

"Yes, sir," Antoine said, "I've had some of the same thoughts. It's important to fight back, to protect the average citizen."

"But I was wrong. There was something I failed to see."

"Sir?"

"That power and self-interest can trump the law, confound and blur the truth, make the righteous the villains and the villains the righteous. Because power is a law unto itself and makes a mockery of country bumpkins like me who did not understand that where power resides, truth, the law, justice, are mere commodities to be bought and sold. The great irony, Antoine, is that even though I now see it, I cannot change who I am. I've spent my life like a Don Quichotte, tilting at windmills, championing a cause only fools believe in. I'm condemned to follow this farce to the end. And what will be my reward? I'll be thrown onto the bureaucratic slag heap, a nameless cipher."

The young officer said nothing. Poussin looked out the passenger window once more. The drizzle had turned to rain. He sank further into his seat. The fear had returned. *What will become of my Emilie? Asterix? My garden?*

89

"*Directeur Boucher,*" the voice on the phone said, "This is General Girard de Plessy, Commander of the Paris Army Garrison."

"Yes, General," Boucher said.

"*Monsieur, Directeur,* I've been instructed by the highest authorities of the French government to secure the Préfecture and place you in protective custody."

"General, am I under arrest?"

"No, not at this moment, but the Élysée Palace is in disbelief that you, as Director of the Préfecture, dispatched gendarmes to arrest the American president without any notice to the Élysée. Now French and Americans are dead, the American president is in great danger and we have a rapidly deteriorating security situation internally and internationally.

President Jardin will shortly issue a declaration of a state of emergency for the city and environs of Paris."

"This is all a terrible misunderstanding," Boucher said. "My involvement was purely incidental. Both the magistrat and Commandant Poussin are guilty of abysmal judgment in this matter. There is no reason for me to be placed in protective custody, I assure you."

"Unfortunately, that's not my decision to make." the General said. "In a few minutes team members from my Special Operations unit will be at your offices. I would appreciate it if you would instruct security at the Préfecture to stand down, and permit my men to proceed to your offices. They will ask you to accompany them."

90

"Where are they?" Poussin said to the SWAT squad leader. Poussin was standing on the subway platform, rainwater dripping from his leaky impermeable. He'd arrived just after the team had raced down the Metro stairway to intercept the Americans.

"Commandant, it appears they were able to get on the train heading East toward the station at Chateau de Vincennes. It's the last stop on the line."

"They have a head start so we should jump ahead Poussin said. "We'll intercept them at *Bastille*."

91

Situation Room

"Admiral," Vice-President Stein said, "what are our options for extracting the President?"

The Situation Room in the basement of the West Wing fell silent as Admiral Gus Edmunds, Head of the Joint Chiefs of Staff, shifted in his seat and looked smartly at the vice-president.

"Limited, Mr. Vice President. We have considerable air assets based in the U.K., as well as units of the One Hundred First Airborne. Naval assets include several frigates with missile capabilities and a contingent of Navy Seals in the North Sea. However, deploying and inserting those assets into Paris is for all practical purposes so fraught with collateral damage, that we estimate our chances of success to be less than ten percent."

"Do you have a recommendation?" Stein said.

"Yes, sir, but it does not include a military operation. We believe the only viable option is to use every diplomatic resource available to us, including the British and German governments, to induce the key players in Paris to bring the crisis to an end."

"I'm afraid that won't satisfy the American people," Stein said. "Besides, that train has left the station. It looks like the key players aren't under the control of the French government. Diplomacy isn't an option. Have another go at it."

92

Yves Marteau, head of Direction Centrale du Renseignement Interieur, France's top intelligence service, was ushered into the secure room of the Élysée Palace, a burgundy briefcase attached to his wrist by a titanium bracelet.

Marteau was big, fast and never subtle. A graduate of the École Spéciale Militaire de Saint-Cyr, France's West Point, his career sparkled with achievement on the battlefield and close quarter combat in the intelligence services. At six-seven, he towered over his peers. His sculptured nose and broad forehead combined with a haughty demeanor, reminded many of the revered former president, Charles de Gaulle.

President Jardin rose from his seat and motioned Marteau to a high back leather chair.

"You may leave us now," Jardin said to his security detail.

Once the doors closed, the president activated the hermetic sound suppressor making it impossible for others to eavesdrop.

"You said it was urgent," Jardin said.

"Oui, Monsieur le Président."

Marteau placed the briefcase on his lap and punched a set of numbers in a red metal pad attached to the bracelet. The bracelet opened with a hiss. Marteau removed the bracelet from his wrist, and punched a second set of numbers into an opaque thin box attached to the side of the briefcase. A stamp- size LED screen appeared. He placed his right thumb on it.

The lock sprang open.

Marteau reached into the case, brought out a digital player, and placed it on the table in front of the president.

"Sir," he said, attaching a pair of ear buds to the device, "I think you should listen to this."

Jardin studied Marteau for a moment, his irritation showing a bit.

"Very well," he said, taking the buds and placing them in his ears.

He pressed PLAY.

After about three minutes, the president pressed the stop button and removed the ear buds. He sat still, barely breathing for a long moment.

He looked at Marteau with an expression of horror.

93

"Find whatever you can and throw it on the tracks!" Poussin said.

He was standing on the quai of the Bastille metro stop as his SWAT team rushed about ripping benches and wall-mounted vending machines from their moorings, throwing them onto the tracks below.

This is where it ends. If there is to be blood it will not start with our weapons. But these people will not be permitted to move beyond Bastille. The American president will be taken into custody, and my work…and my career, will be finished.

Eeeeee! Eeeee!

"Here it comes!" Poussin said. "Safeties off. But do not fire without my direct order."

Brakes screeching, horn wailing, the train emerged from the darkness and came to a jarring stop at the *quai*. As the doors opened, Poussin and the SWAT team bolted into the cars shouting: "POLICE!" "POLICE!" their weapons raised. They tore from one car to the next, checking under the seats and behind the connecting doors between the cars, "Clear"... Clear"...

Then, "All clear, sir."

"Merde!"

Poussin examined the driver's cab. Its controls were set to automated mode. "We have to backtrack. Check stations between Bastille and Concorde. Hurry!"

94

Izzy and Liam were sandwiched into a damp, narrow, utility room located deep in the subway tunnel between the Hôtel de Ville and St. Paul stations. The driver of the train was with them, mouth gagged, hands tied. The president and the others were deep in the tunnel's darkness to avoid detection.

Izzy had stopped the train midway through the tunnel. After they got off, she'd ordered the driver to set it on automatic mode and send it on. "We won't harm you," she'd assured him, though the fear on his face suggested he doubted her.

Izzy turned to Liam who was beside her in a protective stance. She placed a tender kiss on his lips. "I just want you to know how much it means to me that you showed up. I thought we'd run out of luck at Cour Lefuel. Things are still dicey, but it feels good to have a daring knight beside me."

Even in the weak light she could see his familiar puckish smile spread across his face as if to say, *Isn't this exciting!* It was but a brief moment of levity. His expression became more thoughtful. "You're pretty important to me, Izzy. I don't know what I'd do if…"

Izzy gently placed her index finger on his lips. "I know, I know," she whispered.

"Now," she said, all business again. "It'll take them a while to find this location. Should give me enough time to get us out of here."

"Good hunting," Laim said.

She sprinted away, and disappeared into the gloom of the tunnel. Nearing the next metro stop from within the tunnel, Izzy located a maintenance stairway. She climbed the concrete stairs, pushed open the metal door, and was met with a blast of fresh air and cold rain.

She was on rue St. Antoine. The streets were more animated now, and she made her way down the avenue, relieved that her wet, disheveled appearance gave her the semblance of a homeless person, invisible to the indifferent passersby. Reaching the church of St. Paul - St. Louis she turned up the narrow passage that led to the rear entrance of the church, pushed the door open and slipped in.

St. Paul – St. Louis was an elegant church with a rich history. Its first mass had been presided over by Cardinal Richelieu in the presence of Louis XIII.

And the bloody heart of France's most celebrated king, Louis XIV had been granted to the Jesuit Superior of Saint Paul–Saint Louis Church.

The somber quality of the seventeenth century paintings, vaulted ceiling and grand altar gave the church an ethereal, timeless quality.

"It's an early visit you're making," a voice said.

Izzy turned toward the apse. A cassocked priest was smiling benevolently.

"Yes, Father," she said, rainwater pooling from her clothes onto the floor.

"My child," he said, "We know how difficult life on the street is. You are welcome here."

"Thank you, Father."

"You must be cold and hungry."

"Yes, but first I must see Father Seurat. Is he still at this church?"

"Of course." the priest said, a look of surprise on his face. "Does he know you? Father is very busy with morning confessions."

"Not exactly, but I have a personal message for him."

"I can give him your message?"

"Will you tell him that an old égoutier named Jerome gave me his name?"

"Please wait here. I will speak with him."

A few moments later, Izzy heard the sound of beads, muffled tones of conversation, and the slap, slap of sandals rapidly approaching.

A ruddy-faced, heavy-set priest in a floor length, dark-brown cassock approached her, his long robe rustling.

"You were a friend of old Jerome?" the rotund priest said, making a sign of the cross.

"Yes, are you Father Seurat?"

"I am indeed."

"Father, Jerome once told me that if I ever needed help, I should come to you."

The priest came closer, studying her face. He squinted, and angled his head as if trying to recall something.

"Are you the one called 'Izzy'?"

"Yes, Father."

Seurat's large brown eyes lit up. "My dear, he spoke fondly of you.

Welcome, welcome."

The portly priest, who resembled a French Friar Tuck, leaned back and took in her bedraggled appearance.

"My child," he said at last, with genuine sympathy, "I see life has not been kind. The Lord's ways are sometimes a mystery."

Seurat turned to the other priest.

"Thank you, brother. Now we will speak privately. Please prepare a room, clothes, a shower...and hot food."

"Yes Father." The priest bowed and walked away. Seurat turned to Izzy.

"Now, tell me. What can I do?"

"Father, I need a phone? I don't mean a mobile phone, but one that is connected to an outlet, a landline."

Seurat smiled. "I'm afraid that's all we do have. Mobile phones are not in our modest budget."

"I have to make a call," Izzy said. "Then I'll tell you how you can help."

95

Situation Room

"They're alive! They're still alive!"

Bill Hyde, Director of the CIA, was standing in front of his laptop in the crowded Situation Room, elation on his face.

The bleary-eyed crisis group, exhausted from the non-stop vigil, sprang to life.

"Our station chief in London just got a landline call from Izzy Stone," Hyde said, "They're banged up and on the run, but okay."

The vice-president looked at Hyde.

"Do we have a confirm on that?"

"Yessir," Hyde said, his words cascading with excitement. "Langley just spoke with the White House Secret Service. Agent Stone provided Dumbledore's password and a numerical sequence."

"Hooah! Hooah! Yesss!" The SitRoom exploded with cheers, back-slapping and bear hugs as pent-up tension was released and exhausted eyes moistened.

"What else do we have?" the vice-president said, as the room quieted.

"At this point, not much detail. But Stone did specify a rendezvous point and an approximate ETA."

The vice-president turned to Admiral Gus Edmunds, head of the Joint Chiefs.

"It's in your court, Admiral. How will you extract?"

"Sir, following our last discussion, I instructed our Joint Special Operations Command to prepare an extraction plan on the assumption the president was still alive. We have SEAL Team Six members from DEVGRU sitting in three helos good to go at this moment. All told, with three French speakers and two techs on board, it's thirty-five souls. They're positioned on three frigates about thirty nautical miles off the coast of northwest France within striking distance of Brittany and Normandy. In addition, we've deployed two stealth drones. Should give us real time intel."

"Good," the vice-president said. "Nail down the rendezvous point and ETA. Let's move."

96

As the two nuns in hooded habits and five monks in long hooded cassocks with waist cords moved along rue St. Antoine, pedestrians stepped aside respectfully.

"Bonjour, frère, bonjour, chère souer," they said as the group passed.

"Bonjour," Father Seurat said.

Izzy breathed a sigh of relief, grateful that the president's unshaved face was largely obscured by the wimple of the nun's habit he was wearing as he walked alongside her.

Reaching the church of St. Paul – St. Louis, Father Seurat guided the group to the rear of the church where a dilapidated gray school bus with flaking paint and tinted windows waited, motor idling. On each side of the bus were the words: Paroisse St. Paul – St. Louis.

"Father Manet will take you to your destination." Seurat said. "Do not worry about the welfare of the Metro conductor. We will make sure he is safely released as soon as you've left the city."

"Thank you, Father," Izzy said.

"God be with you."

97

Overnight the city of Paris had become an armed camp. Military roadblocks were present at every major intersection the creaking bus approached. Unsmiling soldiers with automatic weapons and attack dogs were checking vehicles. Nonetheless, the parish bus with its cassocked occupants sailed through on its way to the Périphérique, Paris' notoriously chaotic beltway.

"We'll stay on the boulevards until we can join the Périphérique north," five-foot four, wafer-thin Father Manet said to Izzy, in an accented English that sounded oddly Italian. He shot her a quick sideways glance. "From there we'll take the A13 to the coast." Then chancing a sheepish look at the president he said, "Do not worry, monsieur, I am a very careful driver."

He pushed down on the gas pedal with obvious relish, accelerated the wheezing four-cylinder bus to an unnerving high-pitched whine, and raced down the rue du Faubourg Saint-Antoine dodging a meteor shower of delivery trucks, mopeds, cyclists, jay walkers and swarms of interweaving, oncoming vehicles. The absence of marked lanes resembled an anthill that had just been disturbed. Maintaining his animated pace, Manet barreled into the crowded roundabouts at Bastille and Nation, negotiating wild cross-traffic, as the aging springs of the bus strained to keep the vehicle from capsizing. At the Porte de Vincennes roundabout, Manet spun ahead, then pulled sharply to the right traveling counter-clockwiseas he plunged the bus into the roaring Périphérique below, its traffic rushing like a river at flood stage.

Izzy was standing in the stairwell of the careening bus, her eyes focused on Manet. Father Seurat had assured her that the impish priest was the best driver in the diocese. But looking at the diminutive character, his chest up against the steering wheel, hands at ten and two o'clock, eyes locked on the traffic like an Irish Pointer, Izzy wasn't so sure.

Inside the rocky bus, the group discarded their nun's clothing as they wolfed down the bread, cheese and sausages provided by father Seurat. Large bottles of water were quickly consumed as they slaked their thirst.

98

"I want Commandant Poussin stopped," General de Plessy said to his executive officer. "Use deadly force if necessary,"

"Yes, General," the officer said. "But Poussin has gone to ground. We're not sure where he and his men are at the moment. They were spotted at the Tuileries but after that they disappeared."

"Redouble your efforts," de Plessy said. "If Poussin gets to the Americans before we do, France will end up with the blood of an American president on its hands. We'll never live down the shame or the wrath that will be unleashed on us."

99

"They were here." Poussin said, using a large flashlight to illuminate the shoe imprints on the muddy tunnel floor.

Poussin was standing in the small alcove of the subway tunnel where Izzy and the others had been.

He stepped out of the alcove and looked in both directions of the subway tracks. To his left he could see light where the Metro emerged from the tunnel to a passenger *quai*.

"That's the St. Paul station," he said to no one in particular. "It's the closest exit. It must be the direction they took."

Accompanied by his SWAT team, Poussin made his way down the tracks, gravel biting through the soles of his shoes. Approaching the quai, he saw a steep concrete stairway to his left that led upward to an exit door. Already winded from the walk, he trudged up the stairs with great effort and swung the door open. Before him was rue St. Antoine.

Morning pedestrians were taken aback by the sudden appearance of a panting, disheveled, heavy-set man in a weathered raincoat, accompanied by heavily armed men in SWAT attire.

Poussin peered down the boulevard. Vendors were selling newspapers and magazines from their kiosks, while crepe makers prepared oef-fromage crepes at stands consisting of nothing more than a cart on wheels, a small hot plate, and a few ingredients. He saw nothing out of the ordinary.

Poussin turned to his men. "Question everyone. Ask them if they've seen anything unusual this morning, people behaving in an odd way, seeming out of place, injured or carrying weapons. "

100

l'Élysée Palace

President Jardin looked up as his aide entered the room.

"Mr. President, General de Plessy and Magistrat Malevu have arrived."

"Show them in."

General de Plessy entered the room, accompanied by a clearly agitated Malevu.

"Good morning, Mr. President," the general said.

"Good morning, General. And good morning to you as well, *Monsieur Magistrat.*" The president's voice was deadpan.

"Mr. President," the magistrat said, his voice rising, "It is not a good morning for me. I've been brought here under armed guard in complete violation of the laws of the French Republic and my rights as a citizen and member of the judiciary. I demand to be released immediately."

"Calmez-vous, monsieur," the president said, "and sit down."

The steely tone of the president's voice left no question as to his mood. The magistrat sat down.

"General, would you excuse us?" the president said to de Plessy.

"Yes, sir. I'll be in the next room should you need me."

"Thank you."

When the door closed, the president approached Malevu who was now sitting beside a large desk, bare with the exception of a small, black rectangular device. The president walked to the desk, stood in front of Malevu then sat back on the edge of the desk, his right leg dangling.

"Monsieur," the president said, dispensing with name or title. "Your judicial plot is at an end. Through your treacherous actions, you've precipitated an international crisis and caused the deaths of innocent Americans and Frenchmen."

"No," Malevu said. "I merely exercised the legal authority the judicial system has granted me. It is not my fault if the order was improperly carried out."

"That legal authority you speak of," the president said, his voice rising, "does not extend to a jurist who gained his position through murder and conspiracy."

Malevu leaped from his chair. "I'm not afraid of you, Jardin. I demand to be released."

The president brought his face closer to the magistrat so that they were almost nose-to-nose. Fury barely contained, his voice dropping to a low, malevolent register, Jardin said, "You'll go nowhere until you rescind the arrest warrant you issued against the President of the United States. You are a loathsome man who has brought disgrace and near catastrophe to our nation.

You are a murderer and a traitor."

Malevu looked at Jardin.

"I'm not one of your sycophants who tremble in the chambers of the Élysées palace. You forget, *Monsieur le Président,* that I too have powerful friends who will demand that you be removed. You have interfered with the judiciary, and engaged in a criminal violation of our nation's constitution."

The president turned to the small device on the desk and pressed a button.

Malevu's distinctive baritone voice rang out from the device...

"How soon will our young friend attend mass?"

"He'll be at St. Roch on Christmas Eve, Magistrat." a second voice said. "It's the late mass that Abelard always attends during the holidays."

"Do you think he's ready to go through with it?" Malevu's voice was unmistakable.

"He's ready. Told me you had explained everything very clearly to him. He sees it as his patriotic duty. Abelard will soon cease to be an obstacle."

"Good," the magistrat's voice answered.

President Jardin pressed the stop button and looked at the magistrat.

"Early this morning we arrested two of your co-conspirators. They've confessed to participating in the assassination of Magistrat Abelard and have named you as the person who directed the plot. One of them recorded your conversation. They've also confessed to the murder of professor Rene Hachard of the École Supérieure des Arts. You had him killed because he brought you and Emile to the attention of the authorities. It's clear now that you had a plan to arrest the American president on any pretext the very next time he visited. The bombing in Islamabad gave you the perfect excuse."

"Where did you get this recording!" Malevu said, clearly taken aback.

"Monsieur," Jardin said. "Have you ever heard the expression; 'There is no honor among thieves'? "

101

USS Destroyers Gettysburg and Montana, two Arleigh Burke destroyers, and the Zumwalt, a state-of-the-art vessel with a rail-gun were in a high state of alert riding a calm sea thirty nautical miles off the Cotentin Peninsula of France.

On the Zumwalt's deck, a Blackhawk helicopter, rotors slowly turning, was fueled and ready for lift off. The Gettysburg and Montana carried another Blackhawk each. All three Blackhawks had been modified for stealth.

Aboard each helo, elite warriors from SEAL Team Six, Naval Special Warfare Development Group, DEVGRU, sat quietly as they received last minute details of Operation Talon. Armed with specialized communications gear, stealth weapons, and honed to a razor's edge, they were the world's deadliest, best-trained fighters, and they were good to go.

SEAL Team Six consisted of warriors who repeatedly deployed to highly sensitive, extraordinarily dangerous clandestine assignments all over the world. The nature of their missions, always cloaked in secrecy and requiring extreme violence, were never revealed to other branches of the military, much less the general public.

They had been briefed on their destination, the American Cemetery overlooking Omaha Beach at Colleville-sur-Mer, Normandy. Their mission: extract the president of the United States and his security team, and transport them to the safety of the aircraft carrier USS Theodore Roosevelt steaming toward a rendezvous point 120 nautical miles off the French Coast.

The Navy Commander of the SEAL team was waiting for a "Go" from the Joint Special Operations Command operating out of the Situation Room of the White House.

102

Poussin was speeding down Rue St. Antoine, flying into the Bastille roundabout and continuing on Rue du Faubourg Saint-Antioine toward the Périphérique, the city's massive vehicular beltway. Close behind, two SWAT vehicles followed. It had taken an hour to identify the church and interrogate the aging priest, Seurat, who'd assisted Izzy and the president in their escape.

"Père," he'd said, stabbing his stubby index finger toward Father Seurat's nose, "If you do not immediately tell me where these criminals are headed, you will be obstructing justice and aiding fugitives sought by the Préfecture and the senior magistrat of Paris. The consequences for you and your parish will be harsh."

Seurat was unfazed.

"My son," he said, "have you made a good confession recently?"

"I need no confession, Father!" Poussin said. "I'm seeking people who are fugitives from justice. If you know something, you are bound by the law to come forward."

"They were headed to Normandy." Poussin and father Seurat turned in the direction of the voice.

"They were headed to Normandy," the voice repeated.

A disheveled man emerged form the shadow of the apse.

"Last night I sneaked into the church through a window. I was cold. I fell asleep. This morning a woman's voice woke me. She was on the phone. She said something about going to Normandy, but I don't know who she was talking to."

"My child!" Seurat said, appalled, "This is the house of God. We do not betray the privacy of others. "

Poussin interjected and approached the scruffy stranger.

"Normandy is a huge region. Where in Normandy were they going?"

"I don't know," the man said, glancing at Father Seurat with a chagrined expression.

Poussin looked at Seurat. "*You* must know."

"I regret, I do not," Seurat said.

Poussin didn't believe him, but in matters of faith and church he dared not cross the line. Poussin at least knew that they were traveling in a battered parish bus. A flower vendor being questioned said he'd seen the bus rattling away from the church with several people inside.

Poussin also knew that in order to get to Normandy fast, the group would have to exit Paris via the Périphérique and connect to the autoroute. That meant only one thing – they would take the *A-13*, the high-speed highway that traveled westward from Paris, across the length of Normandy, to the shores of the English Channel.

But still, where in Normandy? There were hundreds of exits between Paris and the coast.

103

Izzy's stomach was churning as she looked on in disbelief, standing outside the disabled bus, pistol pressed against her leg, as a surreal scene played out before her.

"*Monsieur*, we will try one more time," Father Manet said to Will.

Will was in the driver's seat of the antiquated bus, his finger on the ignition, clutch depressed, right foot on the accelerator as waif-like Manet, leaned deep under the raised hood, cupped a hand over the exposed carburetor and attempted to coax the vehicle to life.

"You must pump the gas more, more, monsieur!" Manet said.

Through the open driver's door Izzy could see Will pumping the gas pedal as he pressed the ignition button with no success.

"Hold on!" Liam was exiting the bus fast. "You're flooding the carburetor. Let me take a look."

He poked his head under the hood.

"This is a 1970's Renault-Saviem four-cylinder engine," he said. "It's notorious for problems with the accelerator pump. The stem hangs up and fuel can't move."

"Can you fix it?" Izzy asked, remembering Liam had often spoken about his life-long fascination with cars when they were in Washington.

"Think so," Liam said as he worked with a penknife to unscrew the stem. "I'll need some motor oil."

"The bus leaks oil all the time," said Manet.

"Good," Liam said. "Get a small container and put it under the oil pan. I only need a few drops. And I need something narrow to pour with."

"I don't have an oil can," Manet said, "but there are straws in the bus that we give to the children when they have their meals. We also have napkins and paper plates, and….."

"Just a straw! Father. Please."

Moments later Liam was dripping small drops of oil down a straw and into the shaft of the stem housing. Finally satisfied, he slid the stem back into the carburetor and secured it.

"Try it now," he said to Will.

Rrrrrrr…Rrrrrr…..*VOOOM, VROOOM!* The engine turned over with a roar as Will fed gas and revved the motor.

Liam slammed the hood shut and the three climbed back onto the bus. Manet scooted into the driver's seat as Will slid to the side, left foot still feeding the gas.

Manet put the bus in gear and accelerated onto the autoroute.

"We'll arrive in about an hour," he said, his voice buoyant.

104

President Jardin, ashen-faced, eyes blood-shot from lack of sleep, stood at a hurriedly assembled press conference in the press room of the Élysée Palace. It was seven in the morning and standing-room only.

Outside the Élysée an immense electronic village had sprung up along Rue du Faubourg Sainte Honoré as news organizations from around the world converged on Paris. Less than nine hours had passed since the assault on the Hôtel Marly by Commandant Poussin and his SWAT unit. In those hours the city had been transformed from its normal Parisian rhythm to a city under siege.

Every major artery in the city was now dotted with military vehicles manned by heavily armed soldiers. Around the corner from the Élysée palace the ruins of the former American Embassy still emitted the acrid smell of burnt debris.

"*Bonjour,*" Jardin said, his voice ragged and strained, his distinctive runner's jawline taught.

"Last night, shortly after ten p.m., twenty-two hours Paris time, a rogue element of the French judiciary and Préfecture police attempted to place the president of the United States under arrest. The arrest warrant was politically motivated, unlawful, unprecedented in its malevolence, and was issued by a magistrat who is now in the custody of French authorities."

The room erupted with journalists trying to outshout each other.

"Who is the magistrat?"

"Where is President Childs? Is he safe?"

"What was the warrant for?"

The questions cascaded onto the French president.

Jardin raised his hands as if to say stop.

"*Calmez-vous, s'il vous plaît,*" Jardin said. "I will tell you as much as I know, and as much as I am at liberty to disclose. But your questions will have to wait until I complete my remarks."

His words appeared to momentarily quiet the journalists.

Jardin continued. "In addition to the magistrat, several other individuals have been detained and are being questioned in connection with this plot.

Others are still being sought by French military and civilian authorities."

Jardin paused briefly and dropped his gaze to his clenched hands resting on the podium as if collecting his thoughts. Then he looked up.

"As to President Childs," Jardin said, "we have advised the White House that at this moment we remain uncertain of his exact whereabouts or his physical condition, but…

He didn't get a chance to finish his sentence as a shoe thrown by an enraged American journalist struck his shoulder.

"Bastard!" the journalist shouted. "Where's our President? You know where he is, you goddamned liar!"

The reporter was violently knocked to the floor by French journalists shouting, "Your president is a miserable butcher."

The throng of international reporters turned into a wild melee, as security attempted to quell the fighting while others joined in with loud epithets and fisticuffs.

Élysée security hustled Jardin away from the podium.

A few minutes later the French president stood in front of the television cameras again, this time in an empty room while technicians activated the Réseau National d"Alerte, France's national emergency alert system. Citizens across France began turning on their local tv and radio stations to see and hear Jardin.

"Citizens of France, this is your President. As you must know by now, last night the President of the United States was attacked by certain criminal elements. As a result, president Childs was forced to flee and he is now in hiding. The president may be injured and in need of immediate medical care. I am calling on all French citizens to assist your government in locating the president and his staff. Photographs of the president and some of those believed to be with him are available on your local television station and on the internet."

Jardin looked directly into the camera.

"I have a special warning to those who would do president Childs or his people harm. Beware, for the full power of the French government will be brought down on you without mercy."

The airwaves were silent for a moment. Then Jardin resumed but with great emotion in his voice.

"Mr. President, if you can hear me, I'm personally appealing to you to contact us by any means available to you, so that we can ensure your safety and the safety of those with you. I want to say to you on behalf of the people of France, that we are devastated by the nightmarish events of last night. It is true that recent tragedies have stirred strong emotions in both our countries. But we remember our history. The people of France have not forgotten the supreme sacrifices your country made for us when our freedom and very existence were in grave peril. Twice in two great wars your nation's sons and daughters shed blood and fell in battle on the beaches and in the fields of France, not for conquest or glory but to free our people from terror and tyranny. No passage of time or calamity will ever diminish the gratitude and goodwill we carry in our hearts. God be with you, and may God bless the United States of America."

105

"Stay on the A-13 until we have a better idea where they are," Poussin said, as his driver sped down the autoroute.

Poussin's head was pounding, his eyes blurring and he'd run out of *aspirine*. Earlier, the dreaded migraine aura had signaled the onset of the skull-splitting headache, except there'd been no time for anything but the chase. He now regretted not having taken the five minutes to get more when they'd stopped to switch cars at the remote Préfecture vehicle depot in the twentieth arrondissement.

Like the GIGN officers in the two sedans behind him, Poussin's car had no identifying insignia, a necessary precaution, since both civilian and military authorities were now looking for them. His mind returned to his conversation with the homeless man at St. Paul-St. Louis church.

The vagrant told me the American woman said they were headed for Normandy. But where in Normandy? It's a vast area with large cities and hundreds of small towns. She must have been referring to something specific, but what? Where would an American evading arrest go in Normandy?

Poussin had no answer. What he did know was that he'd almost run out of time. Now he was both hunter and hunted, and knew that a massive effort to find him was undoubtedly underway. The French government would be merciless.

He felt the moistness trickling down his left cheek again and used the wrinkled handkerchief to dab it. He looked at the handkerchief. The once-white linen was now blotched with red.

106

"Can no one give me a straight answer?" French President Jardin was exasperated by the torrent of conflicting information pouring into the crisis center, as he and his senior military, civilian and intelligence advisors sifted through hundreds of reports of sightings of President Childs. Callers were sure they'd seen the American president on the TGV train to Metz, the Eiffel Tower, a KFC in Marseille, a hotel in Cap d'Antibes.

The only solid information had come from market vendors at the Tuileries who'd reported that the Americans, to the vendor's astonishment, had thundered out of nowhere on horseback and fled towards the metro entrance at Concorde, demolishing the market pavilion as they galloped through.

Equally vexing to President Jardin was Commandant Poussin, who seemed to always be one step ahead of the Préfecture's dragnet and de Plessy's military cordon.

"Sir, we've located the SWAT vehicles that Commandant Poussin and his men were using."

Jardin turned to the Minister of the Interior, the man in charge of the national police.

"Where?" Jardin said.

"On the street outside the Préfecture vehicle depot in the twentieth."

"And Poussin?"

"Gone, but three unmarked cars from the depot are missing. A video feed from national highway cameras has captured three vehicles speeding on the A-13 autoroute. The cars resemble the one's missing from the depot."

"Where on the A-Thirteen?"

"Traveling west from the péage toll at Buchelay about forty kilometers west of Paris."

"You said they were speeding?"

"Our cameras indicate they were traveling over one hundred fifty kilometers per hour."

"It's Poussin!" Jardin said, his voice filled with alarm. "He knows where President Childs is. God help us." He spun to General de Plessy.

"General, intercept those vehicles. Poussin could be on the president any moment. The Americans will resist, but against the GIGN, we'll have a dead president on our hands."

"I'll immediately dispatch three Tigre attack helicopters and a contingent of our Special Forces to intercept," de Plessy said. He picked up a secure phone, and punched in a number, and looked at Jardin. "Sir, I also recommend we order police units on the A-13 to set up roadblocks."

"Do it!" Jardin ordered.

107

"It's a checkpoint!" Izzy said, as the digital highway display suddenly illuminated, advising motorists to prepare to stop. In the distance, a sea of flashing police lights glowed ominously.

"We'll take the secondary roads," Father Manet said. With amazing dexterity, he yanked the wheel of the aging bus and veered across three crowded lanes toward the exit, while furiously correcting the drift of the loose steering wheel.

Izzy, white-knuckled, watched in wonder as the puckish Manet shot down the exit ramp with the ardor of a driver at Le Mans.

This cleric is a demon behind the wheel, but he's as good a driver as I've ever seen.

All four wheels of the aging bus skidded to a bouncing stop at the unmanned exit barrier. The diminutive priest pulled a card from his cassock, leaned halfway out the driver's window and inserted it into the receptacle, his right leg extended in the cab like a dancer at the barré. The yellow metal arm lifted, but Manet did not move forward.

Approaching panic Izzy said, "What's wrong?"

"I'm waiting for the receipt," Manet said.

"Go, go, go!" Izzy said with disbelief.

Manet popped the clutch, and lurched ahead with a roar.

108

Situation Room

Air Force Brigadier General Peter Piper, Assistant Commanding General, Joint Special Operations, looked up from his computer.

"Mr. Vice-President," he said, "Operation Talon is now wheels-up in helos. Seal Team Six should have boots on the ground at the American Cemetery at Colleville-sur-Mer in approximately thirty minutes."

"There'll be hell to pay with the French government for violating their air space," the vice-president said, "but there's no way we can give them a heads up without increasing the risks. What's the status of our drones, General?"

"Sir," Piper said, "one of the stealth drones we deployed to the Cotentin Peninsula is now transmitting a live video feed from the projected rendezvous point at the American Cemetery. There's an offshore marine layer moving in. We'll be looking at heavy fog pretty soon."

"Let's get it up on the screen before we lose visibility," the vice-president said.

A moment later, through a light screen of wafting fog, an image of the expansive memorial grounds appeared. A breathless silence enveloped the room as the winged observer glided serenely over one of America's most sacred military cemeteries. On the verdant cliff overlooking the gunmetal English Channel and the broad expanse of Omaha Beach, bloodiest site of the D-Day Allied invasion, thousands of pristine-white crosses, each bearing a small American flag, stood in perfect formation against an immaculate expanse of emerald-green grass.

General Piper increased the resolution of the camera lens as the drone dipped below the encroaching fog, methodically sweeping the grounds for signs of the president and his detail. Except for the poignant sea of red, white and blue fluttering in quiet salute, there was no sign of them.

The tension in the room was palpable.

"What's our best estimate of when the president and the detail will show up at the rendezvous point?" the vice-president said.

"Sir," Piper said, silently thumbing the beads of a small rosary in his coat pocket, "our best guess is about twenty minutes to an hour from now. But there's no way of knowing precisely when, because we don't know what they're up against. There could be any one of a hundred complications - interdiction, a fire-fight, mechanical problems, getting lost in this fog...there's no way of being sure, short of contacting French authorities and enlisting their support."

"Can't chance it," the vice-president said. "Even if president Jardin can be counted on, and I believe he can, there's no way of knowing whether someone in that inner circle might be working with the plotters. We have to pray and hope for the best."

The vice-president scooted his chair forward and rested his elbows on the long conference table. He dropped his forehead to his clasped hands and sank into deep reflection. He'd come a long way in his thinking during the course of the mind-bending developments of the last several hours. The enormity, speed and fiendish implications of the events that had struck like a thunderbolt, had caused him to reconsider everything. He now realized that the country was at a historic crossroads. His own political interests were now dwarfed by the existential crisis facing the American government.

Short of assassination, no American president had ever faced such a threat. So improbable, unthinkable, had the legal and physical assault on the president been that it had taken time for the implications to fully sink in.

It was now clear to him that the time-honored notion of sovereign immunity had undergone a profound change. A new, frightening era in global affairs had dawned. No American president, or any head of state hereafter, would be able to freely move about the globe without the spectre of arrest looming in the shadows - a malevolent magistrat from one of America's oldest allies had made that abundantly clear.

109

Poussin saw the police barricade ahead on the A-13.

"They're waiting for us! Take the next exit!"

The three vehicles swerved wildly through the lines of cars already backing up.

Poussin saw police vehicles tear away from the barricade and head in their direction.

As they sped down the unmanned exit, he activated the barrier with an electronic device. The barrier lifted and they sped through.

The Americans must have taken this exit too. They wouldn't have known about the roadblock either until the last moment.

"Stay on this secondary road." he said, "We're probably right behind them."

110

Father Manet was nothing if not intrepid. Barreling down the two-lane D-514 with the abandon of a country veteran he seemed to know every turn, blind curve, cow crossing and hamlet in his path.

Izzy had decided that however meek or frail the priest might appear, behind the wheel he was in his domain, a gifted savant of the highway.

"How far are we now from the American Cemetery?" she asked.

"We're approaching Colleville-sur-Mer," Manet said. "Once we get there it's only about fifteen minutes away."

Izzy heard a distant thrumming of helicopters racing at high speed. She stepped down into the stairwell of the pitching bus and peered through the side window. In the distance she could see a formation of choppers flying in a widening concentric search pattern, nose down, their distinctive profiles and thirty-millimeter guns clearly silhouetted against the growing light.

They're Tigres. We may not have fifteen minutes.

111

Poussin was now in a complete state of mental turmoil. Despite his initial optimism and their speeding rampage through the villages and secondary roads of Normandy there was no sign of the Americans. Fortunately, Poussin had been able to evade the autoroute police who were in pursuit. His instincts told him he'd been very close to the Americans when they'd left the autoroute, yet somehow the trail had gone cold.

Poussin was now on the D-123 moving west, ever closer to the ocean. Soon they'd run out of time, and find themselves facing French police and military units. As they passed the intersection of the D-123 and the D-97, a large billboard flashed by.

"Arrêtez! Arrêtez!" Poussin said to his driver.

The car came to a howling, skidding, stop, and the two chase vehicles behind almost collided with Poussin's car.

"Turn around. Go, Go, Go!" Poussin said, straining to look over his shoulder at something.

Wheels spinning wildly the driver executed a tight u-turn on the narrow lanes. The two other cars followed.

The driver advanced fifty yards.

"Stop here," Poussin said as they returned to the point where the D-97 intersected the D-123, the road they were on. The D-97 ran north in the direction of the English Channel.

The driver rolled to a stop, motor idling. Poussin opened the door, lumbered out, shoved his meaty hands into his raincoat and stared. There in the open field adjacent to the road was an oversized billboard obviously intended for tourists:

VISIT THE HISTORIC GERMAN
CEMETERY
AT LA CAMBE
AND
THE HISTORIC AMERICAN
CEMETERY
AT COLLEVILLE-SUR-MER

"That's it!" he shouted. "They're headed to the American Cemetery."

Poussin hurried back to the car.

Why hadn't it occurred to him before? Short of the U.S. Embassy in Paris, the American Cemetery was the closest thing the United States had to sovereign soil in France. The Americans would have realized this and assumed it would be the safest place to be until they could be rescued.

"Take the D-97 north," he said, "It will get us to Le Grand-Hameau. From there the road leads us directly to the cemetery."

Turning onto the D-97 the motorcade sped north towards Le Grand-Hameau.

Poussin looked out the window, and tried to ignore the pain in his head. He knew the American Cemetery well. He'd grown up in the town of Bayeux, not far from the cemetery. As a child he'd visited there with his grandfather, a disabled former member of the French Resistance, who revered the site. His grandfather had always made it a point to visit a particular grave. Leaning heavily on a cane, *grand-père* would awkwardly navigate the field of crosses until he found it. Placing a small French flag and some wildflowers beside the white cross he'd quietly recite a short prayer.

"Who was he, *grand-père?*"young Poussin had asked.

"An American soldier named James Perkins. He was killed on Omaha Beach the day of the invasion. He was only seventeen. Afterward many of us decided to each adopt an American soldier who died that day. We promised to never let them be forgotten."

"Did you know him, *grand-père?*"

"No, but when a man dies for your country, you become brothers. "

112

"*Monsieur le Président,* autoroute police are reporting a pursuit of several vehicles that evaded the roadblock."

The French Minister of the Interior was in the Élysée crisis room, deep underground, with President Jardin and other key national security members, monitoring the rapidly unfolding events.

"Is it Poussin, or the Americans?" the president said.

"We're not sure. The units in pursuit have lost them, but it's unlikely that it's the Americans. They couldn't have stolen three vehicles without being detected. My opinion, sir, is that it's Commandant Poussin, and the vehicles are the ones taken from the depot."

Jardin saw General de Plessy speaking into his headpiece.

"General?" the president said.

"Sir, I've instructed our Tigre helicopter pilots to get the last coordinates the police had before they lost Poussin. They'll fan out from there, following the secondary roads. With any luck, we'll be able to locate them from the air."

The president turned to Francois Rambeau, his Foreign Minister.

"Francois, is the White House telling us anything helpful about the condition or location of President Childs?"

"No, sir, they've repeatedly rejected our offer of help. Our ambassador in Washington tells us the Americans have put a complete embargo on all information concerning Childs."

President Jardin clenched his teeth.

How can we help if they won't tell us what they know? We're in the dark, with a mad police commandant on the loose, intent on bloodshed. The White House isn't trusting anyone right now. But can we blame them? In their shoes we'd do the same.

113

"Someone's following us," Father Manet said, glancing nervously into the rear view mirror, as he negotiated the narrow lanes of the D-514.

Izzy and the others turned and looked. Three cars, lights on, were about two kilometers, back but were advancing fast.

"How much farther?" she said to Manet.

"Two to three kilometers but there's fog ahead. It will slow us down."

She gauged the distance and calculated how soon the cars would get to them.

They'll overtake us before we can make it.

"Will, Evans, Oberlin," she said, "I'll need time. As soon as we pull over I want you to set up a perimeter and take counter-measures to slow them down.

We'll head to the rendezvous point at the cemetery. You meet up with us there."

"Roger that," Will said.

"I'm in," Liam said.

"All right then," Izzy said, giving her machine gun to Liam, "Do you know how to use it?" she said.

"Special weapons training at Sandhurst," he said.

"Good. Will, you're team leader. Take the point, set up a skirmish line. Let's do it."

Izzy realized she was placing her comrades in mortal danger. They'd be severely outnumbered, outgunned, and had scant ammunition remaining. It would take a miracle. Still, her most sacred responsibility was protecting the life of the president. There were no good options.

"Father," Izzy said to Manet, "find us a good spot to pull over."

Manet pointed the bus toward a small roundabout ahead.

"The first exit off the roundabout leads to the cemetery," he said. "The memorial is only a short distance from there. I'll pull over as soon as we take the exit. There are trees and bushes there, so it's a blind spot," he said.

"Good," Izzy said. "With this thick haze, they won't know anyone's there until they make the turn. Will, that's where you'll intercept."

"Roger."

Izzy looked back to the president. His face was drawn and pale. Yet his eyes and expression conveyed a resolute serenity that seemed to say, *I'm not afraid.*

114

"Take the first exit off the roundabout. It's the road to the cemetery," Commandant Poussin said, as the three cars hurtled toward the small, mist-shrouded traffic circle.

They'd spotted the aging bus only a few minutes earlier, and had now almost completely closed the distance. In Poussin's mind, this would be the end of the line. No pleading, no entreaty, no armed resistance would be allowed to stand in the way of apprehending the American president, dead or alive. The blood of the innocent children killed in Islamabad would be avenged. They exited the roundabout at a fast speed, cars leaning precariously into the narrow tree-lined road.

"Watch out!"

"CRAAAASHH!!"

Poussin's car slammed head-on into the side of the school bus sitting astride the narrow road. The chase cars careened wildly, out of control and crashed into the thick bushes.

It took a few seconds for Poussin to come to. Though he was shaken, the airbag had cushioned the impact. Next to him, the driver slumped, lifeless, airbag deflated, his head almost completely severed by a piece of metal. Poussin saw that the door had detached from the vehicle. Stumbling out, he saw the other GIGN officers unsteadily emerging from the bushes, clutching their weapons.

"They can't have gotten far," Poussin said, checking the magazine of his pistol. "Let's go, but watch yourselves."

They cautiously moved around the bus, now resting on its side, its windows blown out by the impact.

"Pow!"

Poussin instinctively ducked, then quickly realized he wasn't being targeted.

"It's a warning shot," he said. "They'll try to keep us at bay while the president gets away."

He looked at his men. "Safeties off," he said. "We have the advantage in number and weapons, and we're not going to let them stop us." He noticed the men looking at him.

"Commandant," one of them said, "your left eye, the eyebrow...."

Poussin touched the brow line. It felt rough and moist. He looked at his fingers. They were covered in blood. He leaned down and picked up a shard from one of the shattered side-view mirrors. In the reflection he saw that his left eyebrow was gone, in its place nothing but raw bloody skin.

"Let's move out," he said, tossing the mirror shard to the ground.

115

"Five minutes."

"Dodger," the nickname that the gruff, fifty-year-old pilot in the lead Blackhawk had earned dodging fierce incoming while conducting nighttime Special Forces insertions and exfils under withering fire in Iraq, Afghanistan and other hellish places, was keeping the SEAL members in the back of the helo posted, as the stealth chopper approached the "fast rope" point over the American Cemetery. His main concern at the moment was the heavy fog bank moving in. He could always count on something to complicate an operation. On the other hand, the fog made it harder to spot the helo.

Once at the target, Chalk One would quickly slide down a thick braided rope dangling forty to fifty feet from the hovering chopper using the FRIES, Fast Rope Insertion Extraction System. On the ground, they'd proceed with stealth to the hoped-for rendezvous location. There was no point going in with a lot of Hollywood sound and fury. Silence and surprise were always more effective. Especially when killing was a near certainty.

Chalk Two would fast rope at another location on the cemetery's perimeter. Chalk Three would remain airborne off-shore in reserve, just below the bluff for added concealment.

They did a final check of their weapons and backpacks, and pulled their Heckler & Koch 416's closer to their chests. Wouldn't help if weapons got hung up.

Team members were accustomed to pulling off the impossible, so the task before them resembled many prior operations in terms of the inherent dangers and the need for operational perfection – with one glaring exception. This one was personal. Bad people had attacked their president, their Commander-In-Chief. Though the laser-like professional focus never waivered in any operation, this was a mission unlike any other they'd ever undertaken, and God help the man who screwed up.

116

"We're close," Izzy said. "The rendezvous point is at the memorial grounds just beyond this path."

She was trying to be encouraging but her tone carried more bravado than conviction. She could see that the president was in dire straights. There was a deathly pallor to his complexion and his breathing was labored. His body sagged more with each step. Izzy feared he could collapse any moment.

Though she and Father Manet were bookending the president she had been shouldering most of the weight since the short priest, dwarfed by the president, was struggling mightily to support him.

Izzy, beyond total exhaustion, was having to power her way through every step, her right arm wrapped tight around the president's waist, left hand gripping the handle of the "Football," the briefcase containing the nation's nuclear codes.

I hope my message got through to the White House. Will and the others will only buy us a few minutes. After that, it's game over.

"Unghhh!" The president collapsed, bringing Izzy and Manet down in a tangle.

Izzy regained her footing, and knelt down beside the president, now doubled over in obvious pain.

"Sir, talk to me."

Childs looked at her, eyes half-closed, his face a tight grimace.

"Shoulder," Childs said, in a voice that was almost inaudible.

"Let me see," she said.

She slipped the torn, grime-stained suit jacket off his right arm, exposing the shirt beneath. It was soaked in fresh blood. Being as gentle as possible, she unbuttoned the shirt and pulled it away from his shoulder.

Jesus.

The bandage that had been hurriedly placed on the shoulder wound following the attack at the hotel and re-dressed in the parish bus was now a large, weeping red mass. The wound had likely re-opened during the punishing escape at the roundabout. Bright blood pulsed from the shoulder.

He's losing too much blood.

She knew she couldn't afford to panic, but panic was fast approaching.

"Father, grab two handfuls of that tall grass."

Manet scrambled to gather the dry field grass that grew all about them. He brought a bunch to Izzy.

"I need the sash from your cassock," Izzy said.

Manet removed his sash and passed it to Izzy.

She worked quickly to compress the grass into a firm pad, placed it over the leaking bandage and wrapped the sash tight around pad and shoulder to slow the bleeding. It was a makeshift tourniquet that lacked hygiene and wouldn't last long, but it was that or allow the president to die. *Never.*

"Izzy, listen to me," Childs said, his voice a mere whisper. "I'm not going to make it. You need to go ahead, take the Football, make the rendezvous, try to come back with help."

"I'm not leaving you."

"You'll die here. I…I can't do that to you."

Izzy brought her face close to his. She would keep up a brave front, but the truth was, she didn't know how much time they had left. She was prepared for a bloody end. But before that moment came, she wanted him to know what he'd come to mean to her.

"Leyland," she said, "I'm not going anywhere without you," her voice was strong, reassuring. "If we die, we die together. But not here, not now, not so far from home." She placed a palm on his cheek. "Your country needs you…I need you."

Then for the first time since the horror of the attack at the hotel had descended on them, Childs' composure faltered. His stoicism during the attempt on his life, the chase, the pain, the burden of the presidency, had somehow kept his emotions in check lest they overwhelm Izzy and the courageous agents who were desperately fighting to save his life.

But her words had pierced that steely reserve, exposing feelings he'd been reluctant to share with her or even admit to himself. Emotions that had been forged in bloody Amman, then strengthened and deepened in Amman's anguished aftermath. He knew now that, live or die in the next few minutes or hours, she would stay at his side. Izzy wasn't just fighting for the life of her president, she was fighting for the two of them. He would not let her down.

Gritting his teeth, sweating and shaking in obvious pain, the president slowly raised himself up and stood, unsteady but defiant. He looked at Izzy.

"Let's make that rendezvous."

Izzy wrapped her arm protectively around his waist, pressing her body closer as he took a tentative step forward.

By now Father Manet had returned to the president's side, providing as much support as his own diminutive body could handle. Izzy looked at Manet. Tears had welled up in the cleric's eyes, apparently moved by what he'd just witnessed.

Izzy smiled, and gave him a slight nod. He'd proved himself to be a happy warrior in the life and death chase. She felt guilty about having persuaded the frugal priest to straddle the parish bus across the road. Manet had been hesitant. In spite of the imminent danger they were facing, Manet with his impenetrable logic had said: "Madame, there are only two buses in the entire parish."

"Father," Izzy had said, placing a hand on his small shoulder. "The United States Government will buy you a dozen new buses."

117

Situation Room

"Mr. Vice-President."

The vice-president turned to Brigadier General Peter Piper.

"Yes?"

"Sir, JSOC reports our SEALS are five minutes from fast rope, boots on the ground, but are encountering heavy fog."

"Right. Any further from our drones?"

"Negative, sir. Still no sign of the president or his detail, but the second drone is coming online now. We've expanded the search area to the perimeter outside the cemetery."

"What the...?" someone in the SitRoom said.

The hazy image from the second drone showed a large vehicle on its side and several smaller vehicles scattered around it.

"General," the vice-president said, "We need a tighter shot."

General Piper moved the joystick and the drone leaped forward until the picture came into clearer focus. The cratered church bus was now more visible, as were the three vehicles that Poussin and his team had been driving. Several men carrying automatic weapons and assault gear could be seen through the mist, moving slowly down a narrow brush-covered, tree-lined road.

"That vehicle looks like a defensive perimeter," General Piper said. "I suspect the men by the bus are hostiles, sir. Look like French GIGN but can't be sure."

"Where are our people?"

General Piper brought the drone lower, sweeping the narrow road.

"Don't see anyone else. Could be they're concealed. I recommend we immediately dispatch Chalk Three to this location. If our folks are down there they'll need serious help."

"Do it."

118

"I'm hit."

Secret Service agent Oberlin clutched his neck, as he rolled down the embankment, blood spurting from a shattered artery. Oberlin had just crossed to the other side of the path as he tried to position himself alongside the narrow path. The firefight had started almost immediately.

"Cover me," Liam said to Will and Evans who were on the opposite side of the road.

Will and Evans let loose a volley of automatic weapons fire, as Liam ran towards Oberlin in a half-crouch.

Pop, pop, whizzz, pop.

Liam could feel the heat of the rounds overhead as he dove into the shallow ditch. He knelt next to Oberlin and examined the neck wound. The round had severed the carotid artery. Oberlin would die on him fast, and there was little he could do other than put pressure on the gaping hole and tell Oberlin he was with him. He wouldn't die alone.

119

Rat Tat Tat! Pow! Pow!

Poussin could hear the fierce firefight behind him. Heart pounding, clothes ripping, he flailed and fell as he charged forward with great effort, over the uneven ground and mist-covered brush that flanked the road. He'd maneuvered around the bus and the Americans, leaving the GIGN team to deal with them. He suspected the resistance was a delaying action. He guessed that by now the president was no longer at the roundabout.

He's headed for the memorial.

Ahead, the encroaching fog made it difficult for Poussin to discern the visitor parking area. He knew that beyond the lot was the Garden of the Missing and beyond that the towering semi-circular colonnade overlooking the immense cemetery.

He moved forward carefully, until he reached the rear of the colonnade. From his vantage point he could see the twenty-two-foot tall Spirit of American Youth Rising From The Waves at the center of the colonnade. Beyond lay the memorial grounds.

Moving quietly from one column to the next he made his way to the front and looked out. There, in a luminous veil of translucent mist lay endless rows of white-marble stone crosses, the nearest to him distinct, while others merged eerily into the silver-grey fog. The utter silence and consecrated vastness of the scene triggered a powerful memory of childhood reverence.

There was a movement ahead. Beyond the long reflecting pool, three figures were moving deeper into the low-lying fog toward a small chapel situated at the center of the grounds.

It's them!

He made his way down the stairs of the colonnade, passed the reflecting pool, and moved into the thickening mist. As he did, a subdued buzzing sound permeated the air.

120

"Two minutes," Dodger said over the intercom, turning on the red light, his voice calm as he fought to stabilize the chopper against erratic updrafts. He'd been flying fast and low over the surface of the water in order to minimize chance of detection. The Blackhawk, like the other two in the formation, had been modified for stealth and noise suppression. If there were hostiles at the rendezvous site, Dodger would be sitting on top of them before they realized the world's most efficient killers were fast-roping down on them.

In the back of the chopper, the SEAL team had queued up near the open door, doing a final check of gear and weapons, and double-checking the FRIES bar for the fast rope descent.

"Thirty seconds."

The Chalk leader was already sitting at the open doorway of the chopper, his legs dangling over the edge. The chopper slowed to a forty-foot hover alongside the tree line at the northwest perimeter of the cemetery.

The green light illuminated.

"Go, Go, Go."

121

General de Plessy looked at his computer and listened intently to his headset.

"Monsieur le President," he said, spinning around to face president Jardin, "our Tigres are reporting they've located Poussin and, perhaps, the Americans."

"Where?" Jardin said.

"At the D-514 roundabout between Colleville-sur-Mer and the American Cemetery. They're seeing gun flashes. It appears there's a fire-fight underway."

"Mon Dieu!" Jardin said. "Poussin will kill the American president. Can you stop him with the Tigres?"

"Difficult, sir. Heavy fog is preventing our people from making a positive identification. We run the risk of firing on the Americans. We need to immediately insert our Special Forces onto the ground and have them proceed. It will take a few more minutes for the helicopters to get them on the ground but it's safer."

"Then do it, and say a prayer for France," Jardin said.

122

"GO, GO, GO!"

The ten members of the SEAL squad in Chalk Three along with their French speaker and tech were fast-roping forty feet down to the access road where the roundabout firefight was underway. It had only taken three minutes to cover the short distance from the Omaha bluffs to the location of the firefight.

Each SEAL was carrying over eighty pounds of communications, munitions, first-aid kits, power bars, special armor and weapons that included Heckler & Koch MP7's, and Heckler & Koch 416 assault rifles with suppressors; specially designed hand grenades, mortar launchers, 180 degree night vision goggles, 3-D GPS-driven satellite video streaming software, and haptic interfaces that emulated visual hand signals through algorithmic vibration.

The fog had made thermal imaging impractical. As a result the fast-rope descent had put the team farther away from the bus shootout than had been planned. They'd have to move quickly if they were going to do anything other than retrieve dead Americans. Unsure where their countrymen were they did what SEALS do best - they improvised. Shouting "WHO'S THE BOSS! SOUND OUT! WHO'S THE BOSS! GODDAMMIT!" they double-timed along the embankments of the road toward the firefight. It wasn't textbook stealth but it was what the situation called for.

"SPRINGSTEEN, BORN IN THE USA!" came the energetic reply from the bushes ahead.

"SEALS!" one of the squad members shouted. "Hang on, stay low, we're at six-o'clock."

"Special Agent Burgan here!" Will shouted from somewhere ahead. "Hostiles at the bus, left and right."

It was all the SEALS needed to know as they unleashed a murderous fusillade on the bus.

123

"*Monsieur le Président,*" General de Plessy said, his voice filled with incredulity, "our Special Forces are now on the ground, and are reporting a massive counter-assault on Poussin by the Americans."

"How can that be?" Jardin said. "I thought they were outnumbered by the GIGN?"

"Something's changed," de Plessy said. "Sir, should we engage the Americans?"

"No," the president said. "General, I order you to have our Special Forces and the Tigres stand down. If Poussin is outmatched, so be it. We will not help kill more Americans."

De Plessy touched his headpiece and began speaking.

124

Situation Room

All eyes in the cramped SitRoom were focused on the fog draped images of the violent roundabout firefight being streamed live via military satellite from the cameras mounted on the helmets of the SEAL team.

The utter incongruity of a brutal, life-death struggle unfolding in real time several thousand miles away while the occupants of the Situation Room sat in leather chairs, coffees and waters nearby, was surreal. President Childs was in mortal danger, his whereabouts still unknown. People were killing and being killed before their eyes, yet they could do nothing but watch and pray, barely breathing, hands gripping chair arms, bodies inclining forward as though yearning to leap into the battle.

The sole exception in the room was Air Force Brigadier General Peter Piper, coolly orchestrating the video feed and signals traffic coming in from the SEAL teams and the helo pilots.

Inside his guts were churning.

125

Izzy, the president and Father Manet were now inside the small, circular limestone chapel located at the center of the memorial grounds. They were out of breath and exhausted. Izzy checked her firearm…empty.

As her pulse became normal she surveyed the small enclosure. The room contained an altar of black and gold Pyrenees Grand antique marble, bordered by U.S., British, French and Canadian flags. Behind the altar, a tall translucent window with amber coating provided faint illumination. Above, a mosaic ceiling depicted an image of America blessing her sons, and a grateful France bestowing a laurel wreath upon American dead.

Izzy was adjusting the president's shoulder bandage when a shadow entered her peripheral vision. She turned and saw a heavy-set man standing at the entrance of the chapel, a gun in his hand. The man's appearance startled her. He was wearing a weather-beaten raincoat over a torn, mud-stained suit and shirt. His taut facial expression suggested pain. The area above his left eye was bloodied and raw, his heaving chest gurgling with the congested rattle of a heavy smoker.

"Do not move," Poussin said in a heavy accent. He looked at the president for a long moment, taken aback by the appalling condition of the man. He hadn't envisioned confronting the most powerful man in the world under such bizarre circumstances. Yet before him stood a haggard fugitive president, his blood-stained clothing disheveled and filthy. Standing beside him was a tall woman, mud-stained head to foot, yet defiant and alert, her body language in a protective stance as if ready to strike at Poussin. To the side stood a frail priest, his body visibly trembling from fear.

Far from being the monster the arrest warrant had described, this head of state in front of him radiated none of the malevolence he'd expected. Poussin studied the man's face. It was a good face, and as Poussin had learned over a lifetime of police work, a man's face told you a lot.

If there's evil in this person I do not see it. Yet here I am with a crumpled warrant in my coat pocket saying he's a detestable war criminal. What if the magistrat was wrong?

It was all getting too bewildering. He made a concerted effort to push away the pounding in his head, to clear the fuzzines and think clearly.

"Monsieur," he said at last, "You are the American president?"

"Yes," Childs said.

"My name is Poussin. I am a commandant of the Paris Préfecture and though I regret to see that you are hurt and that my English is not so good, it is my duty to inform you that in the name of the Republic of France you are under arrest."

"If I refuse?" Childs said.

"I would not advise it," Poussin said, placing both hands on his SIG-Sauer in a firing position. His hands were shaking and it took effort to keep the weapon steady.

Poussin noticed that Izzy seemed to be judging the distance between them. Her body language was in attack posture. It was obvious she was no mere aide. His gun was at the ready, but he made sure to keep himself just beyond her strike zone. He stepped backward out of the chapel, gun trained on the president.

"This way, please," he said, as he motioned the three out. With Poussin behind, they began making their way in the direction of the colonnade. But the fog had thickened, making it harder for Poussin to retrace his steps. The grass had grown wet and slippery and the enveloping fog was disorienting. The stabbing pain in his forehead had become intense, and he could no longer tell if they were moving toward the colonnade or away from it.

In his mental confusion, Poussin made a misstep, and his feet suddenly slid out from under him. He fell sideways striking his face violently on a cross. He heard a crack and felt a sharp pain as blood spurted crazily from his nose.

Dazed, he saw Izzy coming at him.

With great effort he rolled to his side, propped his gun arm with his other hand.

"*Non!*" he said, swiveling the muzzle toward the president.

Izzy stopped and took a step back. "Okay, okay," she said. "Don't shoot."

Training his pistol on the president, Poussin leaned heavily against the marble stone and slowly raised himself with his free hand. As he did, his gaze fell on the cross. Rivulets of blood coursed down the marble face, tracing the path of the letters etched in the stone.

In the pale light he squinted and came closer to the inscription… then sprang back in horror.

James Perkins
T Sgt 116 Inf 29 Div
Ohio June 6, 1944

Non! It can't be! Out of the thousands. Why this cross? Why me? Why my blood?

Like some past phantom, the image of his *grand-père* was suddenly before him, an old man, head bowed in humble prayer beside the grave of a young American soldier he'd never met, yet whom he'd mourned like a fallen brother.

Is the ghost of the old man rebuking me? Telling me that I've no right to desecrate this hallowed ground by hunting down the American president? Perhaps shooting him dead for the sake of an arrest warrant that might not be righteous?

Am I prepared to kill him if he tries to escape? And the priest, and the woman as well? Am I now God to decide such matters? Will I be the last man to spill American blood on this soil? Who am I to violate this sacred place and dishonor the fallen soldiers my grand-père cherished?

Poussin looked at the three people in front of him. The expressions on their faces conveyed puzzlement and dread. Expressions that seemed to say they were looking at a madman, and had no idea what he might do.

He felt tired, more tired than he had at any time in his life. He wanted nothing more than to be home, working in the small vegetable garden his dog, Asterix, alongside.

It occurred to him that the gun in his hand had become heavy and foreign.

Its purpose, solely to harm, maim, kill. He wanted no more part of it, no longer wanted to see fear in the eyes of his captives. The thought of pulling the trigger was now loathsome to him.

I will end it all now. I will surrender this weapon, leave, try to forget.

He took several steps towards them. He could see their bodies tense.

"*C'est fini*, it is over," he said.

He looked down at his SIG-Sauer to remove the magazine.

A sudden movement. He looked up.

Mid-air in flight, Izzy was crashing down on him hard, grabbing at the gun with one hand, pummeling with the other, snarling, screaming, her face a mask of naked rage. As they slammed violently to the ground…

"POW!"

A single shot rang out.

Poussin's face contorted as he was pushed away by the force of the large caliber round. His body, crumpled and lay motionless, a gaping hole in his head.

"Friendlies," a voice said.

As Izzy peered into the mist, a heavily-armored SEAL emerged carrying a long gun. Behind him several other SEALS appeared. The shooter leaned over Poussin and checked him, then stepped back, apparently satisfied.

"McGrath, SEAL Team Six," he said to Izzy.

"Special agent Stone with the president," Izzy said. She saw the president and Manet approaching, accompanied by a squad of Seal Team members.

"Sir," said McGrath, presenting a smart salute to the president as he neared. "SEAL Team Leader McGrath. We're to accompany you to the USS Theodore Roosevelt. Helo's ready, sir."

The president managed a return salute. "Thank you." He turned to Izzy. "I want you with me, Izzy."

"Mister president," she said. "You're in good hands. I'd like to stay here until the rest of my team arrives."

"Right, I understand." He said.

Izzy turned to McGrath. "The president needs immediate medical attention."

"Roger," McGrath said. "We'll exfil POTUS stat. Medics will be on the chopper with him all the way to the ship." He tapped his helmet mike and spoke quickly into his headpiece.

"We have agents up the road," Izzy said.

"Firefight's over," McGrath said, "hostiles are down."

"Good news, thanks." Izzy said.

126

Situation Room

As the fog gradually lifted, the live feed from the American Cemetery via a hovering drone showed President Childs protectively surrounded by heavily armed SEALS as he half-limped, half-walked, unaided but erect, toward the waiting Blackhawk.

"Hooah! Yesss! Go SEALS!"

The once stoic demeanor of the nation's most senior military, civilian and intelligence officials gave way to loud cheers, hugs, and high-fives. The fear, the uncertainty, the existential threat to the president was over and he was on his way home.

127

Izzy watched as McGrath and his SEAL team escorted the president toward the waiting Blackhawk, rotors spinning. The end of Poussin had been fast and violent. Only then, only when she knew the mortal threat to the president had finally come to an end did she acknowledge her complete exhaustion. She'd almost lost it in that powerful instant of rescue. She'd been at the breaking point.

But she was no weeper and today would be no different. Her only concession to sentimentality had come when she'd placed a comforting arm around the small shoulders of traumatized, trembling Father Manet.

"You're a good man, *Père*," she'd said, "as brave a person as I've ever known. My country will always be grateful to you. You're all alone here. If you come with us we can arrange to have you safely transported back to Paris."

"No, thank you, madame. I can find my way to a village. I know the area well."

Izzy smiled. "Yes, Father, I noticed that much this morning." She gave him a gentle pat on the shoulder. "And we won't forget the new buses."

She looked back toward the president. He was almost at the Helo.

Then to her surprise he stopped, turned around and appeared to waive away his protectors. Her heart skipped at beat as he began to retrace his steps, unsteady and in obvious pain, in her direction. She was standing amidst the white marble crosses, her disheveled clothes in tatters, ruby hair unruly and mud-caked.

Step by labored step, Leyland Childs, President of the United States and leader of the free world closed the distance until at last he was standing in front of Special Agent Isabella Stone, the one who'd been to hell and back with him. The one who'd given every thing she had to protect him, to comfort him, minister to his wounds and take him home again.

He stood before her for a long moment, his head inclined as if in prayer. Then he gently wrapped his arms around her, pulled her to him and held her in a tender embrace. Izzy melted into him. And in that moment Izzy knew that a sacred bond had been forged between them that neither time, nor distance, nor fortune, be it ill or good, would ever break.

After a pause the president whispered something in Izzy's ear. She nodded slightly and looked up at him, a wan smile on her face. Then the president turned and made his way back to the SEAL team - as tears unapologetically fell in the West Wing Sitroom.

The sole person in the room not celebrating or shedding tears was Air Force Brigadier General Peter Piper, who was intently working his computer, monitoring and coordinating the exfil of the president. He wouldn't relax until the Blackhawks were wheels up and out of French territorial waters, and wouldn't consider the president finally out of harm's way until he was safely aboard the USS Theodore Roosevelt. The six Boeing F/A-18E/F Super Hornets he'd scrambled would provide cover for the short trip to the ship.

"Izzy!"

Izzy looked toward the memorial colonnade. Will Bergan waved and smiled as he made his way toward her, protected by a team of SEALS. Walking alongside Will were Evans and Liam. Evans looked fine but Liam had a large bloodied bandage on the right side of his head. She didn't see Oberlin. Her stomach tightened.

The three looked fatigued, their faces were scratched and dirt-smudged.

She met them halfway and gave each a heartfelt hug.

"Good to see you guys."

"Same here," Will said.

"Oberlin?" Izzy said.

"Didn't make it," Liam said, his expression taciturn. "I was with him…it was fast."

Izzy bit her lip hard.

"POTUS is wheels up and we're ready to exfil you guys," one of the SEALS said, pointing to a waiting Blackhawk.

"Roger that," Izzy said.

EPILOGUE

Washington, D.C.
Georgetown

It was early Sunday morning and a light rain was falling. Izzy, wearing a long white silk bathrobe stood barefoot by the floor-to-ceiling windows of her warm "R" street townhouse. Sunday morning was her favorite time, a rare moment when Georgetown still remained in silent repose but for the soft pitter-patter of rain that seemed to sometimes tiptoe in during the night. She loved the effect the rain had on the red brick sidewalks creating shimmering crimson patterns amidst a rich pallette of fallen leaves.

It had been several months since the chaos of Paris and Normandy. In the immediate aftermath, the president, still recovering from his injuries, and French President Jardin, had agreed on a narrative of the deadly events, describing them as a one-off by an extremist judge and a mentally unstable police commandant. As to the victims, a joint national period of mourning was declared, with somber memorials to the fallen children and their teachers, and posthumous citations to police and secret service agents.

Izzy had taken time to rest, decompress and restore herself. Amman and Paris had exacted a heavy toll physically and emotionally. Violent dreams and panic attacks had lasted weeks. Leyland, as she now called the president, had helped her through the difficult days. The two were now closer than ever, talking often by phone, dining privately at the White House residence, sailing Chesapeake Bay, and discreetly slipping away to small candle-lit restaurants or her townhouse with the able help of Will Bergan and other agents. But people were taking note, and a Beltway cottage industry of tantalizing speculation had sprung up. Was this simply a temporary bond born of post-traumatic stress, they asked, or was it something more permanent?

The stupefying shock of the two attempts on the president's life, and Izzy's jaw dropping courage, had riveted the nation. Millions of goodwill messages for the two poured into the White House from every region, walk of life and political persuasion. The entire country seemed to want the president and his heroine to be together. Hollywood could not have scripted a more romantic tale.

Izzy knew she loved Leyland. He was charismatic, brilliant and possessed a profound sense of duty to his country. When they were together she felt serene contentment, a sense of well-being and an intense physical attraction. Since their return to Washington, they'd been intimate, but were careful choosing when and where. He'd told her he was in love with her, and would wait as long as it took for her to make a decision about their future. She knew he had moments of great anguish and guilt over the loss of Meg. She wanted to help fill that void, comfort him, love him.

Then there was Liam. She'd visited him at the hospital where he'd been recovering from his wounds. After two weeks he'd been released, and had returned with typical strapping wit and bonhomie. They'd had dinner at one of their favorite Georgetown restaurants. Liam had been his charming, irrepressible self.

It was true, Izzy thought, their times in Washington and New York had been exciting and passionate. They'd discovered a shared love of sports, Thoreau, and Brahms. Liam had been classically educated, yet he'd chosen a life of intrigue and great personal danger - qualities she had to admit had also drawn her to the Service. Life with him would be a non-stop adventure. She cared deeply for him. But... could he make a permanent commitment? Might he just disappear one day? There was a wanderlust, a certain renegade quality about him that inexorably drew her to him, yet made her hesitate. She knew Leyland would never waiver. But Liam?

Pulling the long robe more tightly around her shoulders she took one last look out the window and walked to the kitchen. The aroma of French-press Columbian coffee was strong and inviting. She poured a large white china mug, made her way to the bedroom and stopped at the open door.

"Good morning," she said.

"Ah, coffee."

He sat up, reclined half-naked against the pillows, and rubbed the sleep from his eyes.

THE END

Made in the USA
Charleston, SC
17 February 2017